DEATH IN
FANCY DRESS

Anthony Gilbert

with an introduction by
MARTIN EDWARDS

This edition published 2019 by
The British Library
96 Euston Road
London NW1 2DB

Death in Fancy Dress was originally published in 1933 by W. Collins &
Co. Ltd, London. 'Horseshoes for Luck' and 'The Cockroach and
the Tortoise' were each first published in *Detection Medley*, edited
by John Rhode and published in 1939 by Hutchinson & Co. Ltd.

Cataloguing in Publication Data
A catalogue record for this book is available from the British Library

ISBN 978 0 7123 5340 3
eISBN 978 0 7123 6715 8

Front cover image © The British Library Board

Typeset by Tetragon, London
Printed and bound by CPI Group (UK) Ltd, Croydon CR0 4YY

CONTENTS

INTRODUCTION

Death in Fancy Dress is a classic whodunit which first appeared in 1933. Lucy Malleson (who hid her gender as well as her name by adopting the pseudonym Anthony Gilbert) was by then already well-established as a detective novelist. She'd begun with a couple of books under another pen-name, J. Kilmeny (a pun on "kill many") Keith, before adopting the Gilbert name for a series of mysteries featuring the Liberal MP Scott Egerton.

Still in her early thirties, she determined to try something different. Two years earlier, she'd experimented with a non-series Gilbert novel, *The Case against Andrew Fane*, and now she decided to write another stand-alone. The result was a country house mystery that, despite its conventional setting, veered away from orthodoxy. The story is narrated by a young lawyer, Tony Keith, and he and his friend Jeremy Freyne become embroiled in a strange case which seems to centre on Feltham Abbey.

"It's bound to arouse suspicion in the official mind," the two men are told, "when a wave of suicide sweeps over a country, as it has swept over this one during the past twelve months… men and women have been committing suicide with alarming frequency; and it's noticeable that they are practically all people in what we term the superior walks of life. Either they're people of rank and position, or they're people with money."

The authorities have discovered a pattern to the deaths: "It appeared that in every case mysterious telephone calls had been received shortly before the death. The victim, even if in perfect health and activity up till that time, developed nervousness, irritability, an increased jumpiness whenever the telephone rang or the post arrived, and then came the final act of despair... In practically every case, money in quite large sums had been raised, sometimes to the man's or woman's ruination."

The conclusion to be drawn is clear: "Blackmail on a tremendous scale." And so the central question is: who is the blackmailer? Before the mystery is solved, a fancy dress ball is held at Feltham Abbey, and someone is found dead in the grounds. The guests at the Abbey form a "closed circle" of suspects in the classic tradition of Golden Age detective stories, and the puzzle is eventually solved in pleasing fashion.

The book met with critical acclaim. Dorothy L. Sayers, in an insightful review for the *Sunday Times* on 2 July 1933, said: "*Death in Fancy Dress* has at least one uncommon merit. It contrives to persuade us that something really serious and unpleasant is taking place at Feltham Abbey. So often in a detective story trivial irregularities like blackmail and murder seem scarcely to ruffle the placid current of domestic affairs... Here, the atmosphere of suspense and uneasiness really does pervade the household." Sayers praised the "remarkably well-drawn and sympathetic cast of characters" and the clever way in which the reader's attention was directed away from the truth.

Unfortunately, in an era of economic misery, the novel did not earn its author commensurate financial success. As she said in her memoir *Three-a-Penny*: "By this time a thing called The Slump was beginning to set most of us by the ears. Books were affected, like everything else. Not only did our sales cease to increase according to expectations, but our American markets began to fail, until for a good many of us they no longer existed... I began to get panicky and cast round for some fresh way of bringing the necessary grist to the mill."

She must have found it galling that *Death in Fancy Dress*, like her two previous books featuring Scott Egerton, failed to find an American publisher. Her career was at a turning point, but she was determined to keep going. She toyed with the idea of writing romantic fiction or a thriller, before deciding on a more ambitious course: she experimented with a psychological crime novel under a new pen-name, Anne Meredith. The result was *Portrait of a Murderer*. This novel was again well received, and it was taken up in the USA, but once again it did not make her rich; ironically, the paperback reprint published in the British Library Crime Classics series in 2017, sold much better than the original edition.

Gilbert didn't give up, and continued to ring the changes with her writing. Scott Egerton was given another couple of cases, and she created a French police detective called Dupuy, who featured in three books. But her breakthrough did not come until she created the rascally solicitor Arthur Crook, who made his debut in *Murder by Experts* in 1936, and established himself as her principal protagonist. During the course of a career that continued until the 1970s, Crook became an increasingly likeable character, and carried a business card bearing the slogan: "Linen discreetly washed in private. Danger no object."

Lucy Beatrice Malleson was a Londoner, born on Ash Wednesday in 1899. At the age of sixteen, she trained as a secretary, and over the years her employers included the Coal Association and the Red Cross. But writing was her first love. In *Three-a-Penny*, published as by Anne Meredith, she said: "When I am not writing I am not more than half-alive. I am miserable, hopeful, and dejected by turns." Her credo was: "It is people and not the things that happen to them who are interesting". She enjoyed writing short stories, and two which she contributed to the Detection Club's anthology *Detection Medley*, "Horseshoes for Luck" and "The Cockroach and the Tortoise", are included in this book.

She was a modest and likeable woman, as was noted by her friend and Detection Club colleague Michael Gilbert in a letter to *The Times* following her death in 1973. She was aware of the limits of her talent, but she made the best use of it. As she said in her memoir, "I don't feel guilty that my books don't sell ten thousand copies, although I should love them to do so... When I was young, I confidently thought they would; when they didn't I was astounded, but it never occurred to me, when my average sales were 1,250 copies, to abandon writing and do something more lucrative... That's one reason why writing is such fun—it's so chancy." I like to think that she would be amused as well as delighted to know that this long-forgotten detective novel is enjoying a fresh life in the twenty-first century.

MARTIN EDWARDS
www.martinedwardsbooks.com

DEATH IN
FANCY DRESS

CHAPTER I

YOU MIGHT SAY THE AFFAIR BEGAN WHEN PERCY FELTHAM put a bullet through his head in 1917; or when Jeremy Freyne and I turned up on that foggy night at the Abbey to find half the household had turned out on to the moors; or even to the scene of the second violent death on the premises a few days later. But I think for my purpose it will be best to begin with the day I cannoned against Jeremy in the bazaar at M—— in India. I had just completed a fascinating but intricate piece of personal inquiry work on behalf of a rich and fanatical client of my legal firm, Hutchinson, Keith and Murray. It had involved a great deal of examination, patience, travelling, time, money and the most minute inquiries, all to establish the falsity of a slander that scarcely seemed worth so much effort. I said as much to my senior partner, but Hutchinson is versed in humanity and possesses, in addition, a peculiar ripe wisdom of his own.

"Tell Desmond that," he said, "and he'll make the obvious retort of the almost fabulously wealthy man who has had to earn his living. He's kept his hands clean all these years, worked colossally hard, achieved most of his aims, and his good name is worth a great deal to him. He can't buy a new one, as he can replace most things. To him this is vital, and he hasn't the advantages of birth that would enable him to shrug the lie aside for the stupid insult that it is."

I had no objection to Mr. Desmond's regard for his good name, since it gave me the opportunity of visiting a country that has always possessed a charm for me even in prospect. Moreover, after chasing from pillar to post, I ran down my slanderer, proved his bribes to certain locals and poor whites beyond a doubt, and was coming back with a fistful of evidence when I collided with Jeremy Freyne.

I had known Jeremy ever since we were small boys together at our first prep. school. He had been a thin, intelligent, good-looking little boy, who had only to nod his head to gain adherents to the maddest scheme; at fourteen, at Eton, he had been coltish, with an appearance of wearing someone else's clothes, but his personal magnetism was greater than ever. At seventeen he came nearer to being expelled, without actually pulling it off, than anyone I have ever met. Three of us held our thumbs for him for an hour while his persuasive tongue tackled its first serious task at diplomacy; and after that he was the rowdiest undergraduate on record to escape being sent down.

Wherever Jeremy was there was bound to be something going on; some madcap had only got to say, "What a lark to do so-and-so," and Jeremy would be up and calling, "Come on!" before anyone could protest. The trouble was that his challenges were always irresistible. And he seldom lost his bet. Whenever I see "The Mikado," I am reminded of Jeremy when Ko-Ko says pleadingly, "When your Majesty orders a thing, it is as good as done; to all intents and purposes that thing is done." I remember during his second year at Oxford he got involved in a scrape that made a certain popular hostess remark that she wasn't going to have that dissolute young man at her house again, a distinct miss for Jeremy, who was accustomed to having a pretty good time there. Three days later, there came to call on Mrs. D—— a plumpish, beshawled, button-booted lady, in black, giving a general appearance of feathers and brooches and carrying a large brocade bag. She had come, she explained earnestly, to apologise for the ill-behaviour of her son.

"He is wild," she acknowledged, "but he has a heart of gold."

Mrs. D—— was so won over by the old lady's skittish and witty conversation, once the question of Jeremy was shelved, that she readily agreed to rescind her decision, and the visitor retired to a neighbouring garage to deal with stays, petticoats, suspenders, hairpins and a lace fichu.

The affair leaked out, though it never travelled so far as Mrs. D——. When Jeremy's mother heard of it, she sent for him. She was a round dimpled dormouse of a woman with a deceptive air of gentleness.

"Don't you be taken in, Tony, old son," Jeremy said, feelingly, to me. "I give you my word that school lickings were nothing to my mother when she'd got her monkey up."

Of course, at twenty-two she couldn't deal so simply with him, but her subtlety made even her victim her admirer.

"Dear me, Jeremy," she said in her charming voice and assuming her most delightful manner, "what a positive godsend you are! Here am I harried to death trying to find a good reason for refusing to attend the local bazaar in August."

"Can I suggest anything?" asked Jeremy, looking puzzled.

"No, dear boy, I shan't have to refuse now. What a pity you didn't reveal your gifts last year. There were several functions I know I should have enjoyed. Fortunately, this is also going to be a busy summer."

Jeremy looked appalled. "But why don't you go yourself?" he demanded. "They're—they're your pigeon."

Mrs. Freyne shook her head. "Oh, no," she replied placidly, "I don't run darning-needles into my fingers for fun, or swallow ground glass, so why should I be expected to catch germs in a number of local halls? Have you a diary, dear? There are so many engagements I'm afraid you might forget some of them."

"My God!" said Jeremy in awe-struck tones at the end of the summer vacation, "never pit yourself against a woman, Tony. You won't have an earthly." But to his mother he said, "Dearest, how can I ever thank you enough? You've given me the most amazing warning. After seeing the lengths to which female brutality will go, and realising the manner in which respectable married women employ their leisure, I have resolved never to place my head in the noose."

"How comforting!" said Judia Freyne. "I was so much afraid you were going to marry that red-headed Australian cat you've been trailing about everywhere this year. What about continuing the experiment at Christmas? There'll be lots more parties then."

We both got into the tail of the war, and I ran upon Jeremy at the beginning of 1918. Mrs. Freyne had died the previous year and he took it very hard. Otherwise he didn't seem a scrap changed by his war experiences. He came through without a scratch, while I took a bullet in the hip that has left me a little lame ever since.

When I came back I was taken in by old Hutchinson, who had always promised to give me a stool in his office when I came down from Oxford. He had lost his son in the war, and in 1926 he took me into partnership. I liked the work amazingly, and Hutchinson was a charming man to deal with. There was another young partner, Murray, who came in two years after I did.

I had a little money of my own, besides what I earned, and no dependants, and I felt I deserved a little comfort, so I engaged chambers in town and advertised for a valet. I saw a good many, ex-servicemen to an applicant, but half of them had never dressed anything but themselves, except one enterprising man who said he was an expert at dressing windows, and I was beginning to despair and wax impatient when a tall slender young fellow, with a brief moustache and gold-rimmed glasses, put in an appearance. I have a habit of going by a man's hands when I'm dealing with him, in practically every capacity. It's a trick lawyers learn very early; people can disguise their voices, control their expressions, remain as unmoved as if they were something out of Madame Tussaud's, but again and again they're betrayed by their hands. This fellow had noticeably good hands, with flexible wrists, and he knew what to do with them. The only thing I didn't like about him was the moustache, and I wondered if he'd agree to shave it off. I asked him, tentatively, and he replied without a shadow of hesitation, "Certainly, my dear fellow. It was a damned nuisance, anyhow," and peeling it off, he dropped it in his pocket.

I felt a little annoyed. No man likes being fooled.

"What on earth's your little game now?" I demanded.

"The moustache?" he asked. "To tell you the truth, I'm temporarily interested in a lady who considers it effeminate not to sport a healthy growth on the upper lip."

"And you can't manage the real thing? Bad luck."

"There are several reasons against making the attempt. One, by the time it's achieved adolescence my interest in Clarice and hers in me will undoubtedly have waned. Two, various other of my lady friends consider a moustache a positive nuisance. Three, it stamps me immediately as an ex-officer, and I'm beginning to discover that we aren't exactly a popular lot. Worthy, my dear fellow, deserving, well-meaning, but—for the most part without the haziest notion of business methods, and so liable to grab a bayonet when we want to enforce an argument. Three—no, four—it limits my capacities. After all, one can always add a moustache when desirable, but one can't so easily detach it if it's permanently embedded in the individual. No, I do very well with Charlie."

"I suppose it wouldn't be so easy to pass yourself off as the new Parish Visitor with that kind of excrescence clinging to you," I agreed. "I get you."

"I hope you're going to keep me," said Jeremy promptly. "You'll find me industrious, willing and trustworthy. And my taste is impeccable. Also, I'm damned hard up, I cannot dig, to beg I am ashamed—and I know you do yourself devilish well."

But I didn't—take him, I mean. Instead I took a fair young man with the manners of a shop-walker, and Jeremy disappeared into the blue. He didn't, after all, embrace any profession. He said he had had one darned good try and luck was against him. He knocked about, gathering experience and having the time of his life, so that presently, when you heard of some white man with the reputation of a lunatic, doing anything particularly futile in some obscure British protectorate, you could bet your boots Jeremy wasn't far off.

His last words to me, as he turned to leave my rooms, were, "I bet the chap you do take in my place will sneak your watch, and I hope he gets your links as well."

2

His first words to me when we met in the bazaar were, "Hullo, Tony. Do I win my bet?"

It was a minute before I realised what he meant; then I recollected, and handed him five pounds. "Though, as a matter of fact," I said, "he didn't take the links."

Whatever he had been doing for the past ten years it didn't appear to have aged him at all. He was the same lean, cheerful, reckless chap, deeply tanned, with the same mad dark-blue eyes (they say that if a male Freyne got born with eyes of any other colour it would be promptly disowned), the same cool way of walking into danger, the same casual manner of trusting to the hour to provide its own requirements.

"One of the lilies of the field, I am," he said, complacently. "I toil not, neither do I spin, but I give you my word, I wouldn't change places with any raven living. Come and spot the sacred ape with me, will you? They say he has to be seen to be believed. Personally, I thought we'd encountered his whole tribe."

He looked at the crowds of people surging all round us; representatives of practically every nation under Heaven jostled and muttered and bargained. We watched them surging to and fro; there was a good sprinkling of English and American tourists, easily distinguished by their expansive topees, white drill suits, that made them look like something on the suburban stage, cigars, wrist-watches, cameras and incredible boots. One couple, clearly sprung from the lower middle-class (probably been lucky in the war, Jeremy suggested, but not rancorously), paused near us. The woman said in a quarrelsome, disappointed tone, "It's what I told you all along, Ern. It's just like the Earl's Court Exhibition, only they do have seats there."

Jeremy collapsed into wordless laughter. "Don't let's look for the ape," he suggested. "He'd be pure anti-climax after that. I've found a place where you can get a God-fearing British drink."

"As British as Earl's Court, I suppose?"

"Or the British bathroom. Has it ever occurred to you, Tony, that the one real contribution of the Anglo-Saxon races towards culture is the bathroom? It's become the most important room in the house. Why do you suppose magnates like to be interviewed at unconventional hours? The number of bigwigs, beginning with Lord B——k, that I've interviewed on the bath-edge, would surprise you. A bathroom is now such a thing of beauty that it puts a mere drawing-room in the shade. Of course, a man can't very well say, 'Cigarette, my dear fellow? Now what about a drink? Oh, and before you go, I must just show you my bathroom,' so he stages the whole interview there. The ghosts of the ancient Romans must be getting a bit apprehensive about the way we're overhauling them. What are you doing here?"

I told him. "Nice job, yours," he murmured, "though it wouldn't suit me."

"What would?" I retorted.

He said contentedly, "Oh, well, I rub along all right. I get what I want most."

"And that is?"

"Adventure, novelty, danger, excitement. Those are at least as justifiable as the goals of other average men. The fact is, we live too much on a money basis. And fail to realise that most of the desirable things can't be bought for cold cash. What about you? When do you ascend the next rung in the legal ladder?"

"Take silk, d'you mean? My dear fellow, I'm not a barrister."

"No?" he asked in surprise. "Why? Couldn't you manage it?"

"I don't want to be. Don't want silk, either, if it comes to that."

"What a rum chap you are. I thought every legal pot looked forward to the time when he raked in the fees and saw his pictures in the Sunday press."

"Ah, but I, like yourself, am that rare creature, the man who doesn't live wholly on a money basis."

"I didn't mean merely money. I know you've wads of that. But there are other considerations... you have such a sordid mind."

"Kudos, you mean? But that's only another name, as a rule, for notoriety. Besides, the solicitor sees what the barrister doesn't, the actual working-out of the drama; the barrister only sees the consequences. Between him and his client stands the solicitor, the insatiable middleman. The barrister gets the fees, but the small fry get the fun."

"My own opinion," agreed Jeremy, cheerfully. "How long are you staying?"

"I go back to-morrow. And you?"

"I'm considering a wildcat scheme for raising ivory. For some reason, I've always missed Africa. It can't be that I've overlooked it. This might be my chance."

It seemed to me it was certainly his chance to lose his capital of three hundred pounds. Wildcats were cautious spinsters compared with Jeremy. The more I heard of the scheme the less I liked it.

"It's all right," he said gaily, "I put my money into this push…"

After that nothing emerged very clearly, beyond the certainty that the three hundred pounds never would. I said as much.

"I dare say you're right," Jeremy speculated. "Anyway, I'd practically decided to change my mind, before you planted these doubts in it."

"Why?"

"You make me feel homesick. I suddenly remember that there are such places as the Holborn Grill, the Nelson Monument and the Twopenny Tube. Do they still plaster them with advertisements? His vests he had discarded quite, since he became a Bovrilite. That's you all over, Tony." He hooked his arm into mine and we moved over to the shipping offices.

3

I didn't see much of Jeremy on the homeward voyage. You might say he was in his element on board ship, if experience hadn't proved that he is in his element wherever he is. He was in perpetual demand: he got up amateur theatricals, organised deck games, danced, flirted, romanced, found rugs and sheltered corners for elderly ladies, and was even roped in by the chaplain to help with the Sunday morning services.

"I offered him my services carte-blanche," Jeremy assured me. "To preach the sermons, read the lessons and carry the bag. I gather I'm to do the second."

So that, taking one thing with another, we didn't have much opportunity for conversation till just before we reached port. There had been dancing on the upper deck as usual, and as usual I'd sat out. At last everything was done, the passengers had gone down to their cabins, and a large number of empty glasses had been retrieved by the stewards. I thought Jeremy looked a shade more serious than usual as he came up, observing lightly, "Too good a night to fug in a bunk. It's almost the last of them, too."

We leaned against the rail in an amicable silence, smoking and watching the blaze of moonlight on the heaving water. Presently Jeremy shied the butt of his cigarette overboard. It described a glowing red arc and expired with a short indignant hiss.

"You know, Tony," his sighs, like that of the Victorian swain, increased the gale, as he lounged with his back to the sea, "it's been pretty good fun."

"The voyage?"

"The last ten years. I shall hate like hell letting it go."

"Why must you?" I asked foolishly. I should have known Jeremy better than that.

"Because one of the basic rules of life is that you can't live on the past, any more than you can live on the memory of paid bills. You have to let it drop, and go on to the next thing. And that, in my case, is going to be out of a very different book."

A swift suspicion stung me. "Jeremy, you haven't let any of these affairs get serious? You're not going to settle down?"

"I believe settle up is a more graphic way of putting it."

The notion of our irrepressible Jeremy led tamely on a domestic leash was anything but consoling.

"Can't you put it off for a bit?" I urged.

He shook his head. "Too risky."

"I thought you appreciated risks?"

"Not where really important things are concerned. This counts."

"Is it anyone I know?"

"You ought to." He produced a tattered snapshot from his pocket-book, and let me glance at it. It was a picture of a girl tying up raspberry canes. She wore a cotton frock and no hat. She was laughing. I knew her at once.

"Hilary!" I exclaimed.

"Well?"

I said impulsively, "But, Jeremy…"

"You're not trying to tell me you're in love with the chit, are you? If I thought you were…"

"But…"

"I don't approve of cousins marrying, and I'm sure Eleanor Feltham doesn't either."

"She's Eleanor Nunn now, but…"

"I wish to Heaven I'd taken you to Africa and left you there."

"But, Jeremy…"

"Though, if it comes to that, there's plenty of nice empty sea, and not a soul in sight."

"I'm not in love with her, you ass," I shouted.

"Well, why not say so at once. And there's no need to sound so pleased with yourself. I don't suppose she'd look at you anyway."

I gave him his head. I was thinking of Hilary, whom I hadn't seen for nearly three years. She had been seventeen then, a tall, fair-haired grey-eyed girl, as reckless as Jeremy himself. She had been an attractive minx, with a fiendish love of making men look fools.

I thought they'd be pretty well matched, if they did make a pair of it. Anyway, neither would be able to complain of the tediousness of married life.

After a short pause, I remarked tentatively, "Bit of a hurry, aren't you? The girl's only twenty."

"My mother was engaged at sixteen and married within the year."

"You won't be allowed to be the ship's flirt once you're married."

"I shall have another and even more entrancing occupation."

I grinned. "That of Hilary's husband?"

"What else?"

"You don't find the word husband a trifle—er—overwhelming?"

"Like Humpty Dumpty, I have educated words to bear my own particular meaning. Unquestionably, in the hands of many men the word husband has a peculiarly revolting significance; it is heavy, solid, like the puddings of the old-fashioned nursery with few sultanas to atone for its suety flavour. But with me the word assumes an air, a fascination, a charm, a delight—in short, the prospect of being Hilary's husband satisfies me completely."

I sighed. "I suppose you know your own mind. It's a pity you couldn't postpone the event, though, for a little while."

"It wouldn't be safe. Too many good things are lost in that way. I remember my mother telling me once about a hat she'd seen in a shop window, a purple felt hat with a black veil, it was priced at two-and-eleven, I think (I wished Hilary could have heard the bland assurance of his tone). Well, twenty-two-and-eleven, perhaps, or forty-two-and-eleven—they're all obscene prices—whatever it was, she decided to brood over a cup of tea, and when she came back the hat had vanished."

"And Hilary's your two-and-elevenpenny hat?"

"Precisely."

"I see." A new thought occurred to me. "Does she know of this—er—arrangement of yours?"

"Not yet. I'm going to tell her as soon as I get back."

"But suppose she doesn't agree? Suppose the idea of being your wife doesn't appeal to her as a position of charm, fascination and delight?"

He swung round, astonished, perplexed, stupefied. "By Jove," he exclaimed. "I never thought of that."

I watched him saunter down the deck, his hands in his coat pockets; he was softly whistling a lilting Spanish air. I found myself wondering if any woman could resist him; so far he'd kept himself free from serious entanglements.

I had already forgotten the moral of the purple hat.

CHAPTER II

W E REACHED SOUTHAMPTON ON A DAY OF FLYING MIST AND grey ribbons of cloud. It was cold and cheerless with a leaden sky, hanging low over the roofs. The docks were sodden and dripping. My heart sank, but Jeremy's spirits rose mercurially as we came ashore. Every mile that the train drew nearer to London his air of debonair excitement increased, though whether he was inspired by the return to his own city, that he knew like an American fanatic, or whether it was because each mile brought him nearer to Hilary I couldn't determine. At Charing Cross he leaped out, greeting the porters as if they were his family come to welcome him home. People stared, laughed, were attracted, startled, amused. He went to buy cigarettes at the kiosk and said something to the girl there that made her exclaim, "Well, you are a one," a remark neither of us has ever been able to elucidate, because, said Jeremy, how could we be a two or any other figure? Then he bought an armful of papers and hung about the station reading them, while I expostulated with a porter about a damaged suit-case. This debate appeared likely to continue interminably, when I felt a touch on my arm. I glanced up, explanatory words on my lips. But Jeremy's face silenced me. All the vitality and fun had died out of it. He was like something locked and impenetrable.

"Sorry to interrupt you," he said, curtly. "But I'm in a bit of a hurry."

"I shan't be long," I assured him, with what appeared to me pardonable irritation.

"Well, good-bye." He held out his hand.

"What the devil?" I expostulated. "Where are you going?"

"To that place in the Strand where you buy passages…"

"Passages?"

"Yes. In a ship. To the East. To-night if possible."

I said stupidly, "But you've only just arrived."

"Well, I've seen my native land. Now I can let her alone for a few more years."

Too much taken aback to attempt to fathom the reason for this amazing volte-face, I could only murmur, "But Nelson's Monument. You told me you were hungering for a sight of that."

"I've bought a picture postcard that I can carry in my waistcoat pocket."

"And the Thames? You've been positively lyrical about the Thames."

"Goodness knows why! I can see plenty of shipping on plenty of other rivers."

I abandoned my suit-case; its battered condition and the probable ruin of its contents became matters of no moment.

"Have you gone crazy, Jeremy? You've just arrived…"

"And am now about to depart. This evening. If possible. By boat. Would you like me to wax lyrical about that? I dare say I could try."

I exclaimed in despair, "But Hilary…?"

"Hilary?" repeated Jeremy in a surprised voice, as if her name had never been mentioned between us, "Oh, she's quite capable of fixing up her own future. She won't need to consult me."

I began to see daylight. "You mean?"

He sighed, like a man afflicted with an idiot son. "Would you like me to spell it out for you?"

I said in my driest voice, "Suppose you let me have that paper for an instant," and he passed it to me with a contemptuous air that made me first resentful and then wretched for him. I knew Jeremy pretty well. It took a good deal to break down his gay nonchalance. Then I looked at the paper. It had been folded back at the picture page. It wasn't a very good likeness of Hilary; there wasn't a picture of the man at all, but the caption under the photograph read, "Miss Hilary Feltham, whose engagement to Mr. Arthur Dennis of the Foreign Office is announced." And in the gossip column there was a further paragraph, saying that Hilary was the only daughter of the late Sir Percy Feltham and stepdaughter of Lady Nunn.

There was, of course, no reference to Feltham's startling career, and I supposed that most of Hilary's contemporaries had barely left the nursery at the time of the scandal. Dennis had held one or two not very important appointments and was now domiciled in London. The wedding was spoken of as taking place during the summer.

I wondered who this fellow was and what was his attraction for Hilary. I said as much.

Jeremy, replying to the first, said, "Fellow she's going to marry, apparently," and to the second, "Why not ask her?"

I said, "I suppose he's all right, as Eleanor's agreed to the announcement," and Jeremy asked if I could think of anything, short of a young tank, that would stop Hilary once she'd made up her mind.

"Still, Eleanor could have refused to sanction the announcement. Hilary's under twenty-one."

Jeremy asked cynically if she had control of her money, about ten thousand pounds saved by Percy Feltham from the wreck. I said I believed she came into it on her twenty-first birthday, in about a week. Jeremy said, "Well, that may be the answer to your questions."

"I wasn't wondering why any man should want to marry Hilary," I corrected him, and instantly fell to pondering on these possibilities. Ten thousand pounds isn't a great sum, I admit, but Jeremy interrupted to say that to the majority of the world, who weren't bloated capitalists like myself, it was a devil of a lot of money, particularly when you got a girl like Hilary thrown in. "Give them my blessing," he added. "I take it you'll be going down to the Abbey."

"I am. I hoped you'd be coming with me."

"Another time, perhaps. Just at the moment urgent pressure of business at the other side of the world demands my presence."

"You can't go till you've had a drink for luck," I urged.

"I doubt if I have time."

"That's rot. A man with your reputation for absorbing liquor can't go back without putting his lips to a glass. Besides, you won't be able to buy a ticket now. All the shipping offices will be shut for lunch."

It was a poor argument, but it served. I beguiled Jeremy out of the station into the usual tangle of people you always find round Charing Cross. The streets were slippery with the kind of ooze you mostly associate with February; churned-up snow made the going difficult for traffic; half-frozen men in thin overcoats sold two-penny canaries and clockwork mice and bunches of violets in the gutters; the crowds pushed, with the febrile peevishness of anxious, overworked and under-nourished men and women, along the greasy pavements or were forced into the puddles in the gutter. They complained weakly and shrilly of splashed stockings and spats and told one another in high voices that So-and-So seemed to imagine he'd bought the whole ruddy pavement; and refined voices chimed in with, "Really, some people seem to imagine they're better than other people, but if it comes to that, some people's manners…"

Jeremy looked at them without pity. "Did you ever see such a rabble? All of them sick of the lives they live, but too dispirited to try and change them. Why, their very physical make-up gives them away. Look at them—spindly shanks and narrow shoulders. Hullo!" He waved authoritatively at a passing taxi, that a choleric city gentleman had assumed was his, and jumped in. This trivial conquest seemed to hearten him considerably. He said in cheerful tones, as the taxi hooted in a vicious manner at a foolish girl in a blue coat who couldn't make up her mind whether to cross or not, "On my soul, Tony, I'm beginning to savour the delights of my own funeral. I always think a corpse must feel very supercilious by contrast with the crowd. Not," he added, cannoning against me as the taxi skidded at a dangerous corner, "that I expect to take my last journey in anything like such gaudy state."

At the Club old Porteous nodded to me civilly enough, but Jeremy might have been the Prince of Wales.

"'Tisn't often we see you here, sir," he said.

Jeremy agreed. "I daren't, Porteous. It's a grim confession but true. This place has a Medusa-like effect upon me. If I came here more than once in a blue moon I should be turned into stone. Let's see, the youngest member, barring Mr. Keith, who doesn't count," he grinned at me affably, "is eighty-four, isn't he?"

"You've forgotten, Mr. Freyne, sir, that Mr. Summerhayes had a birthday last week."

There were no letters for Jeremy, who hadn't announced his arrival, but I found a batch waiting for me. Two of them were important. One came from Eleanor Nunn, who had been Percy's wife, and the other from a fellow called Philpotts of the Home Office.

Eleanor's ran:

"My dear Tony,

"Will you come down as soon as you get this? A ghastly thing is happening, and I must have your assistance. Hilary needs you, too.

"Eleanor Nunn."

Now Eleanor Nunn isn't a hysterical woman; she doesn't transfigure mole-hills into mountains; she faced with the most amazing courage a position that must have daunted ninety-nine women out of a hundred. And she did that without any one's help, so I knew that if she used a word like ghastly the position was likely to be pretty grim.

By a sinister coincidence Philpotts made use of precisely the same expression. He wrote:

> "My dear Keith,
>
> "I see from a note in one of the papers that you are coming back on s.s. *Andalusia* with a number of notables. If you come and see me as soon as you dock, you may be able to prevent a ghastly thing happening. It concerns your kinsfolk of Feltham Abbey. I can't impress too strongly upon you the fact that there's no time to lose.
>
> "Edward Philpotts."

Now, if Eleanor Nunn is not given to hysteria, Philpotts is one of the coolest-headed men I have ever encountered, and if he spoke of something ghastly happening at the Abbey, you could be fairly sure the position was desperate. Moreover, his letter dovetailed with Eleanor's. Precisely what he wanted me to do I couldn't conjecture, for Heaven knows, I'm no sleuth; and in any case I've heard Philpotts observe more than once that though his departmental experts may sometimes make blunders, God help the country if the amateurs had a free hand. I was still brooding over this problem when I heard Jeremy's voice pitched on a new note, saying, "Hullo, old chap. Anything up? Not bad news, I hope."

Mechanically I handed him Philpott's letter. He glanced at it, said, "Your Feltham relations? What does that mean?"

"I don't know. Eleanor—Ralph—Hilary—any of them."

"Philpotts isn't the man I take him to be if he's losing any sleep on Ralph Feltham's account; that chap was born to be hung. But—if he means Hilary, what the devil has the girl been doing?"

I here remembered Eleanor's letter and showed that to him, too.

"Neither she nor Philpotts exaggerates," I said.

Jeremy was frowning over the second letter. "Is happening," he repeated. "Not going to happen, as Philpotts seems to think. Tony, I think I'm on in this, if I have the chance."

"Thank goodness for that. Anything Philpotts wants requires about three men where he estimates for one. He's the most flattering chap I know, in that way."

"The only difficulty is that I don't quite see how I can invade this chap Nunn's house without an invitation. I've never met the fellow."

"Nor have I, if it comes to that."

"Still, the Abbey was your home during Percy Feltham's lifetime, and Eleanor Nunn is—what?—your step-aunt? She married your uncle."

"My aunt proper, I suppose, though she was so much younger than he that we've always been on ordinary Christian name terms. Anyway, you must come. There's so much room at the Abbey they wouldn't notice half a dozen uninvited guests."

Of course, Jeremy intended to come, so long as there was a ghost of a doubt as to Hilary's wellbeing. So we left the club and went along to the Home Office, where Philpotts saw us at once. My first sight of the man gave me a tremendous sense of shock and made me realise more than anything else the gravity of the position. You don't shake men of his experience very easily, and you certainly don't shake them for trivial mysteries. And unquestionably Philpotts had been badly shaken. I remembered him as a rather bulky man, with a high fresh colour and a bland assured manner. His face to-day was haggard, with an unhealthy yellowish tinge to the skin; you could make out the bones of the skull, and there were hollows in the temples; his eyes alarmed me most. They had an expression, not of fear precisely, but of a kind of bitter despair. Now, when a man of resource and cool courage changes like that, it makes the most casual stop and think. Remember, here was a man who had tackled what had caused the most notable of his contemporaries to quail and own themselves defeated; he wasn't disturbed and he never lost his sleep. But he was disturbed now, and I should not care to hazard how much sleep he had had during the past three months.

I introduced Jeremy, and the haggard face grew eager. "I've heard of you," he said. "You're the fellow that brought off that amazing Turkish stunt four years ago. And there have been some other rather pretty tricks whose responsibility lies at your door, if rumour's to be believed."

Jeremy said at once, "If there's a row in the offing, sir, I'm your man. I'm popularly supposed to have been an Airedale in a previous incarnation."

Philpotts smiled, and said, "You shall hear the story. I warn you, it's rotten enough. Sit down, Keith. You're an invaluable link. I've got to have someone down at the Abbey on an apparently unofficial basis. I've got one official there, but he, of course, may very well be suspect. I want another chap behind the scenes to keep his eyes skinned. Recollect, we're working almost entirely in the dark. Of course, if there are two of you, so much the better. You'd better light your pipes; cigarettes won't meet the case, and cigars make me sleepy rather than thoughtful."

We settled down, and Philpotts began, "It's a long story and a grim one. Also it has us for the moment pretty fairly beat. And when I say that it means a lot. I'll confess immediately that the puzzle is a long way from being solved, at the same time assuring you that that reflects no dishonour on the police force. I'd be the last man to pretend that it's perfect—I know it too well—but it does attain a pitch of competence of which the laity have no conception. It's no use asking the man in the street what he thinks of the C.I.D., for example. You might as well ask an idiot child what it thinks of the Greek alphabet. There's another thing to bear in mind, and that is that the police don't like mysteries. The public can't believe that; they think, if there isn't a mystery afoot, the police force is as restless as a kitten, going round trying to scrape up trouble. It's different for the public; murders and suchlike make amusing and exciting reading and provide an immediate topic of conversation. And the press gets a lot of free copy and generally someone receives an offer to go on the halls for a few weeks until the general excitement has died down. I've met men who've told me solemnly that the average constable would rather strike a criminal than put a year's pay on the Derby winner. They'll tell you it means promotion, kudos, publicity, all the rest of it. Don't believe all that trash. In the ideal state there wouldn't be any crime; we should prevent it. The police realise that, if the rest of the world doesn't."

Then he asked me how long I had been out of the country. I said seven months, and Jeremy, in response to a questioning glance, said two years.

"Then probably you won't have realised what's been going on for the last year or more. Unless you were a very assiduous and observant student of the daily papers, it's unlikely you would have noticed much, anyway. But you may have seen from time to time what's called a crime cycle in process. I mean, a crime of a certain type is committed and almost immediately there follows a number of other crimes, more or less approximating to the first. There are various explanations for this. Some people urge that the mere reading of a sensational murder trial, or a bank hold-up, fires the imagination of the weaker-minded members of the community, the type that generally labours under the burden of an inferiority complex, and these forthwith go out to show they're quite as good as the next man. Unstable people, naturally, are influenced by anything bold and ostentatious. You'll remember for yourself the case of a child murder in the U.S.A. followed by another, with no motive whatsoever, immediately afterwards. And we have cases in English crime, Thorne after Mahon is one you'll both remember, where you can at least argue that if the first hadn't taken place, the second wouldn't. But that doesn't account for all cycles of crime, and it certainly doesn't account for a large number of suicides taking place all over the country among people of every conceivable status and profession, in a variety of ways. At the same time, it's bound to arouse suspicion in the official mind when a wave of suicide sweeps over a country, as it has swept over this one during the past twelve months."

Jeremy here interrupted to recall the cases of various millionaires who had, comparatively recently, committed suicide in different ways, without anyone suggesting a linking-up of the separate occurrences.

"I should be quite ready to say that the first explanation covers that," Philpotts told us. "A man, himself very wealthy but liable, like everyone else, in these chaotic times, to find himself suddenly plunged into ruin, reads of someone, whom he has regarded as perfectly safe, cutting his throat or taking poison or jumping out of an aeroplane, and insensibly his imagination sets to work; he sees the colossal odds against him, realises how easily he may be crushed, allows himself to get worked up to a state that borders on mania, and then if the market does tilt a little against him, it's more than the over-strained nerves can bear. But I didn't mean anything precisely like that, in the present instance. What has actually been happening is that during the last year men and women have been committing suicide with alarming frequency; and it's noticeable that they are practically all people in what we term the superior walks of life. Either they're people of rank and position, or they're people with money. At the various inquests, the verdict might be Death by Misadventure or Suicide while of unsound mind. Well, that kind of thing couldn't go on indefinitely without attracting attention. We instituted inquiries in case after case, tracked down half a hundred apparently irrelevant facts, with the result that we're prepared to say that, in almost every instance, we can show that death was due to deliberate *felo-de-se*. I don't by that mean that all the people concerned were sane at the time of their death; there comes a pitch when anxiety and fear rob a man of his normal balance. But before that ground of fear arose, these people were perfectly normal. Among the people—I speak in confidence, of course—were Sir Vere Poynter, who pitched himself out of a window; Admiral Bennett, who shot himself, accidentally, while cleaning a sports gun (a man who doesn't shoot from one season to another, and they brought it in Accidental Death, God help them); Professor Robinson-Bries, who also shot himself and made no attempt to throw dust in the eyes of the world; Lady Millican, who took an overdose of veronal; that girl of Lady Pamela Raine's, just nineteen, who strangled herself with her own silk stockings and left behind her the most pitiful letters to her father and lover I've ever been compelled to read. Then there were some rather peculiar swimming and boating accidents, accidents that ought never to have happened, and that excited more gossip, until it seemed to us as if all these inexplicable deaths might be connected, but we couldn't find the master-key. We did, however, get more and more evidence to show that there was some mysterious agency at work under the surface, and a precious malignant one at that. The devil of it was we never knew where it would strike or from what direction. I began to be nervous of opening the morning paper. It appeared that in every case mysterious telephone calls had been received shortly before the death. The victim, even if in perfect health and activity up till that time, developed nervousness, irritability, an increased jumpiness whenever the telephone rang or the post arrived, and then came the final act of despair. No question of wilful murder, you understand. The devils were too clever for that. But further inquiries yielded something more. *In practically every case*, money in quite large sums had been raised, sometimes to the man's or woman's ruination."

"Must have been a ticklish job learning that," observed Jeremy, thoughtfully, "what put you on the trail?"

"We first got the idea some weeks after Louisa Millican took veronal. Her husband was a good deal older than she, a man of mixed Spanish and English blood, who had unexpectedly inherited the title. He worshipped the ground she walked on, and was absolutely bowled over by her death. In fact, we kept a sharp eye on him, fearing he might do himself some injury. Of course, there was no thought of suicide at that time. Everyone took the affair for a most regrettable accident. It was several weeks after her death that he was persuaded to go through her belongings. In his wretchedness he swore he would have nothing that had belonged to her in the house; he gave away her clothes, sold her silver and tortoiseshell toilet set, and sent her jewellery to X—— to be valued. His first intimation that there was something queer about the business was when X—— informed him that the diamonds he'd always been so boastful about were extremely good paste. When he'd got over that shock, he had the rest of her jewellery examined, and practically everything was fake. Millican went to the man from whom he'd bought the diamonds, but he couldn't help him. He knew nothing of the business of the false stones. So Millican employed a private inquiry agent and some very disquieting facts came to light. The trail of the original jewellery was unearthed, and every piece accounted for. Louisa Millican had acted with a good deal of discretion. She hadn't had more than one fake made at any one house; but she must have realised thousands, for Millican was a tremendously wealthy man and would have taken the moon out of the sky if she'd asked for it. The affair broke him completely. He didn't know what to think, and he had practically nothing to work on. But even an idiot could realise that she'd been at her wits' end to raise money and hadn't dared apply to him. He hunted down every possible avenue for some clue to the situation, but he didn't learn anything. Of course, he was a devil for jealousy and he'd have strangled her if he'd discovered anything in the way of infidelity or deceit. Anyhow, she'd completely covered her tracks so far as he was concerned, nor could anyone discover who was responsible for bleeding her white. She did, however, serve our purpose, by furnishing a link in our chain of evidence. By this time we were sure that there was some connection between all these mysterious deaths, and that one agency was behind them all, though no doubt it employed various principals, considering how diverse was the position of the men and women in question. And there seemed no reason why these affairs shouldn't continue to multiply, if we couldn't trace this devil to his lair. We'd got, somehow, to stop the rot from the start."

"Blackmail on a tremendous scale? I see. A dirty business."

"Loathsome. And the fiend behind it was as clever as the devil. There were certain facts we could determine. One, at all events, of the principals, probably the chief one, was in society himself, and not only society in the limited sense of the word, but a society covering various phases, political, artistic, professional…"

"Wherever, in short, there was money to be picked up?" That was Jeremy again.

"Precisely. And so far as we could learn, not only money. Do you remember the Abernethy suicide? It isn't three months old. There was an important political appointment to be made, and everyone imagined that an obvious candidate called Probert would get the job. It was so certain that the matter was hardly discussed. Then to the universal amazement Abernethy began to talk about a second choice, a man called Fletcher. We knew all about him. He was a rich chap, competent, brassy, but no imagination, no flair, none of the diplomacy such a job would need. Quite clearly he wasn't the man for the position, and at first people were inclined to laugh at Abernethy. They wouldn't take him seriously. Then, when he didn't join in the fun, they became apprehensive. Wondered if he wasn't fooling them. What did it all mean, then? There must be something behind this, and whatever that was, this appointment mustn't be made. It would ruin the new Governmental policy to have a chap like Fletcher in an important position, and Abernethy, being a tried and normally discreet person, he wouldn't have put the suggestion forward if someone behind him hadn't been pushing him pretty hard. He was looking like a ghost, anyway, and his nerves were rotten. At last a personal friend approached him and told him that whatever pressure was being exerted, he'd got to drop this crazy notion of giving the job to Fletcher. Didn't he realise, he was asked, what his position would be if this went through? Everyone would say he'd been bribed. And Abernethy, having tried at first to bluff it out, broke down and admitted that was about the size of it. This friend didn't get the story out of him at the time, but the whole country knew it soon afterwards. Probert's appointment was duly announced, and within twenty-four hours Abernethy had fallen in front of an Underground train. There was plenty of evidence forthcoming that his health had been rotten, that a doctor had certified him as suffering from vertigo, but no one paid any attention to that when one of the more lurid Sunday papers came out with a yarn about some disreputable piece of crooked dealing in which he had been involved some years earlier. The thing was very cleverly done; it would have been worse than useless to attempt a libel action, and very wisely Abernethy's widow and son allowed the matter to drop. But there was another link in our chain."

"Fletcher, of course, was ready to pay something handsome," reflected Jeremy.

"Of course. They're clever, you see, these crooks, and they know how to play a waiting game. They'd had that information about Abernethy for months. So much we discovered. And they might have made use of it to get something out of him. But he wasn't a rich man, and they decided to keep the information till its value rose, and by waiting for their market they could command a much higher price. Sooner or later they would be in a position to insist on favours, and so they were ready to hold their hands for the time being. Well, admittedly they didn't win, but they were in much the position of the pugilist who gets a bigger purse if he goes down than if he keeps on his feet. There were plenty of people to put two and two together, and if the affair didn't swell his coffers, at least it increased the Spider's prestige, in the sense that it put the fear of God into a number of people who might, in due course, be useful in one capacity or another to the organisation. And when you've got a man into a funk, half your battle's won."

"And you don't know yet who the Spider is?"

"No. We adopted that name for him because of the tremendous risk connected with the work of establishing the pest's identity. You see, there are obviously numbers of cogs in a machine of that size, men and women who very likely know nothing of the value of the information for which they're paid, but who are essential, like tiny parts of any technical machinery. We calculate that the Spider must have two-thirds of the ladies-maids and butlers in society in his pay. And probably numbers of other small fry, secretaries, confidential clerks and the like. The very man who brings in the agents' reports may be a spy. We can't tell. So we have to work very obscurely. Ask any man in the street who the Spider is and he'll tell you vaguely that he's the headpiece of this cat burglar gang that's occupying a lot of space in the press at the moment. It suits our book that they should think that. Our telegrams, etc., come in code."

"And the very man who decodes them may be in the Spider's pay?"

"Only four people understand that code. Myself, Detective-Inspector Horsley of the C.I.D., my understudy here, a man called Atkinson, and a fellow from the Foreign Office who's helping us in this case, a chap called Dennis."

"Arthur Dennis!"

"That's the man. Know him?"

"By repute," said Jeremy guardedly.

"He's a clever chap, and he's in this with us because we believe there may be foreigners mixed up with the gang. He did secret service during the war, did Dennis, and he may be deuced useful to us. He's down at Feltham now."

"Does Feltham come into this?"

"Of course it does. I told Keith so in my letter."

"Which of them is being threatened?"

"According to our information, it's the girl, Hilary Feltham. Why, I couldn't tell you."

I put in that she would inherit this ten thousand pounds from her father in the course of the next week or two, and that might attract some scamp.

"But what hold has he got over her?" Jeremy asked. "I don't exactly see Hilary lying down and allowing herself to be blackmailed.

She's much more likely to hit the fellow over the head and tell him to do his bloodiest."

I agreed with him there. I knew Hilary pretty well; as a youngster I'd seen her take any number of falls hunting, and I never remember her either bawling or going home before the kill.

"Are you sure it isn't Lady Nunn?" Jeremy urged. "She'd be a splendid person to get your claws into. She's got a rich husband, an extremely rich husband, I gather. Of course, I don't know what they could get her on. There was the Percy Feltham scandal, but they hardly can be resurrecting that at this time of day."

"We don't know what their hold is," Philpotts confessed. "This young woman may have been indiscreet—there's a lot of foolish behaviour in society these days…"

"Still, damn it all!" Jeremy protested. "I haven't seen the girl for two or three years certainly, but mere indiscretion wouldn't land her in this sort of mess."

It was queer, certainly, to think of Hilary being afraid of anyone. Still, there was Eleanor's letter, and that mentioned her, too.

"Does our dear friend, Ralph Feltham, come into this?" Jeremy asked. "It sounds uncommonly like his line of country."

"I should think most probably," Philpotts agreed, "but Dennis will be able to tell you more about that. He's been down there three or four days, smelling out the country. All I can say is that we do definitely know that the Spider is at work at Feltham. And for heaven's sake, don't make the colossal blunder of under-estimating the power of the gang. You remember my telling you about Lady Millican's jewels? Well, after that, we got into touch with various prominent jewellers and money-lenders, and though, of course, we haven't been furnished with names, we have been assured that a tremendous amount of valuable jewellery is being sold, and paste being employed to disguise the fact, while large sums of money are being raised, through money-lenders, by numbers of people prominent in society. It's a rich time for them, believe me. I could name a dozen men who have never been in a bad scrape in their lives, and to whom the word debt has been practically unknown, who're up against it now, and may be bankrupted and ruined at any moment. And in quite half those cases I'm convinced we have the Spider to thank for the position. It's astonishing, if you come to examine family history, how often the most correct men have skeletons, for which they themselves are not responsible, tucked away in their cupboards. The Spider has made it his business to discover those skeletons and threatens to exhibit them. The ancient Church was right when she named pride the most deadly of the sins; but for pride, men like the Spider would have to go out of business. It's the wound to family pride, not anything personal, that makes that scoundrel a rich man."

"Quite," Jeremy agreed. "Well, I suppose we'd better be off."

"And at once. You may be in time to save another death."

"Another? Whose?"

"Arthur Dennis's."

We were both surprised and showed it. "Dennis? But why that man? Because he's dangerous?"

"He's doubly dangerous. He's in this officially, on our account, and privately, on his own, because he's engaged to this girl, though, if you only landed this morning, you perhaps hadn't heard of the engagement."

"Oh, we'd heard of that. And let me assure you that it won't last long."

"That's what we're afraid of."

"We?"

"The whole Department, and Dennis in particular."

Jeremy grinned. "One man's meat," he murmured. "Ah well. I shall be interested to know what Hilary has done to get into this mess. Unless," he added, the thought striking him, "they're trying to get her on this Percy-Feltham affair."

"Why should they go for her?" Philpotts asked.

"She was Feltham's daughter, so she's involved, just as Feltham's wife was. She has this ten thousand pounds coming in; she's reckless, and is quite capable of refusing to treat with anyone."

"Telling them to do their bloodiest," quoted Philpotts, "without in the least realising what their bloodiest is... Well, it may be that." But he sounded doubtful. So was I.

"Surely that's very ancient history," I said.

"Unless they've produced definite proof. The affair was never allowed to become public. And it would be a tremendous scoop for the papers. This is the age for raking over the muck-heaps of dead men's shortcomings."

"It may be," Jeremy agreed, "but they won't get any proof in this case, because there is none. Feltham was no more guilty than you or I."

"You can prove that?"

"No. It's a matter of common sense, that's all. The man wasn't capable of treachery. Besides, what motive had he? He was a comparatively rich man, rich enough to satisfy himself anyway. The defence took a great deal of money, I know, or he'd have left Hilary a great deal better off."

"Even rich men do incredible things for the sake of getting more money. It acts on them like a disease."

"Not men like Percy Feltham. He didn't care two straws about money. In himself, he was absolutely detached from all the material side of success. He wanted to succeed, because he felt he owed it to himself to succeed. But the satisfaction was on the spiritual, not the material, plane. And he wouldn't have sold official secrets because to his mind that would imply the final degradation; it would make no difference to him whether he was found out or not. I don't believe that man ever cared a rap what people thought."

"And yet he took his life when the crash came?"

"It was that or publicity. And I believe he thought it was just, in a peculiar sort of way. He'd regard death as the penalty life—or his own spirit—exacted from him for his failure. Oh, yes, he failed. He didn't sell State secrets during his tenure of office, but the secrets were sold, and officially and morally he knew himself responsible. And his code was a severe one."

We were all silent for a minute, thinking of that stiff, proud, shy man, whose life had collapsed so ignobly more than a dozen years before. He had been my guardian, but I had never felt I knew him, and I envied Jeremy that power of his of summing up men.

That was all Philpotts could tell us, except that we must realise that whatever happened we couldn't claim any sort of official protection; we might get caught by the Spider ourselves, or mauled about or put out of the way, and it was entirely our own affair. Jeremy and I agreed, he with astounding cheerfulness.

"It ought to be a bit of a lark," he said, "seeing this chap must be a bit of a sleuth himself."

I stared at him; already he was relegating Hilary and Hilary's peril to the second place in his mind. The adventure came first, and I thought it would always be like that, and wondered whether Hilary would care, when she found out. Or whether she wasn't of the same calibre herself, in which case they'd make an excellent couple.

"And remember you have got Dennis with you," Philpotts wound up, in much the same tone as one of the Higher Powers might have used to Tobias, saying, "Remember, you have got your angel."

"Oh, we shan't forget Dennis," Jeremy assured him politely.

"There ought to be someone always keeping an eye on Miss Feltham, you see."

"What else did Heaven cast Dennis for?"

"He does happen to be rather interested in clearing up the mystery and getting this vile persecution stopped."

"A man in love ought to realise his limitations."

"And—er—you?" hinted Philpotts, delicately.

"I have them, of course," Jeremy agreed, "but my sight isn't good enough for me to recognise them at that distance." We all laughed and Jeremy went on, "Do we report to you—or what?"

Philpotts said, "You're forgetting Dennis already."

"True, true. Well, good-bye, sir. You'll hear of us through him, presumably."

"If anyone had ever told me I'd be meekly reporting to a civil servant, I'd have told him I'd see him damned first," Jeremy observed as we came away. "However, I daresay we shall manage to get a lot of fun, even with him cluttering up the ground." He brooded for a moment, then said, "Official securities, indeed. To hell with the lot. I know the kind things the government does to protect you against yourself. You mustn't drink except between certain hours because it's bad for your health; and you mustn't buy your young woman candy after certain hours, presumably because it's bad for hers. Oh, a murrain on all Governments, say I. One moment to drink our jolly good health and then we're off."

CHAPTER III

I

WHEN WE CAME OUT THE FOG HAD DEEPENED CONSIDER-ably. The sky was invisible above the housetops. The city was wrapped in a wet grey blanket. Jeremy regarded it with expert eyes.

"Going to be a nice run," he observed cheerfully. "No time to waste."

"The next train goes at 3.2," I told him. "We've time for lunch first."

"To-morrow, perhaps," he agreed.

"To-morrow be blowed. I'm talking about to-day. If you propose to go down to Feltham Abbey, as I imagine you do, the only train is the 3.2. There's a 1.57 to Rockingham, certainly, but that's a slow train, involving a change, and we shouldn't get in till about seven. Besides, Rockingham's the last place on earth you'd choose to get stranded. There's never a car to be had, and anyhow there wouldn't be on a day like this; and if you're lucky, you may get a lift in a tradesman's cart. I once crawled over to Feltham like that, in my salad days, before I knew the railway line quite so well as I do now. Of course, you might telegraph to the house for a car, but as they all belong to Nunn, whom neither of us has met, I should think even you might think twice about it."

Jeremy said kindly, "Let me point out two or three facts that should be obvious even to a half-wit. One, that Nunn doesn't own every car on the face of the earth. Two, that if this fog gets any worse your 3.2 won't run. Three, that I don't care for my prospective wife to be engaged to any other man an instant longer than is absolutely necessary. Four, that these fiends are after Hilary."

"Are you proposing to fly, then?"

"Don't be more of a fool than the Lord made you. No. Drive, of course. Where's the nearest garage?"

He wasn't asking me, but a convenient policeman, who produced a garage as obligingly as if it had been a match.

"No one's going to drive you a hundred and fifty miles on an afternoon like this," I protested. "The 3.2 is an express. It gets you down at six, so far as I remember. Do show a little sense."

Jeremy retorted pleasantly, "Take your express and go to hell in it. What do you suppose I'm going to do while Hilary, the future Mrs. Freyne, mark you, is mauled by some cad in the Civil Service? It's bad enough she should ever be engaged to him at all. It's intolerable that she should remain so an instant longer than I can prevent."

He waved away the first car offered him, on the ground that it would suit him excellently when he was being driven to the scaffold, and would presumably wish to prolong his journey, and chartered a low, wicked-looking racer that he proposed to drive himself.

"You'll never find the way," I warned him. "They've built a new by-pass since you were down here."

"Then for Heaven's sake, stop behaving like a maiden aunt at a funeral and get in beside me. You'll be useful to point out the way, if nothing else."

And so I got in beside Jeremy, wearing the world's worst Burberry, and we started. I was devoutly thankful I had no dependants when I realised the pace at which Jeremy proposed to take us to Feltham.

"Now," he said cheerfully, narrowly avoiding murder and *felo-de-se* as he rounded a corner on two wheels, "tell me something about the household. Who's Nunn?"

"I only know the fellow by reputation. He's what's called a self-made man. He founded the Nunn Insurance Company. You must have heard of the Nunn Better Policy."

"No insurance company will take me on," said Jeremy, complacently. "I'm too much of a risk. Well, is this chap likely to be concerned in the plot?"

"I shouldn't think so."

"Well, if you've never met him, you're in no position to judge. We don't really know that his teeming millions come from Insurance. They may come from bleeding poor sinners white."

"He'd hardly be bleeding his own wife," I objected. "And what does he stand to gain out of Hilary?"

"That's one of the things we've yet to discover. How long has he been married? I take it, he knew the Percy-Feltham story?"

"I don't see how he could not know it. Everyone knew."

"Not everyone. I admit I developed a certain respect for the Powers That Be when I realised how they can keep secrets if necessary. Oh, I grant you a lot of people knew, but the general public didn't. I doubt if they even realised that our men were walking into ambushes through the treachery of one of our own side. When Feltham shot himself, it was put down to nerve strain by most people. By the way, what did they prove? I wasn't in England at the time."

"Nor was I."

"Still, Feltham was your guardian, and you used to spend your holidays at the Abbey. You must have known Eleanor Feltham pretty well."

"I'll tell you all I know. You'd met Feltham yourself, hadn't you? You know the sort of chap he was, grim, morose, clever as paint and as conscientious as an archangel. But he wasn't the sort of man who makes friends very easily; he had brain but no wit, intelligence but no sparkle. Give him a tough job to do and he'd get his teeth into it and grind out a solution, but he'd put it together with so little imagination that it would lose half its force. It wasn't till after his first wife died, and he found himself stranded with Hilary, a brat of about three, that he ran across Eleanor. People said it was a bit of luck for her. Her father was Lord S—— but they hadn't a penny to their names, and she was really wasting her time with him. She was everything to Percy and the child. From the beginning she overhauled his speeches, put in the light touches that made people sit up and take notice, and then ask themselves what had happened to the fellow; she entertained charmingly, she had a manner that would entice a hippopotamus out of its pond on a hot day. Of course, she was only half Feltham's age, but that didn't seem to matter. Their relationship appeared to be chiefly on the intellectual plane; Feltham was always more absorbed in facts than in people, a farouche sort of chap—you remember. But he was devoted to her, and was very generous. The uncharitable said she'd married him for his money, because the Metcalfes had a very old-fashioned little establishment in Edwardes Square, and all Eleanor's frocks had to last two seasons. Well, she was young and handsome and popular. She had a bad time in 1916 when her baby was born and died when it was a month old. She'd wanted children; but she had Hilary, who was five then, a jolly affectionate brat, and most people thought she'd done very well for herself. She still worked hand and glove with Feltham, and put in a lot of war work as well. That year he got a confidential appointment at the War Office, and was at it about eighteen hours a day. He wasn't a diplomatist by nature, and Eleanor stepped in more than once when his rather high-handed manner lost him his man. There was a row with Sir Rupert Horne, for example, at a time when it was rather important to keep on the right side of the man. And Eleanor stepped in there, and won the fellow over. It was a knack of hers. They said of her that she could make even a list of statistics absorbing, and she talked to Horne on his own subject till he was ready to eat out of her hand. And then Cleghorne came on the scene. He was a queer chap, too, as brilliant as Eleanor, and with more influence. It was necessary to get him in on Feltham's side, and it wasn't easy to secure him. Percy, you see, was in the Coalition Government, and his position would be enormously strengthened if he could get Cleghorne as an ally. Cleghorne was apt to be suspicious; they said there was more than a touch of jealousy in his attitude. Outwardly he announced that he distrusted Feltham's tactics. However, when things were at a deadlock, Eleanor threw herself into the breach, and after a toughish struggle, she won. Cleghorne came in and everyone congratulated Feltham on his tact. That was November, 1917. For several months everything went well. Then rumours started to get about, disquieting rumours. In fact, at first they seemed so unlikely that they were laughed at. Then they were repeated and people remained grave, and at last here and there men spoke openly. They said that information was leaking out through some official in the know, with the result that our moves on the Western Front were counteracted as they were made, by the other side. There was a gigantic scandal in the spring of 1918, when half a regiment was cut to pieces, and that put the lid on things. They started an official inquiry. It was too late now to murmur reassuringly about coincidences and inconsiderable losses, when surprise attacks at dawn were countered by solid massed battalions, and our casualty lists were like a butcher's shop. One of these more scurrilous and unprincipled weeklies came out with a demand to Name the Spies, and though they didn't actually commit themselves to names on their own account, their opinions were pretty thinly veiled. Well, the inquiry began and the results were pretty grim. It was Cleghorne. He'd ratted. Rumour said he got colossal sums for his information. So much was proved beyond a doubt. And his disappearance clinched the matter."

"What happened to him?" Jeremy asked keenly.

"He was never discovered. Some people will tell you that he got away to Austria—that was a current rumour for a long time—but there are others who say he was one of a number of refugees whose unrecognisable bodies were found several months later in one of the German forests some miles from the fighting line. Anyway, it wasn't Cleghorne who bore the real brunt of the affair. Obviously the Government had got to find a presentable scapegoat. They couldn't say airily, 'Yes, we know who did it, but unfortunately he's got away.' So they said that Cleghorne couldn't have been responsible for all the treachery. They decided there were some things he wouldn't have known, and if he had known them, the responsibility was Feltham's, for passing on information he should have kept to himself. The affair for him was calamitous. It was the end of his career, and his career was his life. Even Eleanor was little more than a pawn in his scheme, though he was fond enough of her in his own way. Hilary as a little girl adored him, and I believe she won't let anyone mention his name now. She was only seven, you see, when the crash came, but she was intelligent, not to say precocious, having been so much with her elders. She and Eleanor had a ghastly time. Feltham took the best way out; I suppose they gave him that last chance. After all, they wouldn't want an open scandal, if they could help it, and when the rumour circulated that he'd been overworked, and the strain and the responsibility for young lives had affected his mind, they allowed it to rest at that."

"And what happened to the others? How did his widow collect her millionaire?"

"She went to work for herself and Hilary. She hadn't any money, and what Feltham had left, about ten thousand pounds, was tied up for the child. She wasn't to touch it till she was twenty-one. Of course, there was the income, but Eleanor never touched that for herself. It was a difficult position, because fingers were still pointed at them both. She couldn't send Hilary to school straight away, so she got her a governess, and herself found a job in Nunn's office. I told you statistics were among her delights, and pretty soon her work attracted attention. After 1918 people began to forget the scandal, and Hilary went to school like some ordinary child, and Eleanor went up a peg or two in the office."

"How much does Hilary know of all this?"

"No one is quite sure. She asked me, the first time I saw her after her father's death, if it was true that people only killed themselves if they'd done wrong and were afraid to live. I got out of it as best I could, but that shows you the trend of her thought. When I tried to get back to the subject, she said quite definitely that she didn't want to talk about her father. I asked Eleanor, but she hadn't got any more out of her than I did, except that she said passionately that she loved her father whatever he'd done. I've never heard her mention him since. Eleanor was distraught. She said she'd got Cleghorne in, and without her there would have been none of this mess. And after that she didn't discuss the matter, either. In 1924 I heard she was going to marry Nunn. No, he wasn't a widower, he'd been too busy to think of the domestic side of life, and apparently had been looked after by a widowed sister."

"And I suppose she was thrust into a Decayed Gentlewomen's Hostel?"

"Oh, no. He has, as Eleanor wrote to me, quite Asiatic notions of family responsibility. I don't know whether this woman has always lived with them, but she's with them now, and has been for a long time."

"I shouldn't myself call Lady Nunn fortunate in either of her marriages," commented Jeremy, grimly. "However, I daresay the unfortunate lady herself doesn't trouble them much. She's probably a mousey shrinking little creature, who yearns for the cosy security of Brixton or Tooting Bec. And now, where does Ralph come in?"

"Not at the Abbey at all."

"Not? It's his house, though."

"He's only the landlord at the moment, and his tenant has forbidden him to call. A galling position for Ralph, I grant you, particularly as I believe he honestly does care about the place. He's got a little house in the neighbourhood, hardly more than a shooting-box, I believe. Of course, Ralph's record is patchy to say the least of it. There's queer blood in that family. I've never been among the crowd that thought Feltham guilty, but he was an odd fish himself. Too much blue-blooded marrying, if you ask me. If one of the Felthams had got himself tied up with a bouncing village wench, the stock would have notably improved. As it is, it's hopelessly degenerate. You've only got to take Ralph to show you that, and even Percy—you know, he had a very odd manner and appearance at times."

"Barmy?" asked Jeremy, pleasantly.

"I shouldn't have been surprised if it had ended something like that."

"H'm. Nice little Job's comforter you are. Have you any theories where Hilary's concerned?"

"Hilary, I must say, seems absolutely normal. I hardly knew her mother, but perhaps she's responsible."

"I'm glad you admit Hilary isn't likely to end her days in a mental sanatorium. I should hate to end my life as one of Lord Buckmaster's hard cases. What about Ralph and Hilary? Do they ever meet?"

"I shouldn't think so. They wouldn't have much in common."

Jeremy surprised me by saying, "Well, I don't know about that. Hilary's all right, as you say, but she's got the same strain of recklessness in her that Ralph has. She wouldn't be party to this Spider affair, of course, but she's like a pal of mine who spent a year after the war blackmailing profiteers and giving the money to some service fund. You couldn't make him see he'd done anything indefensible. And Hilary would be in the same boat. When she's married to me, I may be able to drill a little sense into her. Is that the lot?"

"Except the servants."

"I doubt if any of them would be implicated, except as links. Have they been there long?"

"Hook was Feltham's butler, and he returned to Eleanor after her second marriage. There's an elderly housekeeper who has been with Nunn for some time. I don't know about the rest."

"On the face of it, it does look as though Ralph was implicated, though he isn't in this as a one-man show. He hasn't got enough imagination to organise anything on this scale, but he's quite conscienceless and would be an excellent partner. He's knocked about a lot, knows the world from the underside better than most, and has no reputation to lose. And he's not in the least likely to draw the line at blackmail, when he hasn't drawn it at murder."

"That was never proved. In fact, he produced an alibi."

"A dozen, I believe. But that doesn't alter the position. By Jove, though, he must have given that woman a run for her money. Cleopatra they called her, but those in the know say that even Cleopatra didn't maintain the state this mysterious demi-mondaine was accustomed to. I wonder what she saw in Ralph—a new type, perhaps. She'd had lovers enough, heaven knows. And then, after all that splendour, to be found strangled with one of her own gold chains in a hotel bedroom. Yes, I know it was a hotel de luxe, but I shouldn't imagine it made much difference what kind of room you died in, if you had to die, particularly in that very brutal way. In a sense, the affair was proved up to the hilt against Ralph. He'd been with her within a few hours of her death, there'd been a hell of a quarrel over some other fellow in the hotel, he disappeared early that morning. Everything pointed to him. Of course, he showed astounding wisdom in returning as soon as the news of the murder was broadcast, and he came back with his fists full of alibis. Did you notice, though, they were all the kinds of alibis you could buy? Porters and newsvendors and keepers of coffee-stalls. He got off all right. But he did it. Oh, he did it. The devil of it is that a man who can work that kind of bluff wouldn't care what he did to anyone. I'm thinking of Hilary now... She's in danger... I know. Talk of the devil in practically every big city in the world, and you're soon hearing of Ralph Feltham. He knows that's his reputation, and he glories in it. And this job of nosing in other men's dustbins would suit him down to the ground. Offal's his proper meat. He's the sort of fellow who talks of selling his sword, but I wouldn't mind betting he'd sell it simultaneously to both sides. They say he even had a bet about that Victoria Cross he got. The question is, who else might be in it?"

"We don't know that anyone else at Feltham is concerned. And if Ralph is involved, I fancy you'll find the other fellow one of these correct, solid, meticulous chaps who might be shoved into the British Museum as typical of the middle-class prosperity of their time. By the way, where the devil are we?"

It had just occurred to me that such of the road as I could distinguish through the heavy wet mist was unfamiliar. Also I could hear water running near by. One is liable, of course, to hear all manner of strange noises in a fog, but this grew momentarily so loud that I became convinced we were approaching a weir. I said as much to Jeremy.

"Damn you!" he said, politely. "I thought the sole reason for your being here at all was to see we didn't miss the road."

We stopped the car at the first house we came to, and he got out and asked the way. It was some time before we could make ourselves clear. Then it appeared that we had taken a wrong turning some time back, and were five-and-twenty miles off our road. We had just got back to it, travelling at not more than twenty miles an hour (any driver less reckless than Jeremy would have slowed to half that pace, considering the weather) when a back tyre punctured. Jeremy displayed commendable patience. When I observed bitterly that I'd as soon try to find Feltham in this fog as plough over the Sahara, he only said, "You wouldn't talk in that loose way if you'd ever gone astray in the Sahara. Bring one of the headlights round here, will you? This'll be a matter of twenty minutes."

In point of fact, it took forty-five. Meanwhile we argued points of common law. Jeremy said unexpectedly, "You know, Tony, I've always loathed the name Arthur. I don't know why, specially. Little Arthur's England, perhaps. One of the crosses of my childhood. The Princes in the Tower, all got up in black velvet tights, with gold fillets round their innocent brows. I wonder what Hilary sees in him. I'm sure he's a poop."

"Because he's called Arthur?"

"Not altogether. I have—intuitions. A lady of my acquaintance once told me she'd never met any man with such a feminine outlook. Such subtlety, such delicacy, such swift intuition. It wasn't for some time that I discovered she was trying to touch me for her dressmaker's bill. Those were the days when I was very young. However, if Arthur isn't a poop, he's probably a rotter."

"And Hilary's marrying him to reform him?"

Jeremy grinned. "You betray your bachelordom with every word you speak. Seriously, though, Tony, it's ghastly to think that we might spot the Spider and the law of the land doesn't give us the right to squash it."

He lay down abruptly, peering into the vitals of the car, and leaving the punctured tyre on the misty road. I began to explain the principles of common law, Jeremy's voice in argument coming to me muffled from beneath the car. Presently he emerged and continued work on the tyre, arguing all the time, sometimes kneeling, sometimes squatting on the wet road, the fog lying in swathes all about us. Jeremy's memory was amazing. He would refute my most obvious arguments with references to cases I had clean forgotten or had never read. We admitted certain weaknesses and deplored certain judgments; we discussed the possibility of corruption and the obvious inconsistencies of certain parallel cases occurring in different strata of society. On the whole, I didn't come out of it so well as he did. He had the freedom of the independent, the man who is fettered by no creed or following, while I was frequently in the position of the theologian, compelled to defend what he cannot hope to explain lucidly to an antagonist. And I had, too, a sense of disloyalty in yielding, as I often did, to Jeremy's arguments. But, hearing his brilliant, unhesitating parry and thrust, I thought Philpotts was lucky to get such a man on his side.

Our lengthy detour, plus the puncture, had wasted nearly three hours; it was now after five, the hour at which we had intended to arrive. Now we had to go slow along a road with which neither of us was really familiar. Within an hour we had a second breakdown. This was at a peculiarly desolate spot, in the heart of the pitiless moors Hilary loved. We could see them under the curtain of the fog, dripping and impenetrable. I shivered.

"Fancy getting lost here on a night like this! They go on for miles, you know."

"Revolting thoughts you have. Come on. What's the time?"

I said it was about six. Our express had probably reached Feltham by this time, though I didn't make this observation aloud. The evening grew bitterly cold. A sharp wind now and again pierced the volume of fog. As we turned the next corner, Jeremy abruptly stopped the car.

"What's the matter?" I felt a third calamity would be intolerable.

"I thought I heard footsteps. Listen!" He shut off the engine, and we sat, uncomfortably alert, in the dank gloom. Once I thought I heard something that might have been a foot stumbling over roots of heather, but the sound was not repeated, and I decided it was probably due to an over-sensitive imagination.

Jeremy seemed rather put out. "I'll swear there was some one. But if so, where the devil has he got to? He hasn't fallen; we should have heard the crash. Did he hear us and stop dead till we'd gone on? There isn't a cottage or any kind of shelter here where he could conceal himself."

He began to shout but nothing came back, except the faint echo of his voice over those unfriendly miles of moor. The place to an imaginative cold and hungry man seemed definitely inimical; to a superstitious mind, it might have been haunted by all manner of obscene night-fears. As for more concrete horrors, there might have been half a dozen murders going on within as many yards. It reminded me of various things; of the beginning of *Great Expectations*, of parts of *Wuthering Heights*, and sometimes of Flannan Isle, not merely something ghastly, but something beyond human understanding. Jeremy stopped shouting and began to whistle. Then he produced a powerful electric torch and shot the beam over the nearest path and heather clump.

"Have you any idea, Tony, whereabouts we are?"

"None," I confessed.

"Oh, well." He restored the torch to his pocket. "Possibly it's of no consequence. Philosophers tell us nothing is of any consequence really. But, like the police, I don't like mysteries. And I can't understand why a footstep should suddenly be heard on such a night, miles from anywhere, and stop so abruptly when its owner hears a car coming."

"A tramp," I suggested.

"A tramp would have come up and asked for money or a lift—money anyway."

"A man flying from justice?" I spoke jestingly. But in truth the eerie quality of the atmosphere was beginning to tell on me also, and none of the circus tricks of melodrama would have astounded me then—the sudden bright eyes peering out of darkness, piercing shrieks, cold hands on my neck, voices in my ear.

Jeremy settled back in his seat and drove on. We drove for another half-hour and then suddenly the fog began to lift. I knew at once where we were. We seemed to have travelled in a circle, so that when we heard that footstep we couldn't have been very far from Ravensend. At twenty minutes to eight we sighted the rather obscure yet beautiful house of the Felthams, standing with a gracious aloofness in its modest grounds. The house has been rebuilt twice in the last four hundred years, and its appearance is deceptive. It looks a rather small, wandering country mansion, but it has a great deal of space within. The last Feltham to build it had inherited sober Puritan blood. When someone remonstrated with him for the simplicity and lack of ostentation of his design, he replied coldly, "I am not building a house for roisterers and their trulls; I am building a house for a gentleman of leisure and his sons."

2

Our welcome was peculiar. The enormous front door of the Abbey stood wide open. Lights blazed in every room. There was a general atmosphere of flurry and dismay. We rang ceremoniously, but nothing happened; we rang again and a scared-looking footman came hastily into the hall. When he saw us, his face changed. He said quickly, "I beg your pardon, sir. You have news?"

Completely mystified, I said I hadn't, and asked for Eleanor. The fellow looked embarrassed, but took us into a room to the left of the hall. Here we waited for some time. I was oppressed and silent; the memory of that invisible step on the moor remained with me, as though it were knit up with this extra-ordinary arrival.

"Did they know you were coming?" asked Jeremy at last.

"I wired from town. I can't think what's happened."

"It's quite obvious what's happened. Someone or something is lost. You don't leave lights on and doors open unless you want to guide someone home. I want to know who it is."

We waited a little longer, and then the door was flung open and a lady came in. She was middle-aged, with a Victorian figure and an Alexandra fringe. I couldn't at first place her. She seemed breathless with excitement and apologies, turning quickly from one to the other of us.

"I'm so sorry. Have you been waiting long? That stupid man's only just told me. The whole staff is quite demoralised. Let me see, do I know who you are?"

"My name is Keith," I told her. "I'm a kind of connection by marriage with Eleanor. And this is Mr. Freyne."

She barely touched my hand but clung eagerly to Jeremy's. "And you're friends of James?"

I placed her then. She was the widowed sister, of course, but anything less like our expectations you couldn't conceive. Eleanor was brilliant, witty and well-bred; this woman was none of these things, and yet the force of her personality was so strong that it simply didn't matter. I don't know how I can convey her attraction at all adequately. She had nothing approaching beauty or even prettiness; she was short and plump at a time when women were required to be slender and erect. She hadn't, as the saying goes, got a feature in her face; her voice alternated between a delighted squeak and a deep excited bass. She wore the shabbiest clothes imaginable, and colour schemes were unknown to her; she had not even the merit of a short upper lip or a graceful carriage. Yet at a first meeting none of these disadvantages seemed to count. There was about her an inextinguishable charm. Without effort she took handsome young men away from their pretty companions; she walked into a shop and there was a buzz to serve her; she said outrageous things so naturally as to preclude all possibility of affectation. There was some irresistible enchantment about her; she always seemed to be bubbling up at the edge of a miracle. And you felt that at sight; you could no more ignore that quality of hers than you could forget to notice a fire on a cold day or moonlight in a black night.

I was answering her question. I said I was afraid we didn't know James at all, but that the Abbey had been my home years ago, and that Eleanor was a kind of connection by marriage, so that in a sense I had looked upon the house as my headquarters.

"And a very inconvenient house, too," cried the lady, vigorously. "But, of course, it's aristocratic. I've noticed the aristocracy like houses to be inconvenient; no plumbing, if possible, stairs where you don't expect them, and ceilings so low you bang your head every time you stand up. People like James and me—middle-class people, I mean—we like bathrooms and electric fires and windows that shut up to the top, and proper lights—need them, I suppose, to make up for other things. It's just a question of which appeals to you most." She rattled along happily, delighting us both. Then she pulled herself up with a start. "But I'm forgetting—you don't know who I am, do you? My name's Ross, Meriel Ross, and I'm James's sister. It's an easy name to remember, isn't it? That's one of the reasons why I chose it."

"Chose it?" murmured Jeremy, as fascinated as I was.

"Yes. You don't need to spell it on the telephone. Not that I used a telephone when I was Bertie's wife. Women didn't then. They walked to the station with their husbands in the morning, and bought the day's dinner at the butcher's and fetched it home in a string bag. And they saw to it they weren't given equal shares of fat and lean. Butchers had to mind their p's and q's when I was a young wife. Of course, everything's different now. Things come out of tins and cartons, and for all you know your inside's being poisoned seven days a week by the leavings off other people's plates. Like this bottled mustard you get. Oh, and there was another reason—besides the one that Bertie suited me, of course. I never meant to be one of these ticketed widows and there was nothing in the least noticeable about darling Bertie. D'you know what I mean? I wasn't going to have people saying of me, 'Who's that? Oh, don't you know? That's Sir Blank Blank's widow. Wonderful man, wasn't he? Such a brain! Such energy! Such invention! Such foresight! Such judgment! Such courage! Such knowledge! Such enterprise! Such strategical powers!' No, thank you. I mean to be myself. 'Meriel Ross? Oh, my dear, you must know her. She's the woman who wears those awful hats. Gets them at a Jumble Sale, if you ask me.' Now, that's a reputation. The other's an echo." She smiled enchantingly at both of us. "And now," she invited, "do tell me what you think of this one. Be quite, quite candid."

I glanced up and was promptly smitten dumb with horror. I know very little about hats and, to judge from his remarks about the purple felt, so does Jeremy. But I knew instantly I had never seen anything quite so ghastly as the edifice perched on Mrs. Ross's fair fuzzy head.

"Don't compare it with the fashions of the day," she warned us, swaying this way and that so that no aspect of the revolting creation should escape us. "A woman of my age can't be bothered whether women are wearing things like a coal-scuttle or a penny bun jammed on the back of the head. But viewed as an original creation, in short, as a hat?"

I stared, fascinated by its hideousness. It was a tall affair of pale-coloured straw (burnt straw, Eleanor assured me afterwards), trimmed with yards of lace and a drove of plush butterflies, and where there wasn't a butterfly there was a velvet bow.

It rode high like a defiant and nightmare ship on the fair hair that was drawn Alexandra-fashion over the forehead. But nothing defeats Jeremy for more than an instant, not even such a hat as that one.

"It is perfect." He pronounced judgment without the quiver of an eyelash, revolving slowly in the manner of a master milliner. "Ah, Moddom, believe me, it is a dream, an inspiration. There is not another woman in England who could wear such a hat. It is a hat of personality, of chic. It is bold, it has character." He threw up his hands in a Gallic gesture. "One perceives that Moddom is an artist."

"You dear!" exclaimed Mrs. Ross, impulsively. For a delighted moment I thought she was going to kiss Jeremy. I think he rather hoped she would.

She had by this time drawn us into the smoking-room, and was mixing us cocktails.

"Do tell me what you've come down for," she coaxed us, but she wasn't interested in me.

"To put a stop to this ridiculous engagement of Hilary's," said Jeremy, coolly.

"You're going to stop it?"

"Certainly. I've other plans for her."

Mrs. Ross emitted a wail of anguish. "You're not trying to tell me you've come down here to bite the dust at her feet, too? It's too frightful. Every personable man in the place running after that chit. As if she wasn't spoilt enough as it is. I should like to be her mother for just one night. Just one night. Why, you might as well live in a monastery—oh, a nunnery, if that's what I mean—if you tell me you're going out to look for her, too, I shall burst into tears. Even James has gone off on one of these personally-conducted tours through the heather. And Eleanor's gone with him. She'll be a perfect wreck to-morrow."

"What's happened to Hilary?"

"She's disappeared. Well, why not let her? As a matter of fact, I can't think what they're making all this fuss about. Hilary never did notice if she was within an hour or two of the right time for dinner. It's her mother's fault, I understand. She was meant to be a valentine, but she didn't arrive till six the next morning, and I suppose the bad habit has stuck."

"And she's lost? On the moors? On a night like this?"

"Everyone seems to think so."

Jeremy looked about him as if he were inwardly collecting kit. Mrs. Ross saw that glance. "You're not a kind of glorified police-man, too, are you? We've had enough of them."

"Policemen?"

"Yes. All over the house. Asking the most absurd questions over and over again. Does anyone know any reason why she should want to be out at such a time? As if, if we knew that, we should want their help. Breathing ponderously down your neck and going through all the questions in Mrs. Magnus."

"Are there many of them?"

"There seem to be dozens, but of course it might be the same one all the time popping up all over the place. I did notice a resemblance, I must admit."

"If they've got the police in, isn't it pretty serious?"

"No, I'm sure it isn't. If you ask me, she isn't lying about on a wet moor waiting to be murdered, or horribly bloody in a sandstone quarry. She's given us all the slip. And how she must be laughing at us. The fact is, she's always been given her head. And look at the result! Why men should go crazy over her, I can't think. Oh, I know she has a way with her, but look at her want of consideration. Losing that poor man in all this fog—and I'm sure he's got a delicate chest."

"Is this little Arthur?"

"Mr. Dennis. Yes. Well, would any really nice girl take a man out in a fog and then lose him on purpose?"

"That would depend on the man. Being lost in a fog is too good for some of them."

"Well, I call it very wrong. No considerate girl would have dragged a young man out on such an afternoon."

"Any man worth his salt would have been glad to go out with Hilary any afternoon," championed Jeremy, instantly.

"You think that?"

"I'm sure of it."

"Even if he were only going to be shaken off and given his death of cold?"

"He must be a pretty average fool to let himself be shaken off."

"How could he help it? Of course, she meant to get rid of him."

"How do you make that out?"

"Well, why did she try to put him off from the beginning?"

"Did she?"

"Yes. If it comes to that, what reason could she have for going out on such a day if she wasn't going to elope or something?"

"Whom could she elope with?"

"I don't know, I'm sure. There's that delightfully wicked-looking nephew of Eleanor's. You know, I've always wanted to meet a murderer. But I never thought I should do it under James's roof."

"He was acquitted," Jeremy reminded her dryly.

"Of course he was acquitted. What's that got to do with it?"

"A good deal, I should have thought."

"Well, anyway, he's been paying her a lot of attention lately."

"Your idea being that she took her young man out, shook him off—is the fellow a beetle to be shaken off so lightly?—and is now—where?"

"Half-way to France, I dare say."

"Not unless they're swimming," said Jeremy, grimly. "There'll be no boats out to-night."

"Well," she challenged him, "what's your explanation?"

"I don't even know what happened."

"I'll tell you. We were all sitting comfortably round the fire and in strides this young woman and says she wants to stretch her legs. As if they weren't long enough already, and she shows plenty of them, too. A shame, I call it, in a respectable house. All I can say is, I'm glad I lost Bertie before these hussies started going about half-naked. Well, of course, when he saw she meant to go he said he'd come, too. Anyone could see she didn't want him, but she couldn't exactly refuse to let him accompany her. So off they went, and we didn't think much about them till about six o'clock, when the door was pushed open and in comes Mr. Dennis, soaking, poor darling, and saying, with that delicious little stammer of his, 'I suppose the j-joke's on me, is it? Hilary's been in for ages.' Of course, we asked him what he was talking about, and he said they'd had a walk and then had tea at an inn, and when they'd left it nearly half-an-hour Hilary discovered—little minx!—that she'd left her bag behind. And sent him back for it. He's too simple-minded himself to see it was a trick."

"With all due deference to you, and of course loathing the brute like poison for daring to be engaged to Hilary at all, I can't quite see why he should have guessed she meant to give him the slip because she lost her bag."

"Because everyone in the neighbourhood knows the chit, and with good reason, too. If she left a bag at an inn, it would be returned in the morning. And it's absurd to pretend that there was anything in it so valuable it couldn't wait a few hours. If she wanted money, though how people can spend money on a moor I don't know, Mr. Dennis had it. And he always carries a spare handkerchief, I know."

"Oh, Lord!" murmured Jeremy. "Did he tell you that?"

"Yes. He was once in an accident…"

"Quite the Little Lord Fauntleroy," commented Jeremy, approvingly. "Does he wear floppy ties?"

"No. He's in half-mourning for an aunt. He wears a black tie."

"And you blame Hilary for losing this scourge in a fog? Why, Mrs. Ross, why?"

"He might have caught pneumonia," said Meriel Ross indignantly.

"True, true. I'd forgotten the weak chest. Well?"

"He went back to look for the bag, which she'd deliberately stuffed behind some books in the inn parlour, and she promised to wait. The fog wasn't so bad then, according to him, but of course he doesn't know one clump of heather from another. And when he came back she'd disappeared."

"Poor chump missed the path."

"Anyone would."

"Hilary may have tried to get back and missed it, too."

"Not she. That young woman knows the moors as she knows her own face when she meets it in the glass, and that's often enough."

"And that's positively the last that's been heard of her? Did you say everyone had gone out?"

"Yes. And they may be out all night for all I know."

"There may have been something of great importance in the purse."

"There wasn't. I've looked. She'd deliberately hidden it, where it wouldn't be found and brought after her within five minutes. It was all part of a plot. And it won't be any thanks to her if we don't have a funeral as a result. All these people knee-high in mud looking for her."

"Perhaps she's waiting where she said she would, and none of them have hit the right path."

"You think she'd be waiting there at eight o'clock? Not she. Of course they've missed her, and would if she'd been like Lot's wife, frozen in her steps. He's been in once since, and when he heard she still wasn't back, off he went. There are about a hundred miles of moor, and it's pitch black and he's got a candle or something, so how he or anyone else expects to find her I can't imagine. And after that everyone except myself went off, too. Poor Mr. Dennis thinks she may have slipped and broken her ankle. Serve her right, horrid little chit! That young man of hers spoke of chartering an aeroplane, as if he thought the child might be hiding in a bird's nest, only there aren't any, are there, at this time of the year?"

"You can't buy aeroplanes at Woolworths," Jeremy comforted her. "Hullo, here's someone."

Voices sounded in the hall, but I didn't think either of them was Hilary's. Nor was it. The door was pushed open and Nunn came in with Eleanor. Drenched, weary and full of anxiety as she was—and at that moment none of us knew the tremendous burden under which she laboured—there was something about her so striking that she made a mere onlooker catch the breath. Her face had fined without sharpening during the difficult years that followed Percy Feltham's death; she was cool and detached, without having lost any of her zest for the adventure of living. Beneath that mask of composure blazed what ardour, what passion, what radiance, what ability to express and to endure. By a gesture of her fine expressive hands, a movement of the beautifully-shaped head, how she could inspire, enthral and sometimes embarrass an audience! All the old sense of being submerged in a rich flood overwhelmed me as she came forward and took my hand, and I noticed the feeling and life throbbing in hers as she did so. The man with her was a perfect foil to her compelling personality. He was short, square, controlled. His voice as he said, "You're worth a thousand Hilarys and I refuse to allow you to wear yourself out for a worthless young woman like that," didn't betray a trace of anxiety. No one would have suspected that he had been tramping over drenched and concealed moors for the past two hours. In his own way he was as striking as she. It was easy to believe he was what is called a self-made man. There was about him some lack of finish, something difficult to describe, but whose absence was immediately apparent. But, if he hadn't got breeding, which is inborn, he had something better still, and that was personality. You saw how he'd built up his big concern. His face was like one of his own plate-glass windows, displaying the iron resolution, the integrity and courage that had never known what it was to feel dismayed. He'd struggled; there had been a time when, after ten years' work, he had had to abandon his dreams and go into employment with a man whose methods he despised, but he'd gone on building. He wasn't a man you could ever tire or wear down. I could see the irresistible fascination he would have for a woman like Eleanor. In short, they were a fine couple. But with such a man at call I wondered what on earth it was that had induced Eleanor to send me that frantic, despairing note.

Jeremy was just proposing to go out and lend the unknown Dennis a hand when the fellow himself appeared. As Meriel Ross had told us, he wore a grey suit and a black tie. He wasn't, somehow, at all the kind of man I had supposed Hilary would attract; and certainly not the kind I had anticipated would attract her. For one thing, he must have been nearly twice her age (subsequently I learnt that he was thirty-eight), a pleasant, short-sighted, fair-haired chap, not in the least good-looking, but with an attractive voice and manner, an Irishman, casual, irresponsible and cool. He murmured to Nunn, "No luck yet? I should like to shake that child till her eyes drop out. Oh, thank you, sir." That was still to Nunn, who shoved a hot drink into his hand.

"You'd better have something to eat now you are back," his host continued, but Dennis, smiling, shook his head.

"I don't think so, sir. Bad habit to go prowling on wet moors immediately after a heavy meal. B-besides, Hilary m-might think it heartless. And I d-don't want to find her for the pleasure of l-losing her again."

"I should imagine if you want her you're welcome to her," remarked Nunn, and I was astounded at the animosity in his voice.

Meriel Ross had disappeared, and I realised that beneath her surface manner of naïve helplessness was a strong streak of common sense. Now she returned with a plate of sandwiches that she thrust into Dennis's hands.

"You won't go another step till you've eaten all those," she said, sternly, and at once he set to. Eleanor was talking to Jeremy, whom she had recognised.

"It's no use your trying to seduce your young policeman away from me," said Mrs. Ross, instantly. "I've got him tight. And, my dear, do try and cultivate a sense of humour. I really fail to see why Hilary should have all the laughs."

"We haven't come to that stage yet," said Nunn, in a curt voice. "Are you really going out, Freyne?"

"I thought perhaps Dennis and I might go together," said Jeremy. "I know these moors pretty well; I know the short cuts and I know the places where Hilary might conceivably try to shelter if she lost her way."

Nunn didn't want Dennis to go out again. He suggested that, if anyone must go, Jeremy and I might do our turn and give the other fellows a rest. But he might as well have tried to budge a young tank as move either of them.

Nunn looked angry. "I can see I'm wasting my words on you," he said. "It's obvious how it is with you both. But you'll rest here and eat something solid before you go. I don't mean to send out stretcher-parties before midnight."

He and I and Dennis and Jeremy went out of the room together, leaving Meriel Ross and Eleanor alone. Dennis went upstairs for dry footgear, and the rest of us turned into the dining-room.

"There may have been an accident," Jeremy was saying, more urgently than he had yet spoken. I fancy he was a little nonplussed by his host's attitude.

"Serve her right if there is. But I doubt it. That young woman always falls on her feet—or someone else's."

"Oh, come, sir," Jeremy protested. "You aren't really blaming her for missing her road in a confounded fog like this."

"I'm blaming her for being out in it at all, or taking Dennis out. I've seen my wife make herself ill over this young woman, and the rest of you propose to beat the heather all night. Which is what I should like to do to her."

Jerry looked at him inquiringly.

"Yes," reiterated Nunn, in his curt, equable voice. "I consider she's behaved extremely badly. That fellow takes it much too quietly. She's had her head too long, that's the trouble. Comes of not having a father, I suppose. If she belonged to me I'd take a slipper to her for upsetting the house like this. And, of course, all you young poops encourage her."

I was surprised to hear Jeremy chuckle, as he said, "I've often felt that way myself, sir."

Nunn's severity relaxed. "It's a pity you're not going to marry her," he remarked.

"Oh, but I am," said Jeremy, coolly. "You've said yourself that Dennis wouldn't be good for her. And I agree."

At that moment Dennis came back in dry footgear, carrying a rather noisome-looking lantern.

"May I ask how far you intend to go to-night?" Nunn asked him.

"As far as we can. You know the extent of these m-moors? We haven't gone over a t-tenth of them yet."

"Well, Freyne's coming to direct you."

At the name I saw Dennis give a little start, and then he smiled.

"My p-patron saint," he murmured.

For a moment I thought it was a new version of the old expletive, "My sainted aunt!" but it wasn't.

"What the devil d'you mean?" Jeremy wanted to know.

"I beg your pardon. That slipped out. I was brought up in a f-frightfully ecclesiastical home. My father was a p-parson, and when I was a kid every C-Christmas we used to put a p-penny in the box and take a card. And the card had the p-picture of a saint on it, and his p-particular virtue on the back. All that year you had to p-practise that p-particular virtue. My father saw to it that we did, too. You know the k-kind of thing—p-patience or p-perseverance and so forth. And he became your p-patron saint for that year. Hilary's always held you up as a model of all the virtues she admires, and I'm supposed to be trying to m-model myself on you. You see?" His smile was charming. For all his superior years he seemed almost shy. But I had begun to wonder how far this was a surface manner. He wasn't a fool, that was certain. And in spite of my friendship with Jeremy I couldn't help hoping this chap would get his own way. Besides, it would leave Jeremy free for a bit longer, an excellent plan to my thinking.

"You won't be able to feel your feet in the morning," said Nunn, dubiously.

Dennis shook his head and smiled. "I've been on a m-motor-bicycle," he reassured us. "A chap at the garage lent me one."

"Where is it now?"

"It b-broke down," admitted Dennis, apologetically. "It's some-where on the moor."

"Then you can't use it again?"

"I d-don't want to. To tell you the t-truth, I'm rather alarmed by the brute. It slips about so. But now I'm going on foot. It's much s-safer, and I think it's more certain. I've just got this lantern. It never goes out, they say, even if it's dropped in a pond, and the l-light is p-peculiarly brilliant." He flashed it on our faces and we all staggered, looking as yellow as guineas.

"I thought you wouldn't mind my coming with you, as you don't know the moors," observed Jeremy. "Perhaps I ought to tell you that I'm proposing to marry Hilary myself."

"Well, we can't either of us marry her to-night," said Dennis, sensibly. "We might l-let that little matter stand over till we have her back."

"How's the fog?" asked Nunn.

"Oh, lifting," returned Dennis cheerily. "It's been l-lifting for some time. It's begun to r-rain now. Quite nice s-straight rain."

He opened the front door, and we all looked out. The fog was really dispersing at last, hanging in long yellow wisps over the soaked heather, and a heavy rain had begun to fall. Dennis and Jeremy buttoned up their collars and went out. I hadn't offered to go. I knew my accursed weakness too well. That unsound leg of mine would let me down before I'd covered a couple of miles. It lost no opportunity of reminding me that my A1 days were over.

"I suppose that fellow wants to commit suicide," growled Nunn, ringing and telling his butler that what was left of the party would now dine. "Looking over an indescribable area for a problematical corpse. The next thing is they'll both disappear as well. It's a damnable night; the mud sucks over your ankles at every step. And if and when she's found, they'll fuss over her as if she had a million dollars for each of them in her two hands."

I felt unequal to discussing Hilary with him, and he brooded, while we waited for the women. Suddenly he broke out, "I'm not denying there's some purpose in all this. That girl generally has a reason for the things she does. And it's no use most of the time trying to understand a woman's reasons for doing things. They haven't got the same standards as we have, and I doubt if they ever will. I tell you, Keith, I'm always getting the shock of my life at the things perfectly decent women will do without turning a hair. And they raise Cain at what seem to us the merest trifles. That young woman's running a crooked course. If there's anything wrong she ought to tell Dennis."

"Perhaps she daren't," I suggested feebly, trying to think of something that would frighten Hilary.

"Then she's no right to get herself engaged to him. We have a right to expect moral courage in our women. I don't blame them for jumping if they see a mouse, or raising a tired man just when he's got to sleep, because there's a beetle under the bed. That's their nature. But moral courage is one of their natural virtues, like—like long hair. I've sometimes thought it's partly because they're less sensitive than we are, and they have a hatred of being thought like anyone else. A woman will own up at any time to being different from other people; she'd be furious if you classed her with a whole lot of other women. But a man tries to look as much of a sheep as all the other sheep he grazes with. It's the way the creatures are made. Male and female created He them, seeing farther than we. And a damned sight farther, we'll hope." Then his voice changed once more; the speculative tone left it, and he became impassioned. Clearly he felt very deeply on this point, and I wondered where the source of that feeling lay. I couldn't quite believe that Hilary had roused him to this pitch. "If it really is something wrong, then it's something Dennis ought to know. A girl has no right to marry if there's something behind her she daren't let her husband hear. She ought to trust him outright and take her fences clean. I don't like this underhand dealing. It's all wrong, and more than that, it doesn't pay. It doesn't pay in business, and it doesn't pay in love."

Some impulse made me turn my head at that moment, and I saw Eleanor standing in the doorway. She and Meriel Ross must have crossed the hall together, and have heard Nunn's last words. I have never seen an expression so tragic, so terrible, so full of an incalculable despair on any face as I saw on Eleanor's then. For an instant she remained motionless, without colour or even vitality, like some woman slain upon her feet. Then she recovered; slowly one saw the life creep back into the body. It was like watching some marvellous piece of machinery awake to action. She spoke, slowly at first, with gradual movements of her arms and hands; then the blood flowed more quickly and eagerly, until by the time the meal was half over she appeared her normal self.

But not to me. I could not forget that expression, tense, secretly alarmed, that had transfixed her for an instant in the doorway. And I realised then that whatever Hilary's secret was it was in some way bound up with Eleanor's life.

CHAPTER IV

I DON'T REMEMBER, EVEN IN THE TRENCHES, EATING A MORE uncomfortable meal. Humanity is a complex affair, and it is next door to impossible to explain the sudden changes of mood that overwhelm us at every step. Difficult, too, to realise how we determine in our own hearts the things that matter most, differentiate between the significant and the unimportant. Until I saw that expression on Eleanor's face I had been profoundly troubled by the thought of Hilary perhaps hurt or distraught among those endless black ridges, for I was once lost myself in complete darkness, and I know how the loss of sight, which is what such a position amounts to, intensifies the smallest and most familiar sound into a terror and sets the most normal brain flashing with incredible fears. And if, in addition to being lost, Hilary was really in trouble so serious she dared not confide in Dennis, who, by reason of his age and experience and a certain warm kindliness that was unmistakable, was her most obvious confidante, I thought her deserving of sympathy rather than censure. But no sooner had I seen that expression on Eleanor's face, than my feelings did a kind of nose-dive. I almost forgot Hilary or, at all events, she disappeared into the depths of my mind where she was barely perceptible. My interest in Eleanor, that had always been considerable, leapt up and overpowered everything else. I wanted to know nothing, understand nothing, but the meaning of that spontaneous frozen fear. All through the meal I watched her covertly for an instant of self-betrayal, but none came. In her smallest gesture she was once again mistress of her emotions. But it was like seeing for a second some rich tapestry flicked aside by accident, to reveal a treasure-trove of which the merest glimpse kindled the onlooker's ardent curiosity. I waited with an impatience I found it hard to dissemble while we got through the meal somehow, talking a little of Hilary, more of Dennis and Jeremy, and of more general subjects, such as a coming by-election in the neighbourhood and the effect on local rates of the opening of a factory at Ravensend. And all this time, while I bandied words with Meriel Ross or answered Eleanor's casual questions, I was aware of such a storm of feeling raging behind the quiet controlled mask that the very air seemed stirred by its force. I tried not to watch her movements, or observe the changes of her tone; but it was inevitable. The world might have shrunk to no larger than was necessary to hold the pair of us; I was convinced that she could explain this sudden absence of Hilary's. She had, indeed, a look as though some dreadful thing had been accomplished, that she had been unable to prevent, but for which she was nevertheless accountable, something that would shatter the fabric of her own happiness and security, a woman facing ruin yet refusing even so to exhibit her misery to the world.

After dinner she told me the story, and allowed me to see how closely I had identified my version of the position with the truth. We were alone, and, waiting for her to speak, the strain of that artificial silence during which she was nerving herself to tell me the rather horrible truth playing on my nerves, I muttered something about Hilary.

"Where on earth she can be..." I began, and Eleanor said, "Ask Ralph."

Something in her voice, something dull, certain and hopeless, astounded me.

"Ralph?" I repeated foolishly.

"I'm convinced he's at the bottom of this as he's at the bottom of the rest of the trouble."

"The trouble about which you wrote to me?"

"Yes. But I wrote too late. He's struck. I didn't think he'd dare."

"But what hold has he got over Hilary?"

"The same as he has over me. Only I brought my trouble on myself, and Hilary's suffering for it."

"I wish you'd explain."

"Yes. I must start at the beginning. It's a long time ago. It began during the war, when I wanted Cleghorne so badly. There is a lot of nonsense talked about the effect the war had on people who stayed at home, but there's a grain of truth among the chaff here and there; and undoubtedly people did change their standards. Or rather, their standards imperceptibly shifted. In a way, I think that was for the good. Because in most cases they shifted away from the eternal question of how this or that would affect themselves and did, however vaguely and even hysterically, begin to think of how it would affect communities, or, at all events, their neighbours. All this," she added, regaining control over her voice, that had been a little shaken and unsteady, "isn't meant as an excuse for myself. I don't think even at the time I thought of it as that."

I said, increasingly bewildered by these generalisations and unable to link them up in any way with Hilary's disappearance, "But what was it you did that gave Ralph a hold over you? For I suppose that's what you're driving at."

"It has to do with Cleghorne."

"Well, but even Ralph, blackguard though he may be, can know nothing fresh about the man, the time. He can't be threatening to tell people now that the fellow was a skunk and a traitor."

"He was something more than that."

"What, then?"

"My lover."

She spoke the words so quietly, so coolly, almost as if they didn't matter, that for a moment I scarcely understood their tremendous significance. I just repeated dazedly, "Your lover?"

And she said, "Yes. Does it seem incredible to you? Did you know the man? He had a charm—Percy had it, James has it—I recognise it in every man of the same type. A certain power—I can't explain. It wasn't just physical. But he awakened the life in me that couldn't be satisfied by the ordinary people I met. You're horrified, of course. You're thinking of Percy. But, Tony, you aren't a child. I don't know how well you really knew my husband, but for years I hadn't existed for him except as a kind of assistant, a secretary, someone to whom he could turn at any hour of the day and night for interest, for sympathy, for help. I think you did know what a lot I could do for him in his speeches. He wasn't an eloquent man. I loved the work; I liked the sense of power it gave me, drafting sentences that were going to move rows and rows of stolid, practical men. I've always loved playing with words. I got wrapped up in the thought that this was a way of helping, an unique way. I hadn't got a son, I had only myself. The work I did at the hospital could have been done equally well by anyone else. But here was something no one could do in precisely the same way. And it was work that mattered. Or so I was conceited enough to think. Then came the need to get Cleghorne to help us. It was a difficult job. Percy put a good deal of the work on to me. I began for the work's sake; I went on partly for his, partly for my own, and partly for something I can't very well explain; it was as if something in my own life was flowering. You see, though my mind was occupied with my work, we're more than just mind. It matters, but it doesn't absorb all our energies, and at that time I used to have a terrible sense of running to seed, of wasting something that was too rich to be carelessly flung aside. Of course, it was Percy's right, privilege, call it what you like. But he didn't want it. I wasn't piqued. I'd learned to accept the position. And, as I say, at first I was too much absorbed in what I was doing to think of the matter in a personal way at all. But presently—I suppose it was being so constantly in touch with Cleghorne—I began to realise that I was living one-sidedly. Human nature is terribly adaptable, and I believe it grows in the direction we choose to train it. There was a time when the very thought of a lover would have shocked me beyond speech. Now it began to seem perilous, but in a way exquisite. And later still, when it became a tussle to get what we wanted, it was like part of a plan. It didn't seem horrible to me; it seemed inevitable. Cleghorne was a fascinating man; he was cosmopolitan; he had met everyone; he was polished, cynical, intelligent, imperturbable. Our interests were similar; we could talk and we could sympathise. I felt as if a part of me that had been dead for years took new life when I came into intimate contact with him. I didn't feel that I was cheating Percy; I was like two women, a public and a private life, and my private life was my own. To this day I'm not sure whether Cleghorne was simply acting magnificently all the time. I don't think he was. I think it did mean something to him, but it's a proof of my belief that we are two people more often than any of us suppose. It's rather a terrifying thought. He, too, had a private and a public life. No one could touch the first; but it hadn't, in his mind, any relation to the second, the public life. We're complex, Tony. We can't split ourselves up into sections. It sounds unreal to you. But it was like the heart of my existence, beating quietly unseen. The kind of thing you take for granted, but it controls the life of the body. That's how it was with me. I'd been walking very calmly and circumspectly and securely between blank walls, and suddenly there was a break, there was colour and warmth and light. And I took them. I paid, of course. I think I paid pretty heavily. When the truth came out about

Cleghorne, Percy was crushed; he couldn't understand it. He swore he would discover exactly when and how the leakage had started. I don't know how he discovered about us, but he did. And then the whole thing seemed clear enough. Cleghorne and I were lovers; we were in partnership. I was his tool, and we were in this thing together. Nothing I could say could convince him that he was crazy to suggest such a thing; he had a deep mind, but a narrow one. A woman who could betray her husband would make small work of betraying her country. He really believed that, and I couldn't shake him. He hadn't a thought or a gleam of compassion to spare for me; he didn't even see my position, how much worse it was than his. He never had a great deal of imagination. But his brother was butchered in that ambush..." Her voice stopped. Hitherto it had not faltered; now I saw that she was momentarily beyond speech. She sat as erect as ever, those fine hands folded quietly on her knee, a woman lost to hope. "You see my position?" she continued a little later. "If Ralph is allowed to circulate that story—he's got hold of the letters I wrote to Cleghorne—everyone will revile Percy even worse than they do now. There were a good many people then who believed him terribly injured. Now they would say that he was ready to let his wife enter into liaison for whatever Cleghorne was giving him."

"How did Ralph find out?" I asked foolishly.

"I don't know, unless he knew Cleghorne, then or later. He won't tell me, but I think it's very probable. Ralph has never been sound. But you see the strength of his position?"

"He's been blackmailing you?"

"Up to the hilt. I've parted with everything but my good name, such as it is. And that he shall not have. It isn't mine any longer. It's James's." Her voice had altered again, strengthened, becoming not defiant but dominant. There was something heroic about her as she contemplated the devastation her own passion and Ralph's treachery had wrought, and refused to be defeated by it.

"You must see how it is with me. It isn't myself any longer. I haven't a personality anyone can harm. It's all James's now. And Ralph shall not destroy him. As it would, of course. You heard what he said about Hilary. He would condemn me utterly for marrying him and saying nothing."

"Couldn't you have trusted him?" I asked.

"Perhaps. But do you think I wanted him to know something that would have hurt him every time he thought of it? You think perhaps it was cowardice on my part that kept me silent. Don't believe it. It's hurt me more to say nothing, to keep up a pretence that any accident might break down, than to have acknowledged the truth. But it wouldn't have been for his greater happiness. It isn't that I don't trust or believe in him, but I don't see why he should carry such a burden. After all, I know what the weight of it's like; I've been carrying it for years, and there are times when it bows you to the earth, for all your resolution and courage. But now," she added, her voice losing some of its eloquence and returning to more normal levels, "it's Hilary."

"I still don't understand about Hilary."

"Ralph tells me very little, but he's in a tight corner again and wants help. He's had everything I've got, and still he isn't satisfied. He suggested to me some time ago that I should approach Hilary. Percy left her practically all he had, not a great deal, but about ten thousand pounds in stock of various kinds, most of it sound. If I could have prevented his telling her—she, of course, was a child and knew nothing…"

I said, aghast and ashamed on her account, "But you could. You could. You could have gone to your husband. You oughtn't ever to have let Hilary know that story." I remembered her as I had last seen her, a tall, laughing, fair-haired girl of seventeen, grey-eyed, undisciplined perhaps, but with something rather fine and charming about her. She wouldn't, at all events, have let anyone else in on her private trouble.

"Do you think I'd weigh Hilary for an instant against James?" Eleanor asked me fiercely. "I can't divide my heart up into neat compartments as some people seem able to do." I didn't agree with her; it seemed to me that she was deliberately sacrificing Hilary, a young girl in no way a match for her poise, her brilliance, her social abilities; but I was silenced. There was something so compelling about her that I couldn't argue. I knew why men found her irresistible; and whether you deplored her particular point of view or no, you had to admit her burning sincerity.

"And so," I said lamely, after a pause, "your notion is that Hilary gave Dennis the slip in order to meet Ralph?"

"To give him money, perhaps. I've bought back a lot of the letters and proofs. But there were so many. And James won't have him in the house."

"And she's with him now, wherever he is?"

"I—don't—know. Very likely they're right, and she's lost her way on the moors coming back."

All through the evening I had been horrified at the thought of her, perhaps hurt, alone in the darkness and the fog; now that seemed to me a reprieve from the thought that she was with that cruel and treacherous creature, Ralph Feltham. Heaven only knew to what lengths he would go if he had her in his power. I asked abruptly, "Has he ever said anything about wanting to marry Hilary?"

"He did threaten something of the kind once, but it was only a grim sort of joke. He knows it wouldn't be allowed."

"Suppose that's his ultimatum? That if he doesn't have Hilary the world can have the truth?"

Eleanor stood up; she was very queenly and moved with the loveliest grace I have ever seen in any woman. "I refuse to suspect anything so horrible. But Hilary wouldn't have him."

"There's no knowing what Hilary wouldn't do to save her father's name. I know she was only a child when he died, but you know he was her hero and idol, and she's grown up believing him to be a martyr. And you know the strength of feeling of which she's capable. You may be able to reassure yourself that she'd do nothing so wild and wrong as marry Ralph for the sake of a sentiment—shall we say?—but I shouldn't be surprised to find she'd be capable of anything to prevent people resurrecting and in their view proving a hideous scandal." Then I changed my tone, becoming unsympathetic and enraged. "Eleanor, for God's sake, stop this crazy policy of yours. If anyone can scotch this plot it's your husband. You've no earthly right to make young Hilary stand the racket. The very thought of her being in that brute's power would make any reasonable man sick. Jeremy would go half out of his mind, if he knew. Tell him, never mind if he's hurt. Someone's got to meet the bill, and he's more fit for it than she."

Eleanor demurred. I was being more and more impressed by the wisdom of her husband's contention that you couldn't rely on even the most honourable woman you knew to play with a straight bat, according to masculine standards. Here was Eleanor, who had faced trouble enough in her own time and never uttered a complaint, coolly prepared to see this girl of one-and-twenty harried and distraught rather than let the burden fall on James Nunn's shoulders. If I hadn't known from experience the high quality of her courage, I should have written her down one of the most deplorable cowards I had been unfortunate enough to encounter. I pressed my arguments home with a keener and keener blade.

"Look back over your own life," I urged her. "Oh, I don't deny it hasn't been all roses. Life isn't. But it's been a pretty rich affair take it by and large. And there's a law that we shall reap as we sow. But it's monstrous to let this girl's life be blighted at the beginning by forcing her to take your harvest."

I was secretly apprehensive of her reaction to such an accusation; but rather to my surprise she showed signs of horror. I honestly don't think it had hitherto occurred to her that she was taking a cruel advantage of Hilary's defencelessness.

"If she comes back all right," she promised, "I'll go straight to James. You're right, Tony. I should have done that long ago."

"Why do you say all right? What do you think can have happened to her? That Ralph would do anything—desperate? But he couldn't."

"You don't remember him very well if you think that. Talk of the devil anywhere, and within five minutes everyone's speaking of Ralph."

Hearing that, I blamed her more than ever. Woman-like, she could only see one thing or one person at a time, and here it was James Nunn and his reaction to the truth.

CHAPTER V

I

HILARY CAME IN SHORTLY BEFORE ELEVEN. JEREMY AND Dennis were still out, but everyone else was in the house. I had expected, if she returned at all, to see her wild and despairing, and illogically my sympathy for her underwent a sharp reaction when I saw her composure. Except that she was as white as paper, she didn't betray herself at all. She even smiled.

"Did you think I was lost?" she inquired.

"If you weren't lost, what excuse have you got for turning up at this hour?" countered Nunn belligerently.

"I lost my way. Anyone would, on such a night."

"If the percentage of arthritis and pneumonia in the neighbourhood rises a hundred per cent. in the course of the next week don't be surprised," he continued. "A third of the village have also been losing their way in the heather this evening. I wonder you didn't stumble on any of them."

"I didn't." But I detected a faint change, as though a wind of alarm had ruffled her composure. "I hope people haven't really been turning out for me."

"I did my best to dissuade them."

"Where's Arthur?" She put the question sharply, and a tinge of colour whipped into the pale cheeks.

"Where should he be except catching his death of cold out there?"

"How stupid when he doesn't know the way at all."

"You'd have been extremely offended if you'd found him calmly smoking in here."

"You're very solicitous for his health."

"Someone has to make up for your deficiencies, my dear."

Hilary looked suddenly like a little girl who is going to cry. "Why are you so bitter about it?"

"Because I think it's bad manners to keep a guest out in this weather till nearly eleven o'clock."

"Well, I've been out most of the evening myself. But I suppose you don't mind about that."

An odd expression crossed Nunn's face; for an instant, I thought he was going to say one of those things that are never forgotten. Then he appeared to change his mind. I was aware of Mrs. Ross entering the room.

"So there you are. You haven't eloped, after all."

"Who was I going to elope with?"

"You seem to have most of the neighbourhood at your feet. Poor Mr. Dennis."

"I'm sure you saw to it that he took his goloshes."

"I don't think he has any. Anyway, he wouldn't wait for anything. But what made you treat him like that?"

"Like…?"

"Sending him back for your bag, when you knew you'd hidden it. It was only a trick, and a nasty one at that. It was horrid of you to take him out on such an afternoon and then lose him."

Hilary struggled back to her original casual manner. "That's just the point. I didn't take him out. He came. If he would be so tactless as to insist on going where he hadn't been invited, he mustn't grumble at the consequences."

"So you shook him off on purpose?"

"Yes. I had to be alone. You here don't realise; I never get a minute. I said I wanted to go out by myself. I had to think…"

There was something so endearing about the clumsiness of her excuses, the childish defiance of her manner, that I felt I had had as much as I could stand.

"I expect you're dog-tired," I intervened, coming forward and pushing a chair towards her. "And starved. Sit down and let me take off your wet shoes." And at that I caught sight of Mrs. Ross's hopeless face and chuckled.

But Nunn wouldn't let Hilary off so easily. "And have you thought sufficiently?" he asked.

"Yes."

"About…?"

"Whether I'd marry Arthur or not."

A new voice said, "And—w-what have you decided?"

At that sound, the least expected of any at such a moment, we all turned like a crowd of marionettes jerked by an identical string. None of us had heard Dennis and Jeremy enter. Jeremy, indeed, still stood so far back in the shadow that Hilary didn't notice him.

"That I can't. I'm sorry, Arthur, but James and Meriel will tell you you're lucky."

I admired the man at that moment. He didn't stop to argue or protest. He came through us, pushed her into the chair, asked me if I'd ring the bell, pulled off her shoes and put a cushion behind her head before he made any comments. Then he said, "I won't ask you for explanations t-to-night, of course. You're tired out, but perhaps in the m-morning…?" He looked at her with a glance so confiding, so shy and so friendly that Hilary suddenly began to cry.

"It isn't any good, Arthur. I can't do it."

"Well, if you c-can't, you can't, of course. D-don't worry about it to-night. You're all right, are you? L-look here, sir," he turned to Nunn, "I think she ought to go to bed at once. She's worn out, and she oughtn't to be made to t-talk before the morning."

"Hear, hear!" put in Jeremy, and at the sound of his voice Hilary flushed a rosy red.

"I thought you were somewhere on the Equator," she exclaimed. He came across the room and took her hand.

"No, I agree with Dennis that you mustn't be allowed to talk to-night. To-morrow you can tell us what's wrong, and we'll do anything you want. If you should require someone murdered or anything, just let me know."

She began to laugh, a high uncertain sound, the prelude to certain collapse. "Oh, Jeremy, I wish you could."

"Why not?" he murmured. "Just one thing. Tell me, is it that hound, Ralph?"

She drew her hand away. "You'll think me unspeakable, Arthur," she said, facing round to us all, "and I'm sure James won't let me stay in his house. But I'm breaking with you because I'm going to marry Ralph Feltham."

2

After Hilary had gone, I was surprised to find Dennis easily the coolest man of us all.

"Well, of c-course I knew she hadn't been ploughing about on the Downs all the evening," he said. "You've only g-got to look at her shoes."

He pointed to them, where they lay on the floor, as he spoke, and we saw what he meant.

"They're m-muddy, of course. But anyone who walked a quarter of a mile on the cleanest path would be muddy in weather like this.

But compare them with yours," he nodded to Jeremy, "or mine, and see the difference. S-she didn't lose her way at all. She kept to the paths all the time."

"Then she's been deliberately deceiving you," broke in Meriel indignantly. I caught a glimpse of Eleanor's face; it was tragic. She looked as if she were going to speak when Dennis forestalled her.

"What we've got to f-find out is whether she's marrying Feltham, or t-thinks she's going to marry him, because she has to—I mean, because he's g-got some sort of hold over her—or whether it's because she wants to."

"Wants to!" exclaimed Eleanor in a dreadful voice. "Can you imagine any woman wanting to marry Ralph Feltham?"

"Quite a lot have w-wanted to," Dennis pointed out, a little apologetically. "And I d-don't think it's very odd, either. I mean, we live a good deal by the law of contrast. You could hardly f-find anyone less like all of us than Feltham, c-could you? It's pure reaction, I should s-say."

Nunn observed in his curt, unvarnished manner, "Upon my soul, Dennis, you take it pretty coolly. Do you mean to say you're going to stand aside and let a fellow with Feltham's reputation marry the girl you were engaged to?"

"Oh, no," said Dennis, in some surprise. "Of course not. And even if I would, Freyne wouldn't. But I'm just pointing out a second reason why Hilary might be prepared to. He's very picturesque, and there is something that Hilary would call romantic about marrying a man of his achievements."

"He's either being very modest or very subtle," announced Mrs. Ross in decisive tones, "and when men are being modest they're always proudest of themselves. Besides, I dare say he doesn't want to marry the chit any more—unless he's going to be philanthropic on top of everything else."

"Do you call it philanthropic to marry Hilary?"

"It would save her from herself, wouldn't it?"

"By preventing her from marrying anyone else? But I don't agree. I shouldn't save Hilary, as you call it, by preventing her marrying Feltham, though between us that's what we've got to do. I'm only pointing out his probable attraction."

"Over your own?"

"A girl I t-thought at that time I wanted to marry—it's about t-ten years ago now—told me she couldn't t-think of anyone she'd rather have for a second husband. I dare say t-that's how Hilary feels."

Then Jeremy stopped all this senseless badinage by saying in a thoughtful voice, "Whereabouts is Feltham at this moment? I didn't realise he was in the neighbourhood."

"He's not supposed to be," returned Eleanor, "but with Ralph you can never tell. He has a shooting-lodge over at Ravensend, and he comes down every now and again."

"Where did you say Hilary gave you the slip?" Jeremy turned to Dennis.

"At M-Merlin's Wood."

"H'm. I hadn't realised that. Of course, there's a direct short cut to Ravensend. That explains a lot. In fact, it must have been Hilary's footstep we heard. No wonder she stopped dead when we shouted. I wonder if we could get over there to-night. Fog's lifted, hasn't it?"

"I don't c-care if it's lifted as high as H-heaven," said Dennis, in his mild, determined tones, "you aren't going to hunt out Feltham t-to-night."

"I beg your pardon?"

"You aren't going to hunt out Feltham to-night."

"No? Who says not?"

"I do."

"You…?"

"Yes. I'm officially engaged to her still. D-don't forget that. And I won't have the s-scandal. What do you suppose people would s-say if they heard she spent several hours with the fellow and t-then you went and tried to throttle him? B-because that's what it would c-come to. It always does, with hot-headed fellows like you."

"All the same," repeated Jeremy, coolly, "I think I shall go. Just smell out the land, so to speak. No?" as Dennis shook his head. "Who'll stop me?"

"I w-will, if it comes to that." When Jeremy laughed in an unpleasant manner, the tall, casual fellow reached out an arm and with a muscular strength for which none of us had given him credit, had Jeremy's wrists between his fingers and slowly, silently, forced him on to his knees. Jeremy was like whipcord and india-rubber; the rest of us watched fascinated. I could see that it took Dennis every ounce of his strength and atom of skill to hold his man; but hold him he did.

Jeremy yielded with a good grace. "Your trick," he said. "And I wish some time you'd show me how that's done. I thought I knew most of the dodges, but that's a new one on me."

"Asiatic in origin," murmured Dennis. "Sorry and all that. Damned undignified, I know, but you m-must see that if you were allowed to have your crazy way, you'd play straight into Feltham's hands. In fact, I w-wouldn't mind betting most of what I've g-got, that he's sitting up, hoping for something of the kind."

Meriel Ross's plaintive voice broke in again. "But why does he want to marry Hilary, do you suppose? Because she's going to inherit ten thousand pounds next week? But now that we have sensible laws, there's nothing to compel her to give him anything."

"Still, a girl doesn't marry a man with the idea of hanging on to every penny of her own, if he's in a tight corner," Nunn put in. "Anyway, she's reckless about money."

Dennis said, so thoughtfully that we all began to laugh, "We can't tell that that is the reason. He m-may want her for herself."

"Men are odd," Mrs. Ross agreed. "But if that's true, he's in better company than he's been for years, I should imagine. And now I'm going to bed. Really, it's been a most remarkable evening, and I seem to have enjoyed it a good deal, especially this last part." She smiled affectionately at Jeremy and waved her hand to the rest of us.

CHAPTER VI

I

THE AFFAIR WAS GIVEN NO OPPORTUNITY TO SLIDE, EVEN FOR a few hours. Next morning, before the house was properly astir, that is to say, before the guests had turned out to the customary late breakfast, Ralph Feltham rode over on a very fine bay mare. I wondered cynically whom he had bled for that. A man who could afford to own such a beast was not the penniless adventurer I remembered. Nor could Eleanor alone have supplied him with sufficient funds to warrant such luxury. It was ten years since I had seen the fellow, but he had worn well. Beside him, I was bound to confess that Dennis was a pretty poor stick. Ralph had always had the advantage of commanding height, good shoulders, a fencer's hips and flanks. He had, too, the good looks of most of the male Felthams, and instantly I realised all the good points a woman would discover in the man. On the whole, despite the years of dissipation and reckless folly, his appearance had improved. He had what Dennis manifestly had not, the stamp of wide and spirited experience. He had matured, perhaps, but he had also mellowed. In place of the impudent assurance or the bluff insolence for which I looked was a quality of cool-headed resolution that could not fail to be impressive.

But if I was impressed, Nunn wasn't. He was upstairs when Ralph arrived, and he kept his visitor waiting some minutes, during which he and I kept up a desultory conversation. But if it was desultory it was, to my mind, profoundly disturbing. Ralph walked lightly round the hall, pausing beneath family portraits that he astonishingly resembled; his riding-kit emphasised all his good points; his hair was as thick and black as ever; he had trimmed his moustache to the merest toothbrush. He hadn't, as I had half-expected, run to fat. Those fierce, disconcerting black eyes, that he got from his West Country mother, flickered like a butterfly's tongue, gathering up every treasured detail of that hall's beauty. He had been brought up here; I had only spent isolated periods in the house, and I always felt a guest. To him it was home. In spite of the lapse of years, that was evidently the way in which he regarded it, as he touched with a thoughtful hand the moulding on the walls, caressed the old, carved newel-post, stood at the narrow windows to observe the distant enchanted view, while he waited for Nunn to come down to him.

"Odd how these places get you," he murmured to me. "I've hardly been here in fifteen years. The present tenant positively discourages my visits, but I feel as if I'd scarcely ever left its roof. One of these days I'll be back here—with Hilary. A man has to cut loose some time, dig in his roots. It'll be good to be back." He drifted into a jumble of anecdote and legend about the place; the fellow was amazingly plausible. I forgot his errand as I listened. No wonder he'd been able to do much as he pleased as he knocked about the earth. And according to his own account he'd had a royal time. I was genuinely surprised when Nunn's voice interrupted the conversation.

I saw Ralph stiffen a bit at the sight of him. He couldn't forget that, whatever his record, he was a Feltham of Feltham Abbey and this squat, uncompromising little fellow had started life at half-a-crown a week.

"I asked for Eleanor," he said, coldly.

"My wife is unable to see you. She has deputed me... I take it, it's a matter of considerable urgency. You know my views as to your presence in this house."

If he had wanted to insult Ralph he couldn't have chosen a better opening. I thought myself it was rather galling for the fellow, considering the place did actually belong to him.

"If I didn't know them, you couldn't conceivably blame yourself for lack of emphasis," said Ralph, colouring with rage. "Well, I've only come for Hilary. I'll go after that. But before long we shall both come back—here. Not even you will be able to keep us out."

"You're scarcely serious?"

"Certainly I am. Do you suppose I would come out here to meet the kind of reception experience has taught me I may expect from you for a trifle? Hilary told you, I take it."

"Hilary was scarcely in a state to talk of anything reasonable last night. She'd obviously passed through a very severe ordeal."

"You don't spare your enemies, do you? I'm to take it that you're opposed to the match?"

"My ward is engaged to another man."

"But she won't marry him. If she didn't marry me, I doubt if she'd marry him. She's recognised that mistake already."

"You have grounds, no doubt, for your statement..."

"Fellow's too old."

"Not more than a couple of years older than yourself, I believe."

"In every possible way, including years, he's too old a man for her. These Civil Servants age quickly. And besides, he's not her type."

"Nor are you, I believe, hers."

"That's where you're wrong. She's not one of those women who must go all out for security, any more than I'm that type of man."

"Possibly not. Still, in a marriage it's necessary for one side at all events to have a little sense, and a grain of conscience."

"You don't credit her with either?"

"Married to you, her life would be a disaster. She needs a very different type of man to save her from her own foolishness. However, that's all rather beside the point. There is and can be no suggestion of my ward marrying you."

"Because I've led what you might call a racketty life? So have most men, if it comes to that. Or is there some additional objection?"

I was surprised at the amount of control Ralph was displaying. For, though he had his temper in check now, he was strongly moved, and had been strongly provoked.

"Is it really necessary to pursue the matter further? Yesterday's behaviour alone would justify any man in refusing to listen to you. Didn't it occur to you how her reputation would suffer if it became known that she'd bamboozled her future husband in order to meet you on the sly?"

"As I'm proposing to become her future husband, I should hardly suppose that matters. And how else did you expect her to meet me? You've resolutely refused to let us meet openly. You've closed your doors to me. She can't even go out by herself, without that long Irish fellow tagging after her."

"That seems natural enough in the circumstances."

"It may be, but when she's my wife he'd better steer clear of my house."

"When…?"

"And why not? Do you think you'll stop me? I've had all the things I meant to get so far, and I've paid whatever price was stuck down on the label. Oh, yes, you're remembering the Laurine scandal, the fuss there was over that diamond business in South Africa, yes, and half a dozen other things, no doubt. But there's one point you seem to have forgotten, and that is that in each case I wanted something and meant to get it, and in each case I did. When you want a thing or a woman beyond law and convention and what other men think, you've as good as got your way."

"And you've forgotten something, too. In none of those other cases have I been in your way. There's another reason why you can't in any circumstances marry Hilary. Have you forgotten what you are? I'd rather hear you acknowledge that you were guilty of that harlot's murder than know, as I do, that you've even sunk to blackmail." (So Eleanor had told him.)

Ralph laughed. "You can't frighten me with words. Oh yes, blackmail sounds ugly, but what is it that you haven't done yourself, if we get down to brass tacks? Just taking advantage of the folly or the weakness of your adversaries. How did you build up a big business like yours? By keeping your weather-eye open, and profiting by the lapses of other people. You were more intelligent, no doubt, but if your opponents never made a slip and you didn't take advantage of it, you wouldn't be where you are now. And when you make money, and pots of it, by those means, no one calls you a potential criminal. Oh, don't make any mistake about it. I've seen this kind of legal ramp go on in every city in Europe—and in the U.S.A. and Australia and every other place where men meet together and try and outpace one another's fortunes. You see it on the Stock Exchange, and you see it in business, and you see how every man uses every scrap of information he can get about his neighbour's concerns that may be helpful to him—and are you going to try and pretend to me that you're so squeamish that you don't make use of such information? Of course you do; and make money out of it, too. And so do I. You can rebuke that kind of thing, if you like, but don't forget that we're in the same boat."

That gives you some notion of the fellow's ingenuity and his method of argument. I was trying to decide whether he really meant all that or whether it was pure bluff, when he turned suddenly, saying, "I suppose it's no use my asking for Hilary? But I'll get her all the same."

"I doubt it," said Nunn, drily. "Though I acknowledge that, at the last, it's an affair you'll settle between yourselves."

"I don't imagine I shall find this fancy-man of hers much difficulty."

"And after him, there's Mr. Freyne."

If they had been scoring, that would have been a goal to Nunn.

Ralph was galvanised into sudden activity. "Freyne here?"

"He is. He's a guest of mine."

He didn't mean to spare Ralph any more than he had spared Hilary last night. But now Ralph didn't seem to notice.

"Of all the… And he thinks he's going to marry Hilary? He would. He's a damned obstinate beggar, too."

A door above our heads opened and Dennis came out on to the wide gallery. He looked, owing to the construction of the house, slighter and shorter than he actually was, more like a shadow from the ghosts of the past than a creature of bone and sinew.

Ralph took a step forward. "Mr. Dennis?"

Dennis bowed.

"I have been trying to persuade Sir James that Hilary has broken off her engagement, and is, instead, going to marry me."

"It hadn't occurred to you to try and persuade me of that fact, first?"

Ralph tapped his boot with his switch. His voice was pleasantly insolent. "As a matter of fact, it hadn't."

"It's these strategical blunders that ruin more potential generals than you outsiders would ever believe."

Ralph scowled. "Since you've raised the point, may I ask you to accept my assurance that Hilary is not going to marry you?"

"I'm a civil servant, I'm afraid. It's a stiff training. One of the first things we learn is not to accept unofficial information." He bowed again and went back to his room. He hadn't turned a hair.

"What the devil did Hilary see in that chap?" asked Ralph, genuinely puzzled. "He'll be bald before they've been married five years. And I shouldn't be a bit surprised if he wore paper cuffs in his working hours. Cool devil, too. Casually smoking a cigarette as if he hadn't a care in the world."

"Oh," I said, "they teach you that in the Civil Service, too."

Nunn rang for a servant, and I walked down to the gate with Ralph. I don't know why I did it; I don't like the fellow, and I've never trusted him. But all the same he was the owner of the place and every stick and stone there recognised him. He said lightly, as he loosed his mare, "You might try and hammer it into Dennis's thick head that he's wasting powder carrying on this argument. I wonder if he'd be so keen to marry Hilary if he knew as much as I do. Feltham did sell his side, you know. Oh yes, he did. I've got papers to prove it. And anyway, I always thought he had. The race isn't stable; you'll admit that, even where Hilary's concerned. I fancy Eleanor knows the truth, too. It was a rotten pill for her to swallow. Not that I care. If every relative Hilary had had gone over to the other side, lock, stock and barrel, it wouldn't have made any difference to me. You may not believe it, Tony, but I am in earnest about that girl. I can't live without her, and I don't propose to try. What's done is done; there's time ahead, and that's for her and me. I'm only using this weapon because I must. As for Dennis, there are plenty of sensible women with suburban minds and economical ideas for Sunday supper who'll suit him to a T."

He nodded to me and rode off, smiling as though he hadn't a care in the world.

2

I came back to find Dennis, Nunn, Jeremy and Mrs. Ross gathered in the hall, discussing Hilary.

"I think the best thing would be to let her marry him," Mrs. Ross was saying. "She wants to reform him. Most women want to reform some man, and it's better for it to be their own husband than someone else's. They're so liable to be misunderstood, these reformers. That's how martyrs began. Besides, it won't matter what we say. That young woman proposes to paddle her own canoe."

"You'd better keep an eye on her, if you want her," Nunn remarked briefly to Dennis. "Or she'll cut along and elope with the beggar."

"But why should she?" Mrs. Ross asked. "She could go openly. After all, you can't make a woman marry any particular man in these days."

"Still, she'd have some difficult obstacles to overcome," Dennis suggested.

"Such as?"

"Well, there is me. I should be opposed to it, you know."

Nunn's voice thrust into the conversation like the horn of an animal. "And what could you do?"

Dennis turned, half-smiling. "Well, even Hilary for all her enterprise, c-couldn't make much of a marriage with a c-corpse."

We were all startled; even Nunn lost some of his habitual composure.

"A corpse. My dear fellow, talk sense. You can't go about murdering men who happen to interfere with your domestic plans."

Dennis assured him earnestly, "I've never k-killed a man unnecessarily in my life."

"Well, you can drop any plans you may have formulated about murdering people in my house."

He went out, and his sister went with him. The three of us stared at one another.

The door opened again and Hilary came in. She looked excited and breathless. "Has Ralph been here?" she asked.

"Yes, and gone again."

"Didn't he ask to see me?"

"That was one reason for calling."

"What was the other?"

"To ask me to publish a denial of our engagement."

"What did you tell him?"

"That my middle name's George Washington."

"But, Arthur, it's true. I—I'm not engaged to you any more. I told you so last night."

"If it takes two to make a marriage, it takes two to break it off."

"You mean, you wouldn't release me. But you must. You're not that sort of man. And I must marry Ralph."

"Why?"

She hesitated, looking at him imploringly, but Dennis didn't spare her. "It's all right; we're your bodyguard, and believe that three heads are better than one. Go on."

Hilary looked at me. "You know what Ralph knows about my father, don't you?"

"I know it's a lie."

She shook her head. "I daresay some of it's a lie, but some of it's true. And anyway, it isn't really so much what's true that matters, as what you can make people believe. And I won't have anyone believe that about my father. And anyway," she added, unconvincingly, "there's Eleanor, and James. A scandal like this would break up their lives."

"I don't see any reason for being insulting to your host," said Dennis. "Nunn isn't the kind of man who allows his life to collapse so easily. Now suppose you tell us the rest."

"The rest?" She looked at him, startled.

"Yes, the true reason why you're contemplating marriage with your cousin. Oh, I know all the reasons you've given us; they may be true, but it's poppycock that you'd marry a man you detested for any of them. I may not have known you as long as the others, but I know quite a lot about you. Well?"

I couldn't see what the fellow was driving at. I looked at Jeremy; his face was as white as paper, and his eyes were fixed on Hilary. For a minute she didn't speak, then she said in a dead, hopeless voice, "How did you find out, Arthur? Oh, it's true, there is something, I don't understand myself what it is altogether. But he does attract me, as you don't, as nobody else I've ever met does. Even while I know the sort of man he is, he attracts me. There's some curse, perhaps, that touches all the Felthams; you know, there's a legend that none of them is happy. I don't feel I could marry you, Arthur, or any ordinary person, now. In a way, I shouldn't think it fair, not only because of father but because of us as a family. It's different for Ralph and me. We're tarred with the same brush. Whatever the secret is, we're both in it. It comes of being Felthams. Do you understand?"

Her face was so ravaged that I was appalled. She seemed to have changed in an instant, undergone some frightful initiation into horror. But to my amazement Dennis only said, "It's all right, Hilary. I know exactly what you mean." I noticed that this morning his stammer was scarcely apparent. I felt less certain of the position myself; I'd never seen our courageous, high-spirited Hilary look like this. And I thought she really did believe in the existence of some mysterious curse linking her with her infamous cousin.

"It's Feltham," said Dennis, briefly, when she had gone again. "He's magnetic. I knew that when I first met him. Oh, he has undoubted charm of a kind, but I don't propose to allow him to exercise it, not on Hilary. He's a queer chap, you know. If we lived in the ages of faith we should say he was devil-possessed. Nowadays we've done away with the devil and replaced him by complexes and inhibitions. Though dear knows what inhibitions Feltham's ever allowed himself."

"You seem to know a lot about him," said Jeremy. "Is this your first experience of him?"

"Oh, no." Dennis looked surprised. "I doubt if he remembers me, but I was doing Secret Service work during the war and I ran across him then. He'd go anywhere, do anything; didn't know the meaning of fear. He might have worked marvels for us but he wasn't reliable. But he was so damned plausible he could have pulled off anything. Why, any other man who had done what he did would have been put up against a wall and shot at dawn. It isn't just his looks or his manner or his record. It's a gift, like painting or music. Either a man has the seed of it, or he hasn't. And Feltham has. You can see for yourselves how he's captivated Hilary. And she's not a soft school-girl as a rule."

"What's to be done?" I asked. "It seems to me that as long as the fellow's above the earth she'll be unsafe. Even if, as you pointed out, she were married to you, that wouldn't necessarily be a guarantee…"

"Precisely," said Dennis, with so much meaning that we both stopped dead. "Anyway," he continued, in his cool, unhurried voice, "the fellow ought to be put out of the way. He's a public danger. I gather you've both seen Philpotts. You do know what the position is down here?"

We agreed that we had. "Then shall we put our cards on the table? I'm here to try and discover who the Spider really is. It's a magnificent chance, looked at officially, because for the first time we're on the spot before the end of the story. Up till now we've had to begin after the death; this time we're going to prevent it, and in so doing spot the criminal."

"Is he Ralph Feltham?" asked Jeremy bluntly.

"It's no use going at it like a bull at a five-barred gate. I don't want to get hold of one principal and let the gang generally go. I want to scotch this thing for good and all. You may think me sentimental, but I tell you there are nights when I can't sleep, thinking of that crowd at work, and the havoc they've produced, and the worse havoc they have in mind."

"I don't want to be offensive," said Jeremy, "and I only ask in order to get the position perfectly clear. But your engagement to Hilary—is that part of an official campaign or something totally apart?"

"Totally apart. I admit I would strain a good many nerves to run this fiend to earth, but getting a girl to give herself away and then politely restoring her to the shelf, with a 'Thank you so much. That'll be all for to-day,' is too much even for me. No, as you suggest, my engagement is quite outside the official sphere."

"I only thought it might clear the air a little if it hadn't been," Jeremy explained. "And it would have simplified things all round."

"For yourself?"

"Yes. If I could think of you as that sort of cad, think how much more pleasure I should experience in robbing you of Hilary. Whereas I shall probably suffer hideous pangs of conscience, if you really need her..." He smiled one-sidedly. But Dennis didn't seem embarrassed.

"Charming of you, I'm sure. And very handsomely put. Like the parent who chastises his child to the tune of

This hurts me much more than you,
A thing I simply hate to do.

But to come back to Feltham. If he's in earnest about Hilary, as I think he is, the sooner he's put out of the way the better. Of course, there mustn't be any scandal. It mustn't look like suicide. Still less must it look like murder. It must be an accident, with nothing whatsoever to connect it with this house. Remember, Nunn is a big man locally, and we owe it to him, as his guests, not to get him tied up in anything discreditable. He'll be in the Lords one of these days, and he won't want to take his seat with the flavour of murder attaching to his name."

"Have you forgotten that Keith here is a lawyer?" Jeremy asked, honestly scandalised by Dennis's cool assertions. "And lawyers, like actors, are professionals first and human beings second, and a long way second, too." He turned to me in some anxiety. "If Dennis should prove to be in earnest, Tony, remember this conversation is without prejudice."

Dennis got off the table where he had been sitting. "It wouldn't matter," he murmured in his soft Irish voice. "I'm not such a fool that I should leave anything to chance. I wasn't in the Secret Service for nothing."

"It's difficult to believe you're serious," I said.

"I'm serious enough. But, as I assured Nunn this morning, I've never in my life killed a man unnecessarily. I'll tell you this, though. There'll be a good many hearts beating more easily all over the world when Ralph Feltham is in his grave. And even if that weren't true, and this was the only household he could damage, I should do the same. He isn't going to smash up Hilary's life, believe me."

He went out through the French windows into the dreary garden, where the first snowdrops were beginning to prick up in the stone bath beyond the library windows. Jeremy whistled.

"We seem to have our work cut out," he observed. "One of us had better keep an eye on Hilary and the other on that chap.

At the end of this adventure we ought to be qualified for first-rate nursemaids. By the way, does your fountain-pen write?"

"I expect so. Why?"

"Because I want to borrow one. I don't think Dennis is the sort of chap to beat much about the bush, and the papers will pay handsomely for a really lurid biography of a man like Ralph. And me knowing more than most, it might be my chance to make a touch. So long."

And he followed Dennis through the French windows.

CHAPTER VII

I

I WAS NOT LEFT ALONE VERY LONG. FIRST, MRS. ROSS POKED her head in, looking for Jeremy. When I said I couldn't tell her where he was, she looked at me suspiciously.

"I don't trust people who say they can't tell; it's the Puritan conscience evading the lie direct. It means that they know, but feel themselves bound to keep silent. It's ridiculous. I want him to help me. I've been roped into doing some work for this ridiculous bazaar of Eleanor's. I offered to dress dolls, it's the only kind of bazaar work they taught girls when I was young, and I want to dress a grandmother, but I haven't got a white-haired model. I thought Mr. Freyne's so clever with his fingers he might have cut a little bit out of the sheepskin rug, where no one would notice, and we could glue it on."

Within five minutes of her departure Eleanor appeared; she looked a complete wreck this morning, and her first words confirmed my impression that, whoever was having a bad time, no one was suffering more than she.

"I want your advice, Tony," she said. "It's about Ralph. Now that he's top dog, as he certainly is at the moment, what do you think is our best policy? Shall we go on vetoing him and perhaps drive Hilary into his arms, or shall we give him carte-blanche to come and go as he pleases, in the hopes of putting off the evil day, if nothing more."

I asked what Nunn thought about it. After all, it was his house so long as the lease lasted.

Eleanor confessed, "I've no key to James's real feelings at the moment. You can guess a little how he takes the position, because you heard what he said about Hilary the night she was lost. I don't believe, as a matter of fact, he minds so much about Cleghorne as the fact that he's been kept in the dark while all this racket about Hilary has been going on. It's very difficult for men to understand why we do what we do. I hadn't a thought, except for him."

"That's just where you were so unfair," I pointed out. "In a sense, you put the responsibility for the business on his shoulders, and even I, who have seen very little of him, could tell you that he isn't that sort of man. He'd have tackled Ralph at once. Has he suggested doing it now?"

"Not to me. But he did say that no breath of this story should be known beyond these walls. I don't know what he's going to do. I'm more frightened than I've ever been in my life. Much more frightened than when Percy shot himself, and I didn't think I'd ever have to go through anything worse than that."

I said, superfluously, that it was a pity she hadn't told him earlier. Eleanor agreed.

"All my life, Tony, I've envied people who had the courage to risk everything. What's called complete surrender. To step over a cliff, absolutely assured that you won't crash on the rocks but that by some miracle you'll be sustained—I'd give all I've got to be able to do that. But I can't. I can stand on the edge and brood over it, but I can't take the final plunge. I must feel solid earth under my feet. And I couldn't plunge this time, either. It's a question of courage, I suppose. But now things are worse than I had imagined. If I keep Ralph out, then we may force the issue with Hilary. If I let him come here, I'm afraid of the consequences."

"To him? Or to your husband?"

"To him, of course. There was a queer look about James when he said he'd make it all right. He's a clever man, he's shrewd, he's daring."

"And you think he's planning to bump Ralph off? Well, in that chap's place I should give the Abbey a wide berth. That's three people ready to finish him when opportunity offers."

We couldn't say any more, because Mrs. Ross came trailing disconsolately in again. She hadn't found Jeremy, and she didn't dare tackle the rug on her own account. When she saw us she said in a vexed tone, "Everyone seems to have a young man but me. What ideas are you putting into his head, Eleanor?"

"I'm talking about this ball we're having for Hilary's twenty-first birthday. We've been planning it for a long time. It's going to be a Fancy Dress affair, and the prize will go to the best and cheapest. That's James's idea. He says so many of the nicest people round here are hard hit that it's blatant snobbery to ask them to compete for the most gorgeous or striking affair, irrespective of cost."

"Mine hasn't cost me anything," said Mrs. Ross, complacently. "And I'm trying to persuade James to borrow a policeman's uniform, and then his won't cost anything, either. There's a dear little tubby sergeant at the local office, who'd be delighted to oblige him, I'm sure."

"And it's quite time, Tony, you settled down," Eleanor continued, "unattached men are wrong, somehow, out of place, like—like…"

"Floating kidneys," beamed Mrs. Ross. "I hope you've picked him someone nice, Eleanor. Because he's very, very innocent and he'd be sure to go wrong if he were left to himself."

I was startled, and not flattered. "I doubt if I'd make more of a mess of it than anyone else," I said, a little mettled.

"Oh, you're no judge of women," said she, gaily. "Who is it, Eleanor?"

"I shan't tell you because he'll simply set his feet like a mule, and refuse to look the girl in the face, if he thinks we have designs," said Eleanor.

"And is that mysterious nephew of yours coming? He'd brighten up any party, I'm sure."

"I don't know," said Eleanor, simply.

"He'd better, I should think, if you want to stop gossip about that gawky girl, anyhow. Oh, there's Mr. Freyne." Through the French windows she had caught sight of Jeremy, strolling along the path, his hands in his pockets, and she pounced on him forthwith.

2

It appeared to be taken for granted that Ralph would come to the dance, to which most of the county were coming, some on Eleanor's account, for she was a brilliant and unusual woman, and even the scandal that had once enveloped her, and her marriage with a man you couldn't expect the county to notice, could not dim people's interest in her; and some, frankly, on Nunn's account. He was a big man in his way, and he had the sense never to pretend, even to himself, that he was other than he was. He liked the work that had given him his present position; more, he was proud of it, and so he succeeded in making these neighbours of his see something rather fine and honourable in it. There was no question about his popularity; just as there seemed no question that he could get the constituency at the next election if he wanted it.

I had a few minutes' conversation with Hilary the night before the dance.

"I feel like a man who's going to hit a nail into a tenpenny bomb, to see what'll happen," she confided to me.

"You wouldn't be there to bother," I consoled her. "Is it Ralph?"

"It's Arthur more than Ralph. I'm afraid something horrible's going to happen, and I haven't any idea what."

"But you should know if anyone does," I urged. "The whole position hinges on you."

"But it's Arthur who will solve it. You may not think he looks much, but he's got a will like—like the Will of God. Only worse. You can't move it even by prayer."

"He's very affable to Ralph these days," I suggested. "Doesn't that chap realise this isn't a healthy spot for him?"

"Ralph's like me as I was a little while ago. He underestimates Arthur. You know, at first, seeing them together, it does look rather a case of the wolf and the lamb."

"And now you're discovering the rôles may possibly be reversed?"

"I don't think, whatever happened, I'd think of Ralph as a lamb. But Arthur's frightfully deceptive. He looks so meek…"

But I only said, "Then he ought to make you an excellent husband," because I was troubled and perplexed myself, and didn't want to show my hand.

3

The day of the party came. Personally I never had breathing-space the whole day. And the household seemed to me to go to pieces. Except for Nunn, no one was quite natural, and he went about in a business-like but forbidding manner that might have augured any disaster. Hilary came down full of excitement, covered the breakfast-table with disembowelled envelopes and gaping sheets of brown paper, ate nothing and jumped up as soon as the rest of us had finished, exclaiming, "Tony, I want you this morning. I simply must go into Munford to get some things for the party. We can have the little car, can't we, Uncle James? Thank you so much. I'll be ready in five minutes, Tony." And she had flashed upstairs again.

"What does that girl remind you of?" Jeremy asked, as the door closed.

"A mouse," said Mrs. Ross, promptly and unpleasantly. "It leaves its traces behind it wherever it goes." And she began noisily to bunch up paper and string.

I waited for Hilary in the hall. It wasn't half-past nine yet, and I thought if she was going on at this pitch all day, she'd be a rag before night, and ready for any kind of folly Ralph might suggest. Because that was the way fatigue took Hilary; she never owned up to it.

Nunn came through the hall and put a lot of letters into the clearing-basket. He was one of these energetic chaps who're down by six in all weathers, and do half their work before breakfast. Hilary saw him as she came down the stairs, said cheerfully, "What energy, Tony! And what an example for you! Come on!" and we went out to the waiting car. Fortunately the day was fine, though cold. What with buying Hilary's miscellaneous wants, that included a Teddy Bear and a bright-coloured silk scarf, and having the cup of chocolate the English people seem to have added to an already ample schedule of meals, it was one o'clock by the time we returned, to find everything at the Abbey at sixes and sevens. There had been a domestic row on some minor affair, and one of the parlour-maids was marching haughtily out of the house as we arrived.

"It'll upset the whole of to-night's arrangements," said Eleanor, in despairing tones. "And these scenes do irritate James so. Having managed a large staff satisfactorily for years he can't understand any woman not a complete imbecile having difficulty with half a dozen women. I wonder, Tony, if you could drive me into Munford this afternoon? It's maddening for you, when you've only just come back, but there's just a chance of getting hold of a temporary parlour-maid for a few days, if I go in myself. They won't send people out on chance."

"My dear, you'll be a wreck," I protested. "Can't the other maids manage?"

"It isn't so much that they couldn't as that it's against their principle. I suppose at the back of their minds is the idea that once they start doing anyone else's work, we shall reduce the staff. And if I don't make the effort and go to Munford, they won't put themselves out a scrap. Oh, I know servants, Tony. I've been dealing with them all my life, but give me servants in the town every time. They're far easier to handle, and easier to get. In fact, if it weren't for Hook, I sometimes should be in despair. Mrs. Ridley is a most obstructive woman; unfortunately she's too capable to dismiss. But Hook's my stand-by in all these minor crises. You know, when I married James he threw up a better job to come back to me. Yes?"

That was to Hook, who came in at that moment. Mrs. Ridley would be glad if she might see her ladyship for a minute. Eleanor flung me a What did I tell you? glance and disappeared. Mrs. Ross came in. "Is there a mystery or something?" she asked.

"One of the maids has given notice, and Eleanor's got to go into Munford to try and replace her," I explained. "She looks ghastly, as it is."

"She looks all to pieces," Mrs. Ross agreed. "In fact, she is all to pieces, and I can't do anything, because nothing infuriates servants so much as taking orders from two different women. And they'd much rather take them from Eleanor. She speaks to them so much more tartly than I do."

"Tartly?"

"Yes. They don't a bit appreciate being asked if they mind doing things. Well, it is insulting, you know. I used to be asked them years ago before I married Bertie, when I was companion to a catty old lady in Beckenham. Do you mind putting the coal on the fire, Miss Nunn? she'd ask me. Do you mind closing the window? fetching my shawl? cleaning the parrot? kicking the cat because it's tearing up the cottons? going out in the rain for more scones (she was a perfect hog)? And so on. Of course I minded. Doesn't everyone mind being hounded out in wet weather? Or disturbed and sent up to an icy room for no good reason just when you've settled down by the fire? But I couldn't say so. And the maids mind doing things, too. The only possible thing is to say Do this and get on with it, but I can't do it. I was virtually in their place so long it doesn't come natural. It's different for Eleanor."

"I wish this infernal party were over," I said.

Mrs. Ross began to speculate. "I wonder whose life will have changed when it is. Anyhow, I'm sure Eleanor and James agree with you. She'd better go for a holiday for a few days. You know, I've never seen her like this, and I've lived with them all their married life. I always admire her calm; I couldn't be like that myself, it wouldn't amuse me, and I get nearly as much fun asking for a lost parcel, even if I don't get it back, filling in forms, you know, and exchanging experiences about the parcels they've lost with complete strangers at counters, or shop-girls at inquiry desks, as I should have got from the thing itself, so it wouldn't be any use me thinking of cultivating the philosophic mind; but Eleanor's like me to-day, all flurried and anxious. She could have kept that girl if she'd been her own self. Of course, she was pert, but show me any girl who isn't. However, she's gone now. Here's Eleanor. Eleanor, if you're having a joy-ride, and you haven't anything very private to say to Mr. Keith, couldn't I come with you? This house is like a Zoo with all the animals let loose."

So the three of us motored into Munford, and Mrs. Ross was very conversational and Eleanor was very quiet. Mrs. Ross even asked if I wouldn't give her a driving-lesson when Eleanor went into her first Registry Office, but I drew the line at that. The notion of that bright, haphazard, fearless creature with her hands round the steering-wheel chilled my thoughts.

"You won't?" She was taken aback and manifestly disappointed. "How detestable of you. There would have been one thing in which I could crow over Eleanor; because she can't drive, either."

It was, of course, a wasted afternoon. Eleanor went to three Registry Offices, and came down the steps of each looking whiter than before. At last she said, "That's all I can do. I don't know anywhere else to go. In the old days, when I was married to Percy, one's cooks and upper housemaids always had nieces who were only too glad of a chance to get into County service. Things are different now."

"Even the County's different," agreed Mrs. Ross. "Perhaps if James were Sir Percy, it would be easier. Where are you going now?"

Eleanor said she must telephone Mrs. Ridley, and would I please find a place for tea and somewhere to park the car? Mrs. Ross said she'd buy a postal order for two shillings for the upkeep of one child for one day in some anonymous home, and I put the car away and found a tea-shop and booked a window table, and then went back and picked them both up. Mrs. Ridley, it appeared, had been distinctly chilly about the parlour-maid, but Eleanor by this time was beyond minding what any housekeeper said.

The general unrest seemed to have affected everyone. Hilary rushed into the hall to meet us, looking distraught and flushed; she said nothing had happened and no one had been, and that Mrs. Ridley seemed annoyed about something. Presently the cook came up to say some of the creams hadn't arrived, and Eleanor had to go and telephone about those; and at the last minute Hook said there'd been some mistake and they'd run short of cointreau. Eleanor said, "We can't do anything now. How did you let it happen?" and Hook looked shamefaced and said he'd run over to Feltham Major and get the stuff from Reynolds, who was reliable, and would let him have it by the back way, friendly-like. No, there wouldn't be any fear of getting into trouble at this hour; he and Reynolds would manage. When he came back I was alone in the hall; he looked extraordinarily grave, even perturbed.

"There's some nasty rumours going about the village, sir," he told me. "I don't like to mention them to her ladyship, she being so put about as it is, but it seems Sir Ralph's been talking, and talking with a pretty wide mouth. Swears he's going to get his own back to-night, and so forth. Be damned to these jumped-up gentry, if you'll excuse the expression, sir. That man of his seems to have been spreading a lot of back-chat, too. I don't know him myself, relations being what you might call strained between the two houses. But if you could put in a word to Sir James, sir. He'd take it better from you than me."

"I've nothing very definite to go on," I demurred.

Hook looked more upset than ever. "'Tisn't only that, sir. You'll excuse me, I'm sure, but being in the family so long and seeing Miss Hilary as just a little thing…"

"What are they saying about her?"

"All kinds of foul talk about her and Sir Ralph, sir."

"That seems to be Mr. Dennis's job to scotch."

"They're not leaving him out of it, neither. 'Tisn't natural, they say, for a gentleman that's engaged to a young lady to take things as mild as he does. That affair of the other night, you see. Well, there's no denying Mr. Dennis did take it very mild, and they say it's being made worth his while."

"Oh, that's absurd," I exclaimed. The notion was so ridiculous it didn't even make me angry.

"Yes, sir, but it sounds bad just the same. And if no one takes any notice, it sounds worse. Mr. Dennis has never so much as been to see Sir Ralph since that night, and to folks like the folks round here that looks odd. And you can trust them to make the worst of it. It's more interesting, I suppose."

I promised to get hold of Nunn if I had a chance. Then Mrs. Ross came down, and looked round in unfeigned surprise.

"Where's everybody else? Has the party been put off? It's a quarter-past nine. And it's supposed to begin at nine."

I explained that we didn't really expect anyone much before ten.

"Oh, of course," my companion agreed, "I'd forgotten that among the upper classes it's bad manners to be punctual. Though, goodness knows, Eleanor is always trying to educate me. She won't be down for ages. Still in her bath she is, with the sort of scents coming through the crack that we used to think nice women didn't know. It's funny how things change, isn't it? All this red finger-nail business. Now, in the East, James says, only bad women stain their nails, but here you're thought low-class if you don't. Not that I bother, because I know I couldn't deceive people into thinking I was born to the purple anyhow."

"I wanted to have a word with Sir James," I said, uneasily.

"Well, you won't be able to. I don't know when he'll be down as it is. Poor darling, hanging about outside the bathroom door, and then having to plunge into all those smells. Unless he likes to wash in his room, which is what I should do, only Eleanor's bought him one of those glass basins, and somehow it doesn't seem decent to be washing in glass. Not to me, anyhow. It makes you seem to need washing so much more, if you know what I mean."

I asked if the unfortunate man couldn't commandeer a second bathroom.

"More than one bathroom for one married couple?" Mrs. Ross demanded. "How ridiculous. Besides, I don't think it's proper. James's father and mother only had one room altogether for everything, and not a very big one at that. Married couples ought to share something, even in these days, and James is like me, he's old-fashioned. You know, Eleanor ought to have been brought up in a family like ours, where you took it in turns to have a scrub-down on Saturday night, ten minutes each, and then out you came, never mind what state you were in. And my father had strict views on decency, too, and saw to it that we learnt them."

Here, at length, Eleanor did appear, dressed as the Family Ghost, in trailing white draperies, with diamonds in her hair. Nunn followed her, in his ordinary dress suit, carrying a table napkin. It was an ingenious dress, and a courageous one, for, with his square blunt features, the stolidity of his bearing and his general lack of distinction, he looked exactly like the head waiter he represented.

Eleanor whispered to me, "Is Ralph here yet? I wonder what he'll wear."

Mrs. Ross overheard her. "He ought to come as the Co-respondent," she suggested, wittily, referring to the play that had taken London by storm. "He wouldn't need to buy anything for that. Just a file of papers to represent the writ, and a button-hole."

The rest of the party began to arrive. Hilary, in vivid silk pyjamas, carrying a Teddy Bear, came as Tantalising Tommy, though for most of the evening I think she was taken for Christopher Robin, with Pooh. The others showed a marked originality. Mrs. Ross was wearing shabby black and was, to my thinking, the success of the evening. She wore a very old and voluminous skirt of black bombazine (I think), with a ruched train, and with it a boned black bodice, with braid down the front, and two rows of tiny, close, black buttons, like boot buttons, a cameo brooch at the throat, a second brooch of twisted hair at the bosom; a very handsome lace scarf was twined round her neck and she wore a tiny black bonnet, with a jet butterfly on the crown, and long black crepe streamers. She carried an enormous black lace fan and wore a very handsome old necklet of garnets. And with this appallingly lugubrious get-up, she presented the most roguish and demure face conceivable. Her eyes sparkled as if she had treated them with atrophine; her smile was irresistible. She exchanged odd glances with her partners, contrived gestures that enchanted the least susceptible. The contrast between this mood and her appearance made her easily the most popular figure in the room, and most people guessed without difficulty that she represented the Merry Widow.

"I," she observed to me, with smug satisfaction, "am the only person daring to appear in true colours. I am a widow and a merry one. My mother always taught me that a widow's lot was the most enviable in the world. It absolved a woman from the sad necessity of explaining that she was not neglected in her youth, and yet left her as free as air. And experience is always wisdom."

Dennis came in a morning suit, as a plainclothes man, with a badge concealed under his lapel, a device that Mrs. Ross declaimed as unsporting. And Jeremy arrived after all the rest of us, disguised as a policeman. He said he had borrowed the outfit for the occasion from a friend, who was rather a dab at amateur theatricals. Mrs. Ross looked at him suspiciously.

"Is that fair? I mean, we have to say how much our dresses cost, but if you get one lent you…"

"You're so much to the good," said Jeremy, cheerfully. "I shall count the carriage I had to pay for it, and the stamp I used for the original letter. But you needn't worry. I shan't get the prize. There are far too many people here whose clothes haven't cost them anything."

I had had a little difficulty about my own get-up, but Dennis had solved that. I am not one of those enterprising men who have only to don a scarlet smoking cap to be instantly transformed into the Sultan of Turkey. But Dennis said, "Why d-don't you borrow the skull in the hall (I think it had originally belonged to a noble Feltham ancestor, but nowadays it was used to hold visiting-cards, a piece of flippancy that sincerely shocked Nunn and his sister), and wear your ordinary clothes, and c-come as Hamlet in modern dress?" So I did that, though I fancy I found my skull even more cumbersome than Hilary found her bear, with the added disadvantage that if I let it go for an instant, I was accused of birking the issues and not giving the guests a chance.

The party had an original appearance, since Nunn had virtually barred the expensive costumes that normally grace these affairs. The women were all right, of course; they can do so much with kilted frocks and silk scarves, and the majority of their accessories appear to be interchangeable, so they did well enough. But a man on these occasions generally climbs into a suit his wife has hired for him, and comes as Henry VIIIth or a cavalier or courtier of the time of the Stuarts, and these can't very well be manufactured out of a swallow-tail and a boiled shirt. One enterprising guest did appear in sandals and the drawing-room hearthrug, as S. John the Baptist, carrying a locust in a glass case, and another dared the probabilities and came as Moses, in a leonine white woollen beard, a night-gown belonging to his wife, and the Books of the Law very beautifully transcribed in gold. But the rest either had to put on dressing-gowns and carry magnifying glasses, as Sherlock Holmes (I counted four of these), or ragged overcoats and carry trays of matches. And one coward donned the red suit his wife had made him last Christmas and came as Santa Claus. As for the women, they wore every conceivable costume, from the girl who borrowed the housemaid's rig and appeared as Nippy, to people who hardly played fair, and put on handsome silk and satin clothes on the ground that they had bought them for some other party, and so could claim not to have spent a penny.

Mrs. Ross stood at my side and commented on the arrivals. She would, of course, have preferred Jeremy, but he started the fooling with the arrival of the first guest. He stood outside the door rapping out instructions and asking questions, and a good many of the people didn't realise that he wasn't there in an official capacity. I heard some whispers about unpleasantness, and "If Nunn thinks it wise to have the police on the premises..." So that the story about Hilary and Dennis and Ralph seemed pretty common property.

"I think," said Mrs. Ross, with candour, "they ought to give me the first prize. Oh, do look at that woman with a head like a turnip. It's Mrs. Stringer; well, really, she needn't have bothered about the disguise; she's always like that. Who's that man, Mr. Keith? Is he one of the servants—I never can get accustomed to all James's retinue—or is he a guest? Has it occurred to you how easy it would be to steal jewels at a party like this? Almost anyone could gate-crash. There's that child Hilary in nothing but pyjamas. You know, I simply can't understand—not the morals exactly, but the outlook—of people like Eleanor and her set. You seem just the same. Of course, people like me and James are different. Because you make a bit of money in middle-age you don't change suddenly, and James was earning ten shillings a week at fifteen and I went into a shop. And it used to horrify us to hear of the goings-on of the upper classes; the evening frocks the women wore, and the way they didn't leave much to be guessed at. But there doesn't seem to be any limit nowadays. That child hasn't got so much as a vest on, I daresay. Why, I remember being whipped by my father at fourteen for running downstairs in a petticoat with bare arms and no stockings on. There'll be no indecency in this house, he said. But you all take it for granted. All I can say is, it's as well for Ralph Feltham if he doesn't marry her."

"I thought you wanted him to," I protested.

"I've changed my mind. A man like Ralph Feltham wants a woman, someone with a steadfast personality. That girl's like a caterpillar; one minute it's on a blade of grass and the next it's humping itself off goodness knows where. She'd never hold him; she's too much of a flibberty-gibbet. Where is he, by the way?"

I said we were all wondering that. "I should keep an eye on Miss Hilary, if I were you," said Mrs. Ross, grimly. "If you don't want her slipping off by herself. In fact, that's probably why she's wearing pyjamas. She doesn't need any luggage now."

I said shortly I thought she was being unnecessarily romantic, but she only laughed. "An affair like this makes me feel romantic. Besides, I'm beginning to admire that man. He is consistent, and he hasn't changed his spots just to please James, which is a good point in his favour. He stands up to him, too. Lots of men will change anything if they think they can get cosy with a rich man, but Ralph Feltham just goes on his own way. And, you know, women do like a man who's different. Really, most of the men here could change places with one another, and even their wives would hardly notice any difference when they woke up next morning."

A man wearing the costume of the Uncle who murdered the Babes in the Wood sauntered past, with Eleanor on his arm. I saw Dennis standing against the wall, his eyes, apparently leisurely, watching Hilary. But there was a gleam in them that didn't go at all well with his pose of courteous indifference.

The dance went on; it was a gay affair, and all the visitors seemed to be enjoying themselves. As the clock hands travelled round, I heard Ralph's name mentioned more frequently; apparently, people expected him to be here, and when he didn't turn up, they speculated as to whether he had been refused admittance. And they gossiped with dubious discretion of the difficult position in which, as a family, we found ourselves.

I began to have a shrewd suspicion that the girl in the Nippy costume, whose name was Doris Yule, was my aunt's choice of the future Mrs. Keith. She was a blonde of the appealing type, with enormous eyes, the sort that make a man dream first of the infidelities of which he hasn't been guilty but of which they perpetually accuse him, and later of the subtle way in which wives can be persuaded to die without arousing suspicion. Hilary danced a good deal with Dennis, but when she was with other men she seemed completely reckless, flirting and sitting-out in a way that seemed to me in the worst possible taste. My partner remarked on it. She had been telling me that she was often asked why she didn't go on the films, and I'd asked, of course, why she didn't. She'd have been a treasure-trove to any manager in close-ups, with those eyes, though the vapidity of her personality would probably close the doors of any intelligent calling to her. She said, "I can't do it; I'm too sensitive. I know there are women who don't mind admitting the whole world into intimacy with themselves, but—oh, well, I suppose it wouldn't do for us all to be alike. We—some of us, that is—have a feeling that—that feelings should be sacred. You see, it wouldn't be just acting for me. It would be living the part. It would take too much out of me." And then she saw Hilary and asked me with a languishing air if I didn't think it simply too disgusting.

"She's one of those girls who can't leave men alone," she said. "Personally, I'm amazed at Sir James giving a party, considering what happened the other night. If I'd spent a night like that with a man of Ralph's reputation, I'd want to hide my head."

"The fact that Miss Feltham doesn't surely argues something interesting," I suggested.

She stared. "I don't know what you mean," she panted. She was on the fat side.

I wasn't any too clear myself, and I was relieved when the Wicked Uncle came in sight, with a questioning look on his face, and I shook the young woman off on to him.

But it became increasingly obvious that not only strangers but Hilary's own family were becoming anxious about her. Coming into one of the ante-rooms just before eleven o'clock, I surprised Nunn and Jeremy and Dennis and Mrs. Ross, all talking together. None of them seemed to know where she was, and it wasn't only Mrs. Ross who was conjecturing that she might be meeting Ralph somewhere. Somehow, none of us could believe that he was going to let a magnificent opportunity like this one pass him by.

"You've only got to see how she's behaved all the evening," said Mrs. Ross, in her sweeping way. "It's been absolutely outrageous. If I'd been Mr. Dennis and she'd treated me as she's treated him the whole evening, I should jilt her publicly."

Eleanor came in and joined us. "Hilary isn't here, I suppose. Quick, we mustn't collect like this. People will begin to wonder what's up. They're talking enough as it is. Mr. Dennis, when did you last see her?"

"Hilary? She was dancing with Freyne."

"And I handed her on to that long chap in a fish-tail dressing-gown."

"Well, she isn't with him now. I caught her creeping along the hall in a most suspicious way. I begged her to tell me what was wrong, but she would only say 'Nothing.' She was dying to get rid of me, I could see that, and at last I had to let her go. I had a faint hope she might be with one of you."

She went away again, and Dennis went with her. The rest of us stayed and wondered what on earth had happened to Hilary.

"She's mad to-night," said Nunn, in a curt voice, "capable of anything. For everyone's sake, I hope Feltham has the sense to keep out of the way. There's been trouble enough in that direction."

We were still talking when the French windows at the end of the room swung open and Hilary came in. She was breathless, wild-eyed, defiant, as her glance met ours. Her fair hair, that was being grown, and curled on her neck, giving her the appearance of a child of twelve, was tumbled and her face was flushed; her eyes were brilliant, but she was clearly in a towering rage.

"What's happened?" she demanded, seeing us gathered in a little group at the end of the room.

"We thought you'd eloped," said Mrs. Ross, coolly. "And it would never do to cheat the villagers of their wedding at this stage."

"Well, I daresay you could console him," cried Hilary, almost beside herself. "And the villagers won't mind whose wedding it is, so long as they get plenty of beer."

Nunn said sharply, "Hilary, what are you saying!" I tried to patch up the affair by remarking that my prospective match was off, and Jeremy pushed his arm through Hilary's, and marched her off, saying, "My dear, you're spoiling for a row to-night. Come and have an ice. It'll cool you down."

Mrs. Ross said, "I didn't know you were going to be married," and I said I thought there had been some notion in Eleanor's mind that I should rent a cosy little villa at Putney or Ealing Common and devote myself to the next generation.

"Do you mean in company with the lady of the lustrous eyes?" questioned Nunn. "I'm inclined to agree that she might make life rather too much like a perpetual Day of Judgment."

"She ought to have come in feathers, as an owl," contributed his sister, helpfully. "I've been wondering all the evening what she reminds me of."

Jeremy came back without Hilary, and said, "I hope you don't mind your house being turned into a private lunatic asylum, sir. I don't know what's the matter with Hilary. I can't do anything with her."

"Then it's a good thing you aren't going to marry her," said Mrs. Ross, who was determined to play Job's comforter that evening. "Though if it comes to that, can you afford to marry anyone? Have you a career?"

Jeremy turned to Nunn. "Perhaps you could find an opening in your office for me, sir. I'd try and earn my daily bread. Pure nepotism, of course, but it's the way most big business is run these days, I'm told."

"The way it's ruined," amended Nunn, grimly. "Well, what can you do? Accountant?"

"Not quite up to your standard, I'm afraid," Jeremy confessed. "Couldn't I go touting? They tell me there's a lot of money in that. Salary and commission, you know."

"Try and sell me an insurance policy," Nunn offered.

Jeremy assumed an appearance of grotesque briskness. "Good-morning, sir. Are you insured?"

"You think it wise to begin so baldly?"

"Most certainly I do. It's the only way. I'm a plain man. Besides, you have to get your oar in before the door's shut in your face. Good-morning, sir. Are you insured?"

"Thank you. I am."

"No doubt. But from what? Fire? Quite so. Burglary and accident? Precisely as I had conjectured. But what does that accident policy cover? Injuries, fatal or otherwise, from motor-driven vehicles, trains, other steam-driven vehicles, bicycles or other foot-driven vehicles, such as scooters, miniature cars, lap-dogs and so forth, collapse of buildings, storms, falling slates, accidents in reference to airplanes or parachutes. But are you insured, for instance, against death from wolf-bite?"

"There are no wolves in England, I believe—not at large, that is."

"Suppose one escaped from a menagerie?" suggested Jeremy, resourcefully. "And chased you down the High Street? Or through the Cathedral Square? There was a wolf of some note living in a city called Assisi at one time, and not all of us are S. Francis. Suppose you went to Whipsnade and the elephant had an accident and stepped on you? What of your widow? Foresight, my dear sir, foresight all the time."

"I don't see, James, how you can let him go," said Mrs. Ross, enchanted. "I know I shouldn't, if the chance were mine."

"You can come to me if you want something in due course," Nunn agreed. And then Dennis came in and said, "No sign of Hilary yet? I must say, like the King in the Fairy Tale, nobody can call me a fussy man, but in a gathering like this, all eager to manufacture scandal if there's none on tap, I think she might put up some show of behaving as though we were going to be married, if only for appearances' sake." He walked to the windows and looked out at the garden, the long lawns black in the heavy dew, the colourless lines of the borders, the circular beds where the geraniums were too dark to be distinguished from the pervading gloom, the mysterious effect of pollard willows standing in a long rising line, blacker than the sky. He was clearly angry, and I thought Hilary would be wise to risk vexing any other member of the household for preference, even Nunn, if she must be a nuisance at all. I knew Dennis's kind of rage, the slow-burning wrath that takes long to kindle, but longer to quench, and is apt to do such lasting damage before it is finally put out.

Jeremy said, "I should leave her alone for a bit, if I were you. She seems all to pieces to-night."

Dennis swung round. "You have seen her, then?"

"Yes. She came in by that window a few minutes ago."

"Came in from the garden, did she? Why, I wonder."

"Like the hen that crossed the street because it wanted to get to the other side of the road," combated Mrs. Ross.

"I didn't mean I wondered why she came in. I wondered why she went out."

"It's one of the things gardens are made for, to go out in, for air and recreation, you know," Jeremy told him blandly.

Nunn, appearing to lose his interest in his ward, sheered off. Mrs. Ross said, "Still, a girl doesn't go out alone at this hour of night in only a pair of pyjamas for nothing."

Dennis looked at her sharply. Then he said, "P-please, Mrs. Ross, don't s-say things like that about Hilary when other people are p-present. We all understand what you mean, but s-strangers might not." And he, too, moved off.

Mrs. Ross said in her downright manner, "What nasty minds men have. I suppose, though, if you're in the Government, you're always looking for something indecent. It's what you're paid for, and if there wasn't anything, you'd lose your job."

A little later Jeremy said to me, "Young Hilary's making a pretty average fool of herself. If she wants a split with Dennis, she might at least engineer it privately. All this publicity is damned bad form. Particularly considering his position here. He can't concentrate entirely on her; he's got this jolly little gang to round up as well. Wonder if he's discovered anything yet."

"I wonder how far Hilary's in earnest when she says she's going to marry Ralph," I countered.

Jeremy shrugged his shoulders. "She won't do that."

"I shouldn't be too sure."

"What would you like to bet me that Feltham neither marries Hilary nor comes to live at this house?"

"Who's going to prevent him?"

"I once began a short story," observed Jeremy, with apparent irrelevance. "It started: 'There were twenty-eight lamp-posts on the Highbury Road, but the only important one was the twenty-ninth.' Similarly, the really important factors in life are the unexpected ones."

"Meaning you'll put a spoke in Ralph's wheel?"

An odd expression crossed his face. "You can put it that way, if you like. At all events, Hilary will never marry the chap."

"Or only over your dead body, I suppose?"

"Not even over that. I've taken chances a-plenty in my time, but when I come to anything serious I don't, as they say, leave a stone unturned. Though I've seen a lot of things under stones," concluded Jeremy, "that would compare favourably with a fellow like Ralph."

I felt vaguely uneasy. Jeremy has lived so long in countries where might is right that I wasn't sure where he'd draw the line to achieve his end. I stayed on the landing where we had been speaking for a few minutes after he left me, thinking. And then, almost sub-consciously, I noticed that the curtain behind me was moving slightly. The window itself was shut; there wasn't a breath of air; a scrap of swansdown, masquerading as ermine, that had been torn off some pseudo-queen's dressing-jacket, lay motion-less on the polished floor. But the curtain continued to move. I went up the stairs, wishing the wretched affair were over. From the flight above, I saw Miss Yule extricate herself and go quickly along the corridor, with that expression women wear when they have something interesting to impart. I only wondered who her confidante would be.

4

I had someone rather more restful as my partner at midnight, when we went down to supper. Hilary had reappeared, and went down with Dennis. She seemed now in the wildest of spirits, bandying words with everyone.

"When are you going to be married?" I heard someone ask.

"I don't know," she returned. "I had an idea that was for the bridegroom to settle. The fact is, this is my first engagement, and I'm feeling hopelessly unsophisticated. Next time I shall have experienced all the ropes."

Dennis, smiling, said, "I'm in the s-same quandary as Kipps. I can't find an elegant turn of ph-phrase for the question, 'Didn't you ought to name the day?'"

But the supper was not to pass without incident. I knew Hilary better, I chose to think, than Dennis did, and there was that in her expression that warned me she had some madness in her mind. Her partner didn't get much of my attention, I am afraid. Fortunately, her next-door neighbour and her own plate seemed to satisfy her, and I kept my eyes on Hilary. Presently I saw her deliberately tip some mayonnaise over her pyjamas. She jumped up, "I must change," she cried. "The wretched stuff's soaked right through." But to my amazement Dennis stopped her. I don't know what arguments he used, but he wouldn't let her out of the room. A new look came over her face. From anger she changed to a kind of withering fear, and when I saw that I was convinced that somehow, even without being present among us, Ralph was exercising his influence.

5

The party was over at last. The final guest shook hands, became effusive, stifled yawns, drew a velvet cloak more securely about her conception of Boadicea in night attire, threw a final riposte to the engaged couple and went. As soon as the door shut, all light died out of Hilary's face. It was grey, pinched and without beauty. Beauty, strictly, she never had, but there was a charm, a vivacity and ardour that illumined all her words and actions; and suddenly that was as dead as the false gaiety of a moment earlier. I'll swear that all of us were aware of a definite change in the atmosphere, a sense of cold dejection. I looked up, indeed, thinking someone had opened a window and let in the wild and cheerless night. The room itself looked gaunt, cold and untidy; Hilary was drooping with weariness; Dennis looked stern, Jeremy watchful. Hilary said, "Has anyone any aspirins? I want to sleep."

Dennis said something I couldn't hear, and Lady Nunn said, "I'll send you some, Hilary. You look tired out."

But it was Mrs. Ross who had the courage, as Hilary turned away, to voice the question in all our minds. In Eleanor's, as, white and troubled, she stood by her husband, in Nunn's, who was looking stubborn and unsympathetic; in Dennis's, pale and controlled, and Jeremy's silent and alert, in mine, too, for that matter.

"What devilry has Ralph Feltham been up to to-night?"

CHAPTER VIII

I

W E DIDN'T PRECISELY GET AN ANSWER TO THAT IN THE
message that came to us next morning, but we did get a
reply to our question as to what could have kept Ralph away from
the Abbey. A little before seven o'clock two labourers, making use
of the right-of-way that runs through the extensive grounds of the
property, found the body of a man in the deep pool near the western
boundary. They took him out, but discovered him to be a stranger.
He was shabbily dressed in very ragged clothes, was unshaven,
with an untidy little mess of beard, blue cheeks and thick streaming
dark hair. His nose was thickened like that of a prize-fighter, and
one shoulder was slightly higher than its pair. They went up to the
house, leaving the body lying in the long grass by the side of the
road. Hook was the first to see them, and he demanded in some
indignation what they thought they were doing, coming into the private part of the grounds, just because Sir James was good enough to
concede his predecessor's privilege of the right-of-way to the village.

The elder of the two said, with an expressive jerk of his thumb,
"We've found a body down there. In the pond. It's his estate, so I
reckon we ought to bring the body here."

Hook stared at them. "What are you talking about? A body…"

"That's right. Tramp or something of the kind from his looks.
My missus allus has said it was dangerous not to put a paling round
that there pond. Right on the high-road it is, and as deep as hell.
Any chap coming back a bit muzzy might go lolloping into it, and
not know where he was till it was too late."

"That sort of chap isn't any great loss," said Hook, jealous for the reputation of the estate. "Wait you here, and I'll tell Sir James."

I suppose the emergencies of an insurance office make a man cultivate both a philosophic and an impassive outlook. Nunn said, "A tramp? In the pond? What have they done with him?" with rather less excitement than Eleanor showed when a sapphire dragon-fly got into the greenhouse and filled the place with iridescent beauty.

"The men said they'd left him in the grass, if you please, sir; he was a biggish man, and dripping-wet. They hadn't got a hurdle or anything of that sort, but if they could have a barn-door, say…"

They went down to collect the body, and Nunn went with them. They brought it up to the house, with Nunn's handkerchief over the dead face, and Nunn himself walking like the chief mourner in an ancient funeral, beside the bier. The body was put in the barn, on a long trestle-table that Hook had arranged impromptu. There was no question about the fellow being dead. He was stone cold, heavy and stiff; the water streamed from his shocking clothes.

"Must ha' missed his footing," one of the labourers volunteered. "Hunger makes a chap a bit light-headed…"

Nunn said unsympathetically that the fellow didn't seem to be underfed, and indicated that it was more likely he'd called at the Blue Boar. Hook stood by, saying nothing, but frowning, till Nunn asked sharply, "What is it? Do you know who he is?"

"No, sir. But I can't help thinking he must be a stranger. I mean, otherwise what was he doing on the right-of-way at all? If he was a native, he'd know it didn't lead him anywhere that would be any use to him. But p'raps he thought he'd find some barn or house where they'd let him sleep."

"Much wiser if he'd gone to the casual ward," said Nunn. "And that's why we pay rates to keep it going. But perhaps he isn't a stranger, and he was aiming at something special."

The two men went off, full of a placid self-importance, and the news percolated through the house. We had all come downstairs, except Eleanor and Hilary, who were having breakfast in their rooms. Hilary reported an appalling headache; Eleanor was simply played out. Mrs. Ross wore the expression of a sensible woman whose life has never admitted such possibilities as breakfast in bed, when she heard that.

Only Dennis seemed particularly interested in the unknown man. He asked where he was.

"In the barn," said Nunn.

"Could I see him, sir?"

"Of course you can. Why? Do you expect to find a friend of yours?"

"It occurred to me I might be some use in identifying him," Dennis agreed, unruffled by the other's brisk irony.

Jeremy and I went with him. The figure, when the handkerchief was removed, was not an attractive one. The head lolled and the blue patches on his cheeks seemed discoloured already. Dennis behaved very queerly. He took out a handkerchief and carefully applied it to the sodden flesh. He didn't rub it, he patted it gently with very soft careful movements. When he removed the handkerchief, he said quietly, "I wondered, you know…" and held it out for us to see. It was stained with some bluish dye that had been on the face of the corpse.

"I don't know if all this is highly irregular," he went on, "but I have both of you here as my witnesses, and Keith is a lawyer, so I'll take the chance." And moistening the handkerchief again, he began to rub, softly but firmly, on the stubbled chin. He worked for some time, and presently we saw the stubble peel off like the mask it was, revealing a prominent chin, tanned and powerful, and strongly shaved.

"The hair's his own," I heard him mutter, "but what the deuce is wrong with the nose?"

I began to speak, but Jeremy's hand touched mine, and I stopped at once. It was an odd sensation, watching this silent man at work on a corpse. But he was justified in his suspicions, though, by the time he straightened himself, we were both prepared for what he had revealed to us, the face of Ralph Feltham under the stubble and the crooked nose and the wild sweep of wet hair.

"You knew it was going to be him?" said Jeremy, ungrammatically.

"I thought it probable. At all events, I was convinced something very grave had happened to prevent his appearing at last night's show. It was a magnificent chance for him. He had everyone of any importance in the neighbourhood turning up, and he'd only to breathe a whisper of his coming marriage with his cousin, to set all their dovecotes aflutter."

"You have to remember that he was proposing to live at the Abbey afterwards," I reminded him, "and there are some things that even the relaxed manners of these days won't swallow. After all, Hilary is publicly engaged to you."

"Quite right, but all the same I was expecting something final this morning. Of course, we know very little at present, not even why Hilary rushed into the garden at eleven o'clock and came back in that frantic mood; nor why she tried to get away again during supper—she threw mayonnaise over her clothes on purpose, but I'd had about enough by that time, and I made her stay. A lot of people will sympathise if she announces a broken engagement, I fancy."

"Do you think she went to meet Ralph?"

"I don't know, but she didn't go out into the garden on a February evening in that ridiculous rig without some definite purpose. Mrs. Ross is right, too; she ought to be well smacked, running about with hardly any more on than those ridiculous pyjamas, even if she did wear a coat, as she swore she did. You have to remember that Nunn is a straitlaced sort of fellow, who wouldn't countenance anything unconventional, either. I suppose, now he realises that Feltham has or had a hold over his family, he had to be superficially genial. The question now is, how to keep the most damaging truth out of the coroner's way."

"You keep forgetting that Tony's a lawyer," Jeremy reminded him.

Dennis smiled. "Ah, but he's a connection of the family and Hilary's friend. That more than weighs down the scale."

"Who is the coroner?" Jeremy was asking.

I answered. "A fellow called Wellington-Andrews. A pursy presumptuous sort of devil, as difficult as his own name. He'll get every ounce of juice out of the affair. It'll be a God-send to the villagers and the county generally, who'll come in their hundreds to hear how Feltham, who knows his own lands as he knows his own reputation, on an ordinarily clear night, contrived to fall into his own pond. One thing, they'll decide he wasn't sober, and there they might be right."

"There's something I want to know," said Jeremy. "Are you by any chance associating Hilary with any of this?"

"My sole intention is to try to prevent anyone else doing so. I'm afraid she's cooked her own goose to some extent. A lot of people noticed her manner last night, and some of them may have noticed that she disappeared. Anyway, they've been bracketing her name with his ever since she disappeared on the evening of the fog. Still, I doubt if they'll try and suggest she shoved him in. One of us is more likely to get that compliment paid him."

"Meaning...?"

"It might easily be me. I've been saying that come what may Hilary shan't have anything to do with Feltham. So have you. Nunn hasn't been as discreet, I fancy, as usual. Anyway, Lady Nunn's been going round looking like a shell that may explode at any minute. And she's been as nervous as ninepence in case of an open split. And everyone has commented on the geniality with which the Abbey has been thrown open to Feltham since an occasion when one might well suppose all of us would feel less inclined than usual to be amicable. There'll be a great deal of amateur arithmetic indulged in locally during the next few days, and two and two will present more astonishing totals than ever before."

"Are you," I asked, "assuming there's been foul play?"

"I'm assuming nothing, till we have the findings of the coroner's jury. But on a commonsense argument, a man like Ralph Feltham doesn't fall into a pond on his own territory when he has so much at stake. Yes, I've read as many detective books as the rest of you, and I know that some of the besotted neurasthenics you find therein do pitch themselves into ponds solely for the pleasure of getting innocent men hanged, but I never believe in the reality of those people. It's too damned risky. You'd probably get an Open Verdict, which would completely defeat your aim, and if you didn't, you wouldn't get any satisfaction, whatever you might anticipate. No, I'm afraid we may as well face up to the fact that we're all in for a very unpleasant time. And it's no use thinking we can camouflage either this affair or the affair of the other night. Plenty of people will be only too happy to testify to the fact that Hilary was missing for several hours, and that the next morning Feltham rode up as bold as brass, and was admitted. Oh, they will stir up a lot of mud, though they'll very likely obscure the issues in so doing. But none of us will be let down lightly." Then he replaced the handkerchief over the changed face and asked me if I'd get hold of Nunn and break the facts to him.

"I want to get hold of Hilary," he added, "and try and shake a little of the truth out of her."

His tone was grim. I noticed this morning his stammer was scarcely perceptible.

2

Nunn asked me if I'd drive over to Feltham Major and bring Dr. McKenzie back with me. The local doctor had been called out on a labour case that might last all day. "And since we are in for a scandal, I should like to be associated with men I have met," he said. "McKenzie's line seems to be out of order; these country lines are shocking. But the sooner we get hold of him, the better."

I took a car and drove out. McKenzie had heard that a body had been found in the pool, and didn't seem much interested when I told him whose it was.

"Oh, aye," he said, placidly. "Feltham's, is it? I heard they'd found someone. Well, well, a fellow like that was bound to come to a bad end." He collected one or two things into a little bag inseparable from the man. "Something for the County to talk about for a week or two. They might be grateful to the chap that did it."

"That did...?"

He caught my elbow. "Don't try and bait an old fox. Do you think I don't know the sort of reputation the fellow had locally? Why, I helped to get a lad to Canada not many months ago, whose name isn't Feltham, but who carries the stamp of his parentage all over the world with him. And he'll start making trouble as his father did before him. There are a good many people who'd be glad of a chance to put a bit of lead into Ralph Feltham, male and female. A thorough bad lot. Well, it's better than dying in prison, which is his normal end."

He asked for details as we drove back to the house. When I told him about the tramp's disguise, he said quickly, "Why was that? Trying to escape notice?"

"There was a Fancy Dress Party at the Abbey last night."

"Oh, aye. Fancy Dress. Y' know, that's one of the things I can never understand, putting on the kind of clothes people wear who cadge for coppers in cheap watering-places, and not because you must, but because you choose. It's like these ridiculous new sports—cockroach racing, for instance. There's no sense in it, but other people do it. Well, go on. Instead of putting on evening dress, which is revolting but civilised, he donned rags and a faked chin, which is revolting and barbarous, and fell into a pond and was drowned. Somehow that doesn't seem to fit very well. He might, you see, so easily wear the rags and still walk safely. Or do you think he was pushed in?"

"We know nothing about it, except that he's dead," I replied non-committally; because, whatever I said to McKenzie now, I should have, no doubt, to repeat at the inquest later, and then I wanted to say as little as possible.

Nunn was waiting for us when we reached the Abbey, and took McKenzie along to the improvised mortuary. They didn't invite me to accompany them, so I went into the morning-room, where several members of the household, though not Hilary, were standing about, talking in the aimless manner people do at times of crisis.

Mrs. Ross was saying, impressively, "I knew all last night something dreadful was going to happen. Who did it, do you think?"

Dennis replied smoothly, "There's a thing known in the affairs of men and nations as an act of God."

"Oh? Is pushing people into ponds an act of God? If he'd been hit over the head with a hatchet, would that have been an act of God, too?"

Jeremy, catching the infection of her absurd mood, said in irrepressible tones, "There was once a little girl, who came in from the garden, and said to her mother, 'Mummy, there was a red rose in the circular bed that was going to blossom, so I blossomed it.' Helping God along a bit, you see."

"That's very ingenious. Which of us do you think they'll suspect of helping God where Ralph Feltham's concerned?"

"I don't know, I'm sure."

"Well, are you going to tell the coroner that?"

"I don't suppose they'll want my opinion. They don't pay much attention to tramps and outcasts. If I were a householder, now…"

"Oh, of course James will be very important. But I don't think you should say that about tramps. I wonder how much Hilary knows."

"Why should she know anything?"

"She knew a lot about Captain Feltham none of the rest of us knew, and she certainly saw a great deal more of him than the rest of us did. And she seemed to think she was going to marry him. Oh, here's Eleanor."

Eleanor looked more ghastly than I had ever seen any woman look. Even Mrs. Ross seemed startled, and dropping her tone of idle frivolity, she said in earnest tones, "It's not your fault, my dear. No one can blame you. They can't blame James either, because I've seen the lease, and it says he isn't to make any alteration in the grounds and general lay-out without permission in writing from the owner, and I'm sure Captain Feltham would never have let us fill in the pond."

Dennis asked "Why" in an interested tone, and Mrs. Ross said vaguely, "Oh, well, a pond's a useful thing to have in a place like this. It's very deep, they say. And in old days people had dungeons, and they're out of fashion now. They do need something."

Eleanor remarked wearily, "It isn't a joke, Meriel, and I don't think it will help things to treat it as one."

But it was difficult to quench Mrs. Ross. "But, Eleanor dear," she expostulated, "Mr. Keith agrees with me it's absolute Nemesis. He strangled this unfortunate French girl, and—oh, well, you all know about the mills of God. And Mr. Dennis says it's called an act of God. No one holds you responsible for that. Not even insurance agents. You ask James."

I don't think Eleanor was listening. She was as white as paper, her eyes oddly dark in that ravaged face. She looked, in fact, like the ghost she had represented last night. She was moving slowly round the room, touching one object after another, without realising the nature of any of them.

Presently she turned towards us. "It's too clever to be an accident," she said in despairing tones. "Considering how many people wanted Ralph out of the way. Things don't pan out as simply as that in real life. It's like a play." She sat down at last, folding her beautiful hands in an attitude of despair. "I suppose everything will come out now. Have you ever noticed, Tony, the complete detachment of justice? James has done nothing—Hilary has done nothing—but they'll suffer." But I couldn't believe she was troubling very much about Hilary.

Meriel Ross spoke in rousing tones. "Nonsense. Of course, if you go about looking like a ghost, or a woman with a crime on her conscience, everyone will believe the worst. As a matter of fact, if I'm asked, I shall say the Captain was in the habit of drinking too much, and I'd heard him threaten suicide if Hilary wouldn't marry him. And Hilary had better tell the same story. It's always as well to have everybody telling the same truth, especially when they're on oath."

"And, of course, he'd choose the night of the ball, when Hilary was letting everyone congratulate her on her engagement, so as to make things more unpleasant," agreed Jeremy. "You ought to have been a novelist, Mrs. Ross."

Dennis and I felt more serious; at least, we couldn't joke in this hilarious manner. It looked to both of us as if the affair was going to be an extraordinarily unpleasant one for us all. I couldn't myself see much hope of saving Eleanor's good name, unless Ralph had destroyed every scrap of clue, which didn't seem to me likely. And Hilary couldn't escape, anyway. The trouble was, you couldn't get at her these days, as it had been possible to do even a year ago. She'd been a nice, candid child then, but now she evaded your questions with a smooth aloofness or a wild burst of spirits that baffled you. In fact, unless McKenzie was prepared to sign a death certificate for simple drowning, and the coroner pronounce a verdict of Misadventure, there seemed little hope of hushing any of the scandal; and everyone in the county would want to hear the details, and contribute titbits of local gossip.

3

At last McKenzie came back, and a single glance at his face, and at Nunn's, that was pale and drawn under its square impassivity, confirmed my worst fears. Nunn was saying, "You'll give evidence at the inquest, of course? And I take it we may expect further inquiries."

"Oh, bound to," said McKenzie casually. "Matter of fact, I'm interested professionally. I've never known a case of simple drowning where there was so much congestion in the lungs as there is here. But it'll be good to get another opinion. I dare say Gudgeon, the police surgeon, will be along later."

When McKenzie had gone, Eleanor said softly, "The police, James? We're to be spared nothing."

Nunn said in common-sense tones, "You rationally expect the police when you have a mysterious death. It looks to me as though the whole thing will turn on medical opinion. And finally, it'll rest with the coroner's jury."

"What can they do?"

"Bring in a verdict. If this isn't an accident, it must be foul play. They're going to help to decide which. Unless they can suggest another alternative. You can't be sure. There's no end to the things juries will suggest. They feel they're on their mettle in a way, you know. They talk about sifting the evidence, and truth being stranger than fiction. Not that they've any special qualifications. Has it ever struck you how odd it is to leave a man's fate in the hands of twelve casually-appointed strangers, all of whom may be dolts for all we can tell? Or prejudiced. Well, that's English law, and if we have to live under it, it seems a natural corollary that we should die under it, too. Eleanor, my dear, you'd better rest, if I may suggest it. You'll want all your strength when the inquiry proper begins."

I had never heard him talk so fluently; I thought it was to give Eleanor a chance of pulling herself together. Perhaps, like myself, he was afraid that she would suddenly collapse, and the notion of that fine, enduring woman going to pieces alarmed us all. Eleanor took his advice and went off, with Mrs. Ross to look after her; Nunn excused himself and disappeared; Jeremy said, "I wonder what Dennis is doing to make Hilary confess. Gosh! The police! What a racket!"

Whatever Dennis had been doing to get the truth out of the girl, he didn't seem to have accomplished much, beyond upsetting her completely. She came to find me presently, saying in frantic tones, "Tony, have you any influence with Arthur? I don't know what he's driving at, but he obviously doesn't believe a word I say."

I asked her what she had said, and she told me, "He wants to know what I was doing in the garden last night. I told him I wanted to be alone, and get a breath of fresh air. Of course, you know he was annoyed to start with. He thought I was making myself cheap with my partners. He doesn't seem to realise that my stock's gone down since that evening with Ralph. People aren't quite the same, and I made a fool of myself, I know, and felt I couldn't stand it any longer. But on my honour, Tony, Ralph's death is nothing to do with me."

"I believe you," I tried to console her, "and I'm sure Dennis does, too."

"Arthur thinks I'm nothing but a liar. He as good as told me so. And he caught my arm so hard I shall be black and blue to-night. I thought he was going to try and shake some sort of admission out of me."

I said, "I don't want to bother you, but tell me one other thing. Why did you upset mayonnaise over your pyjamas at supper?"

She blushed rosily. "Did you see that, too? I was being chaffed in a way I didn't much like, and I thought suddenly I was going to cry. I wanted to get out—like a small girl who's afraid of being sick in the drawing-room."

Even for Hilary that was very thin, and I wasn't much surprised at Dennis's attitude. But she had plenty of staying power. Even when the police got hold of her and asked her again and again about that visit to the garden, she stuck to her ridiculous story. (I had wondered how they knew of it, but it appears that Miss Yule had torn down with her tongue hanging out to confide in some girlish friend of hers that there was an awful row imminent between that Feltham chit and her admirer, and she'd be surprised if that wedding ever came off. I fancy we were indebted to the same young woman for some of the coroner's other leading questions, as to Hilary's relations both with Dennis and with Ralph.)

4

The inquest was a gruelling affair. Wellington-Andrews had a large, ponderous, unintelligent face, with long moustaches; he spoke weightily and felt his own importance. As a rule, he had nothing more interesting to adjudicate than the death of a man employed on one of the neighbouring farms, with some perfectly simple solution like an attack by a bull, or strain following a hard day; or a road accident, when he could air his views on the heinousness of motor-cycles, and this affair of the Felthams, with its soupcon of scandal, was much appreciated by that tilted Roman nose.

I take my facts of the inquest largely from the local press. It's always easy, in detailing an affair like this, to lay undue emphasis on what contributes very little to the conduct of the case or the solution of the mystery, with the possibility of slurring over facts that do eventually prove of first-rate importance. Anyhow, here they are, for whatever anyone can make of them.

CHAPTER IX

N UNN HAVING GIVEN EVIDENCE OF IDENTIFICATION, MCKENZIE
was called to give medical evidence as to cause of death.
He said that he had felt some difficulty in giving a certificate of
death from accidental drowning, as in his experience, and he had
at one time held a sea-coast practice and had a good deal of work
in connection with drowned persons, he had never known such
a degree of congestion from simple drowning. If a man were
forcibly held under water, he said, congestion would ensue, and
the longer he were kept submerged, the greater would the degree
of congestion be. There were no injuries to the face or bruises on
the body, which seemed to argue against the likelihood of a struggle; deceased was a strong, healthy man, not likely to have had a
sudden fit, and had clearly been in his normal health a little earlier
in the evening, as he had set out with the intention of attending
a party at the Abbey. He, the witness, had considered the possibility of his having slipped into the pond, but it seemed to him
unreasonable that a man who was a notoriously good swimmer
should have collapsed without making any appreciable effort to
save himself. In reply to a question by the coroner, he said that
the body was not entirely free from marks of injury. Blood had
flowed from one ear; this might have been the result of congestion, but there was a wound to the left ear which appeared to have
come in contact with some sharp material or object. And some
time prior to death there had been a bruise on the back of the
head. In his opinion, this bruise was not sufficient to render a man
unconscious, though he admitted that it might induce a certain

degree of vertigo, during which time the subject would be more or less helpless.

"Is it your opinion that, having been rendered giddy, he could have been thrust into the pond?" Wellington-Andrews asked.

"It's possible, of course. But the shock of the cold water would undoubtedly have revived him."

"But if he had been held under the water…"

"That, of course, is a different consideration. But you must remember that in that case whoever was responsible would be bound to bear traces of the affair. For instance, the sleeves and arms of such person or persons would be immersed."

"You don't consider that the deceased was dead before being put into the water?"

"In my opinion, it's a practical impossibility for any medical man to answer such a question with certainty. But if he was dead, then there's only one way, I think, in which he could have met his death, and that is if someone had put a wet cloth over his head, choking the nose and mouth, which would produce the same effect as ordinary drowning."

"Have you ever known such a thing to happen?"

"Not within my own experience, but there is a classical criminal case in which that precise thing is supposed to have been done."

"And, in your opinion, death could not have been due to an accident?"

"I should have said not. I can't account for so much congestion in a person who had not recently had a heavy meal, and who was not liable to apoplectic or epileptic fits. But I should add that I am open to conviction on this point. It's always difficult to lay down any hard and fast rule that will govern all cases."

"Did you know the deceased?"

"I had known him for years, and had attended him once or twice for minor ailments. In my view, he was a perfectly healthy man."

Then they called Gudgeon, the police surgeon. It was unfortunate for everyone that Nunn hadn't had his opinion instead of McKenzie's at the outset, for he declared roundly that in his view death might well be due to accidental drowning. The amount of congestion did not appear to him excessive.

Several of us pricked up our ears at this, and hoped the coroner wouldn't take the matter further. But he wasn't disposed to let the matter pass so easily. He wanted the jury, he said, to have every possible chance of determining a very odd case, and possibly if they knew something of the dead man's circumstances and his position in the neighbourhood generally, it might materially assist them. He called Dennis.

Dennis looked cool and collected. He gave his name and address, and said he was a civil servant, who was paying a visit to the Abbey as the fiancé of Miss Feltham.

"For some reason I c-can't fathom," he added, "civil servants and p-plumbers are the b-butt of the nation. But they are the b-back-bone, too." As soon as he spoke, it was obvious to anyone who knew him that he was like a cat on hot bricks, inwardly shying away whenever Hilary's name was mentioned. We supposed he was hoping to avoid any mention of Hilary's ill-starred visit to the Cottage ten days earlier, and her mysterious venture into the garden on the night of the party.

"I understand that it was you who discovered the identity of Sir Ralph?"

"Yes."

"You were suspicious as to his whereabouts?"

"Yes, I was. You see, I kn-knew he'd been invited to the party and meant to c-come. And when a man d-doesn't turn up when he's expected, and within a few hours a b-body is found on the p-premises, you are apt to p-put two and two together. And in my youth I was intended for a ch-chartered accountant."

"I see." Wellington-Andrews obviously wasn't going to like this witness. "You had met Sir Ralph?"

"Oh, yes. I'd seen him at the Abbey m-more than once."

"What were your relations with him?"

"Really," protested Dennis, "I hadn't any. I hardly knew the m-man."

"You had no reason for cherishing ill-feeling against him?"

"It isn't v-very easy to cherish ill-f-feeling against a man you d-don't know," returned Dennis, reasonably.

"Isn't it a fact that you had had several arguments about him with Miss Feltham within a few days of his death?"

Dennis smiled. "Oh, I d-daresay. I was generally arguing with her about s-something."

"Please keep to the point. You were objecting to the amount of time she spent in the deceased's company."

The old fox hadn't lost any time in collecting local gossip, and he meant to have his pound of flesh, with a bit over, if he could secure it. I heard later that he disliked Nunn, and was glad to make things as unpleasant for him as possible, but I daresay that was no more than another scrap of malicious local rumour.

Dennis was composedly answering the last question. "I objected to all the t-time she spent in anyone's c-company, but mine."

"Is it not a fact that she threatened to marry the dead man?"

"Oh, I expect so. She was always th-threatening to marry someone else when she was c-cross with me. My m-married friends tell me it's quite usual. Nothing to get hot and b-bothered about."

"You had assured her that she would never marry him?"

"Well, she w-won't, w-will she?"

"What precisely did you mean when you told her that?"

"P-precisely what I implied. That I didn't intend to let her m-marry Sir Ralph. I didn't intend to let her m-marry anyone but me, if it comes to that."

"I see. I believe, though, I am not being over-emphatic when I say that you had a grudge against the dead man. About a week ago, half the neighbourhood turned out to look for Miss Feltham, who had disappeared in mysterious circumstances."

"I never heard a fog called a m-mysterious circumstance before," Dennis objected. "Miss Feltham got l-lost in the fog and very sensibly went to her c-cousin's house for shelter. I c-call it the dispensation of P-providence that there was a house for her to go to. I was out in the fog myself for m-most of the evening, and it was devilish cold. She might have got frost-bite."

"You had no angry words with the dead man in that connection?"

"Why on earth should I? He c-came over next morning to apologise for not b-being able to let us know she was with him. He hasn't g-got a telephone."

"You saw him on that occasion?"

"Only for a moment from an upper landing. We hardly spoke."

"And yet, knowing him as little as you did, you had no difficulty in recognising the body, although I understand it had been identified by no one else?"

"There hadn't been m-much time. No one had seen him except the butler and Sir James, and he's t-told you they weren't on exactly intimate t-terms."

"But you, who had only had casual glimpses of him up at the Abbey, recognised him at once?"

"I've been in the S-secret Service, you see," explained Dennis, apologetically. "You get up to all the t-tricks of the trade there, the wig and the mask and the shaping of the nose—all the b-bundle."

"I see."

"B-besides, there were the hands. You c-can't disguise hands as easily as you can faces, and he h-had a little scar on the wrist…"

"You noticed that, too, during your desultory meetings?"

"You g-get accustomed to that kind of thing, t-trained in it, you know. If you stop and th-think for a minute, you'll see how important it is to memorise d-details like that. It's not so hard to change your f-face and your c-colouring, and you can pad one shoulder, as he did, to make it look higher than the other, but sc-scars and birthmarks are much harder to get rid of. That's why observation of them c-counts for so much."

Obviously, he wasn't going to get any change out of Dennis, and presently he realised it, and told him he could go. Then he called on Nunn, and put him through his paces. He said he understood that Ralph was not a constant visitor at the Abbey.

"He isn't at all a constant visitor to Feltham," Nunn told him.

"But when he does come, he doesn't stay with you?"

"He has his own establishment in the neighbourhood. My only relationship to him is that of his tenant, and he's only a very distant connection of my wife's, and that through marriage. In the circumstances, it appears to me unreasonable to suggest that I should offer him hospitality."

"Is it a fact that you and he were not on the best of terms?"

"Sir Ralph and I moved in different circles and had different views on most matters. Again, it would be unreasonable to expect us to be intimate."

"Is it not a fact that at one time you refused him admittance to your house?"

"I am a busy man," said Nunn, urbanely, "and I have frequently refused admittance to visitors. The fact that Sir Ralph was on his way to an entertainment given by me, and at my invitation, surely indicates my attitude towards him."

Wellington-Andrews disliked this able evasion and showed his displeasure, but he scored no more with Nunn than he had with Dennis, who met most of his questions by the repeated avowal that he had known the dead man very slightly, and was not in a position to give information about him. He had last seen him alive a few days before the party. He did not consider it strange that he had not recognised him in fancy dress.

"You haven't any reason for supposing that he would take his own life?"

"I'm convinced he wouldn't. Why should he?"

"Then you can't offer any assistance?"

"I can only say what everyone present knows about him, that he was a man with many enemies, and that he never took any steps at conciliation. He thought it weakness."

"And your theory is that he was followed and murdered by some anonymous person with a grievance?"

"Murderers mostly remain anonymous as long as they can. As for theories, I have none. I should have thought it an accident myself; the pond is on the roadway, and a night in February is dark. Of course, I'm not disputing the medical evidence of Dr. McKenzie. I'm no authority at all in that direction. I can only assure you that I know nothing of the affair."

That finished Nunn's evidence, and Eleanor added nothing new. There was no mention of any hold Ralph had had over her, and it seemed probable that we could prevent that, at least, from becoming public property.

The coroner seemed trying to show how many men there were at the Abbey on the night of the 15th who were eager to see Ralph in some other world. He didn't, as I expected, call Hilary next, but asked for Jeremy. Jeremy was cool and untroubled. He said he'd known Ralph on and off for several years, but never at all intimately; he had never been inside his house.

Wellington-Andrews said, "I believe it to be a fact that on the night of the dance you were heard to observe that you would move heaven and earth to prevent a marriage between Miss Feltham and Sir Ralph."

"I don't think anyone could seriously have linked Sir Ralph and marriage. It wouldn't have been suitable. Certainly, I should have done everything in my power to prevent it, if it had been mooted."

"May I inquire why?"

"Because I'm proposing to marry her myself."

"I see." The foxy old man was pleased, even delighted. He had provided his audience with a sensational motive, and he saw that his moment was being universally appreciated.

"Are you sure you see?" Jeremy asked, pleasantly. "Because, if the idea has flashed through your mind that I had anything to gain, as things stand at present, from Sir Ralph's death, you're inaccurately informed. If I'd meant to occupy the front seat, I should have pushed Mr. Dennis into the pond. He's the real obstacle in my way."

The coroner observed sardonically that perhaps Mr. Dennis would take this as a warning. Then he asked me a few questions that I hadn't any difficulty in answering, and then at last he called on Hilary.

"You were on intimate terms, I think, with Sir Ralph Feltham?" he began without preamble.

"He was my cousin."

"And there were times when you contemplated marrying him?"

Hilary said sweetly, "There are times when one contemplates marrying anything, one's so bored."

"But he was in earnest, even if you were not."

"Of course he was. Men are."

"And ladies are usually flippant?"

"I don't know about that. It depends how keen they are, I suppose. But it stands to reason a man doesn't talk about getting married unless he's serious, because he might be taken seriously, and think what a fix he'd be in then."

"So that he was serious in wishing to marry you?"

"To the extent of being very jealous of Mr. Dennis."

"And you agreed to break off your engagement?"

"No, no." Hilary's face whitened at that unexpected thrust. I wondered how that had leaked out. Through one of the servants perhaps, the girl Eleanor had dismissed a couple of days earlier. Hilary had certainly given the Servants' Hall plenty of matter for gossip during the past few days. Or Ralph might have broadcast the news himself. It would be quite in keeping with his general attitude, and he had enough sense to realise that when a whole community begins to expect a certain course of action on the part of any individual, it is much more likely that that course will be followed up, than if the most constant pressure is privately brought to bear on the victim.

Hilary said, "I could name half-a-dozen people who will agree that we were actually discussing possible dates for the wedding at my party. That doesn't look much as if I had thought of marrying Sir Ralph."

The coroner was obliged to let that go. "Still, you felt very friendly-disposed towards him? Otherwise, you would hardly have remained so long at this house a short time ago, when you realised the anxiety your friends and relations would be experiencing on your account."

"He was my cousin," said Hilary, indifferently, "and I'd have sheltered in an upturned bucket on a night like that. I thought my people would probably guess where I was."

"Did they know Sir Ralph was in the neighbourhood?"

"I don't know. That didn't occur to me."

"You don't think Sir Ralph had any grounds for believing you might change your mind and marry himself?"

"It's never very easy, as I daresay you know, to convince a man he can't have his own way, when he sees no reason why he shouldn't."

I don't think, on the whole, Hilary made a very good impression; most people seemed of the opinion that she'd played dangerously near the edge with Feltham, and probably involved her fiancé in a nasty mess; anyway, they agreed that Dennis had ample grounds for jealousy.

The coroner's last question to Hilary related to the last time she had seen Ralph; she said it was at the Abbey a couple of days before the party, and she had only seen him for an instant. There had been no serious discussion between them. Yes, she admitted she was surprised when he didn't turn up on the 15th and perhaps relieved. She had not heard from him in that connection.

Any of us could have endorsed that last fact. You can't mistake Ralph's notepaper; it's one of his glaring extravagances, huge square white envelopes of a roughish cartridge paper with the seal in black on the flap. He was tremendously proud of the seal, and I think he liked to flaunt it at Nunn, who hadn't one. They say he even had it impressed on his scribbling blocks. And no such envelope had arrived at the Abbey during the week preceding the party. Hook, the butler, who sorts the letters, bore out my own impression about this.

There was only one other witness, but from a spectacular point of view he was able to eclipse all the rest combined. This was Baynes, who had been Ralph's batman, and was afterwards his servant in civil life. Baynes was a thin, well-spoken, superior sort of man, who answered questions readily. I wondered how many of Ralph's shady secrets he knew, but it seemed obvious that he wasn't going to tell anything that didn't suit his book.

He was asked whether Ralph seemed in ordinary health on the night of the 15th. He said, "He was in very good spirits. He had been looking forward to the party. He thought it was an opportunity."

"For what?"

"He said for re-asserting himself, sir, whatever that might have meant. He'd talked a lot during the week, as plenty besides me can tell you. He'd taken a lot of trouble over his costume, and I believe he was going to speak to anyone he met on his way over, in the hopes of making them think he was the genuine article. He left the house a bit after ten."

"He didn't say anything that led you to think he might be going to take his own life?"

"Oh, no, sir. I'm sure such a thought never went through his head."

"He was sober?"

"Yes, sir. He hadn't touched drink all day. As a matter of fact, he did say one very odd thing just as he was leaving. He turned back at the door and said to me, 'Good-night, Baynes. I have an idea I may be going to my death.'"

"What on earth did he mean by that?"

"I did ask him, sir, but he wouldn't say much. But I gathered he was afraid of some sort of trap."

"Why should he be?"

"Well, sir, it's common knowledge that he hasn't been over-popular at the Abbey these last two years, and then this past week or two he's been going in and out pretty well as he pleased. It makes a man a bit suspicious."

"Of what?"

"What it means."

"He didn't consider remaining at home?"

"No, sir, though I did my best to urge him. I said it was running his head into a noose, but he said that whatever people could say about him, at least they shouldn't say he funked his fences—his expression, sir. Anyway, he'd been putting it round the neighbourhood for some days past that this was his chance; they'd been top dog long enough, but they wouldn't forget this night."

"And what did he mean by that?"

"Sir Ralph didn't confide his affairs to me, sir."

The coroner looked angry; it was galling to be snubbed like that by such a witness.

"You can add nothing that may be of assistance?"

"Only this, sir, and I don't know that it makes any difference, except perhaps it might throw a light on the way Sir Ralph was regarded up at the Abbey. About a week ago Miss Feltham came to the Cottage…"

"Ah, yes, the night on which she lost her way on the moors."

"I wouldn't have said lost her way myself, sir. I understood from the Captain that he was expecting her."

A wave of sensation ran through the court. It wasn't that the news was any surprise to us, because we'd all realised from the first that Hilary had deliberately shaken off Dennis for her own purposes, but it was fresh to most of those present or else bore out what had at most been suspicions up to date, and it kindled their excitement to a white heat.

"You're sure of that?"

"Yes, sir. The previous day the Captain told me he would be expecting a lady between four and half-past the following afternoon. He told me to get in some cream cakes and chocolate biscuits and gave special instructions about flowers and so forth. She might be a bit late, he said, and he was a bit fussy himself. But that didn't surprise me. Even when the lady hadn't arrived at half-past five he didn't get upset. Well, I thought most likely something had prevented her, a husband perhaps. It was often that way with the Captain's parties. Of course, there was the fog, but when I asked the Captain how long he'd wait, seeing the kind of afternoon it had become, he smiled and said, 'Oh, we'll wait, Baynes. We shan't be disappointed. She won't dare stay away. Of course, there may be difficulties.'"

"What did you take that to mean?"

"As I've said, sir, I thought the Captain was referring to a husband. It isn't every gentleman that would like his lady to be visiting at Ravensend without himself, and, of course, in a neighbourhood like this they do gossip a lot. There's no pictures palaces here, or anything like that, and they must do something to amuse themselves. Well, about six o'clock the lady arrived. I hadn't known who she was, and it was a bit of a shock to me to see it was Miss Feltham, because I understood she was going to marry Mr. Dennis, and, things being as they were up at the Abbey, I wouldn't have thought of her coming down like that, all secret-like. The Captain was as excited as a boy, and that was odd, too, because he'd often given me the idea he was fair sick of women. Like sugar, he'd say they were; pleasant enough at first, but they made your gorge rise after a bit. It was a long time since there'd been any coming to the Cottage. The lady was a bit muddy, of course, and I thought she was a bit upset. She said she'd had no end of a bother getting over. The Captain said, smiling and quite composed, 'Late hours don't worry me. In fact, the later the better.' I heard him say that as I brought in the tea. I don't know what else they talked about, because, except when he rang for hot water and later to have the tray taken away, I wasn't in the room. I did think, though, Miss Feltham looked a bit worried. It wasn't the first time, not by a long chalk, I'd seen ladies that had come to visit the Captain look like that. There'd been a mort of them one way and another, but generally he treated 'em all alike. Angry he'd be and very short in his manner, and he'd talk of school-girls and women being able to look after themselves. Like a granite rock, if you take me, sir. But that evening he was quite changed. As kind and as pleased as if he'd like to spend the rest of his days comforting the young lady. One other thing I did hear, sir, and that was when I went in to take away the tray. 'How can you, Ralph?' she was asking him. 'Doesn't it make you feel an utter swine?' If you'll pardon the expression, sir. And the Captain said only a fool threw away his weapons when his life was at stake. She softened a bit then, and said was it as bad as that, and he said he generally got what he wanted, whatever it cost; and there wasn't any need to make the bill too heavy. She said, firing up, 'You mean I'm to pay it, whatever it is,' and he said if he wasn't so fond of her he wouldn't be warning her now. He'd run so many debts in his time that it gave him pleasure to see other people having to pay."

In reply to another nauseating question from the corrupt old man, he said that Miss Feltham didn't, after the first, look at all scared, or as if she wanted to get away. "Quite cosy and amicable they seemed together, and when she was really going she said in the hall that perhaps this was the best way out. 'There's something about all of us,' she said, 'and he'—meaning Mr. Dennis, sir—'would soon have found me out.' Even her father, she said, had had to talk to someone; and that the Felthams couldn't stand on their own feet."

"And that was all you heard?"

"From the young lady. Afterwards, when she'd gone, the Captain said, 'That'll be a nice mouthful for Master Dennis to chew. Don't tell me the whole parish won't want to know where she spent the evening. Not that it matters. I'm going to marry my cousin, Baynes, and we shall live at the Abbey.' I asked him when the wedding would be, and he said, 'No need to wait much longer. I can get possession within the year, if I want it. I'd never have leased the place to a parvenu' (if you'll pardon me, sir, they're the Captain's own words), 'if it hadn't been rotting for a bit of attention, and I thought, if it was a matter of going to the Jews, I might as well give my relative's relative first refusal.'"

There was by this time something so nakedly cruel and gloating about Baynes that I began to wonder whether the neighbourhood might not shortly be startled by news of a second death. Nothing could be calculated to do Hilary more harm than this type of story, told in this particular way, while the man's deliberate emphasising of Ralph's disreputable tea-parties thrust her into a category of women whom Nunn wouldn't have had at the Abbey on any pretext. I looked across at Jeremy; he was sitting next to Mrs. Ross, and she had one hand on his knee, and was whispering urgently to him. I have never seen Jeremy so obviously moved; and when I saw his face a new fear smote me. I wondered whether it had yet occurred to anyone else.

Dennis was more impassive; you couldn't tell what he was thinking; he sat with his hands clasped and swinging between his knees, but certain almost imperceptible movements of his head, as the coroner piled one question on to another, assured me that the elements of storm weren't lacking here either. And when that broke it would be a holocaust enveloping everybody concerned.

The coroner asked if Ralph had again referred to the matter of his marriage.

"Only casually, like when he said, 'We shall want that at the Abbey.' And, 'When we're settled at the Abbey'—never 'if' or 'perhaps.' He'd made up his mind all right."

"Now, when he didn't come back that evening, what did you think? That he'd come to some mischief? Were you alarmed?"

"Well, no, sir. I can't say I was exactly anxious. I thought he might be spending the night at the Abbey—it's a big house with a lot of empty rooms to it. Or perhaps he'd gone on somewhere—I'd known him be all night before. Got plenty of friends, the Captain has…"

The original urbanity of his manner was rapidly falling from the fellow; his last words were the equivalent of a wink at the Coroner. There was no doubt in the mind of any man present of the type of roisterer Ralph had been. Hilary's stock dropped with every word he said.

"You don't think, then, that any harm had actually befallen him?"

"I've been with the Captain a good many years, sir, and I've never found him the kind of man to put his head into a trap of his own accord, not knowing it was a trap, I mean. He liked his life, and he saw a lot of fun ahead. That I do know. And I never saw a man so difficult to wear down. What they call whipcord and indiarubber. Nothing tired him or got him finished… not scenes nor threats nor being short of money, nor being in danger, and when I say I didn't think anything really bad was going to happen, I mean to say I didn't think it was going to happen to him."

The court was tense enough now; you could hear the soft sound of breath that has been held, because none of us dared make so much noise as a gasp, whistling suddenly through dry lips. Here was drama and the least significant of us was moved and involved.

Baynes could offer us nothing further and the evidence for the day closed there. The position was highly unsatisfactory and everyone knew it. The Coroner rose and weightily explained their duties to the jury. If, he told them, in the face of everything they'd heard, they could conscientiously say that Ralph met his death by accidental means, then they must do that. If they weren't satisfied, they must say so.

The jury seemed to have a good deal to talk about, and were away a long time. When they returned the foreman said they weren't satisfied as to the actual cause of death. Medical evidence had conflicted, and in their view there were too many additional factors in the case for them to come to any conclusion with an easy mind. They didn't think it possible, even if accidental death were ruled out, to bring in a verdict against any particular person, since, although they had good reason to believe that several people wished the deceased out of the way, no evidence had been offered to show the movements of any of these people during the important hours. They considered that the case warranted a great deal more inquiry, and regretted their inability to bring in a definite verdict.

And there, for the day, the matter had to stand. The funeral was fixed for four days ahead, but long before that took place the police were in possession, nosing about, as Mrs. Ross remarked, like jackals in search of offal.

CHAPTER X

I

THE POLICE AND I HAD LITTLE TO SAY TO ONE ANOTHER. THEY asked me a few obvious questions, and seemed satisfied with my replies. At no time did anyone suggest that I had any motive for the crime, and from the official point of view I faded out from the beginning. We weren't, of course, taken into their confidence, and we didn't know what line they were following. But Jeremy and I got together and decided we might do a bit of sleuthing on our own account; we were in the know in certain things that the police knew nothing about—Ralph's blackmailing activities, for instance, and Hilary's flight to the garden.

"Besides," said Jeremy, "we're not wholly unofficial. We are here by request of your friend, Philpotts, and we ought to be singing for our supper. Let's have our shot at putting two and two together and see what they make. To begin with, where was Hilary making for when Lady Nunn stopped her on the night of the party? What time was it?"

I said it was almost eleven when Eleanor told us, and she seemed to have been talking to Hilary for ten or fifteen minutes. So that eleven o'clock seemed a fairly safe guess for Hilary's appointment. But where and with whom?

"We might assume it was with Ralph. Anyway, let's see where that supposition gets us. What time did Ralph leave the Cottage? Some time after ten, his man said. He's two miles off, call it half-an-hour's walk for him, so if he left about ten-thirty, and Hilary was leaving this house at ten forty-five, where would they meet?"

I exclaimed, "Of course. The summer-house. Why didn't we think of that before?"

The summer-house was a very ancient ramshackle structure well hidden in the wooded part of the estate, about a hundred yards from the pond where Ralph was found. At one time it had the reputation of being a favourite rendezvous for the young bucks at the Abbey, who used to meet their village wenches there, but for a long time now it had fallen into a very bad state of disrepair, and practically no one used it. I remember going there as a lad, when there were visitors I wanted to escape, taking my books with me, and it had quite romantic associations for Hilary, who used to hide there from the wrath of governesses or when she wanted to shirk her lessons. But the younger people in the village would hardly know of its existence. It seemed a likely place for Ralph to fix upon for a meeting, and the fact that the pond was so close made us pretty sure we had hit on the truth. This pond had nothing in particular to differentiate it from a dozen other ponds on the estate, except a withered thorn tree that had been brought a couple of centuries earlier from the Holy Land by a devout Humphrey Feltham. In flower, the tree was extraordinarily beautiful, tall spikes of very pure creamy blossoms thrusting upwards; and there had been a time when people made excursions to see it in full bloom, and brought their children there. But that was long ago, and the tree had now been dead for years. A number of legends had sprung up about it, having their source no doubt in the devout fables of the time. It was said that the thorns had mystic healing qualities; if you broke one of them off the bough, and dipped it into the pond, and then laid it on a sick person, that person recovered at once. If he didn't, then he was in league with the Evil One, and should be left to die, and there are even stories told of people refused Christian burial on no better ground than that they obstinately persisted in

succumbing even after treatment by the holy thorn. Another legend
I often heard recounted was that it was the thorn of love; break off
a thorn and prick your arm, then with the blood still warm upon
the point prick the arm of him or her whose love you desired, and
you would attain happiness. Legend doesn't say what happened
when this failed; presumably it never did.

The present generation hardly knew these stories, though little
boys sometimes broke off the long sharp thorns and carried them
away for the purpose of tormenting their companions; even Hilary
knew very little, but there was a phase when Percy Feltham was
deeply, even passionately, interested in this folklore, and during one
of my school holidays I helped him to arrange various papers and
letters, and picked up a lot of stray information in that fashion. To
anyone else, I fancy these stories had little more significance than
those bogeys of childhood (when one has outgrown them), the
Bathroom Guggle, the Tiger on the Stairs, Tommy Dodd in the
Nursery Cupboard. The village accepted the pool as they accepted
every other pool in the neighbourhood. There were a number of
them, frequently on the edge of the public way, deep, still and
green; occasionally, they were decorated with duckweed; more
rarely, you saw water-fowl there, and occasionally lilies, but none
of them excited comment any more than they suggested to the
average countryman, as they certainly did to inexperienced town
cousins, like the labourer's wife, quite unjustifiable dangers. They,
poor creatures, wanted to see them ringed round with red lights
or white palings for the protection of the populace. Imperilling
human life, they said. And indeed the townsman was right to have
his misgivings. It would be easy enough for him to lose his path
and his life on one of those dark nights on a road that, unlike city
highways, had scarcely an illumination from end to end. And yet
it's very rare to hear of accidents of this nature in a countryside,

nothing like so frequent as the accidents in traffic that happen in well-lit, secure, suburban roads.

2

Jeremy and I went secretly down to the summer-house. It was very dark and dirty, and the steps leading to it were broken and eaten by beetles and so forth. Inside there was a very much stained rustic seat, with rounded ends, and several sharp splinters in the wood-work; the floor was covered with dust and shavings and had been disturbed very recently. Jeremy went round like Sherlock Holmes; he said the naked eye wasn't enough, and produced a magnifying glass. I was inclined to laugh at him, until he exclaimed, "Shut up, you damned fool! Come and look at this."

I came, and saw a darkish stain on the end of the rustic seat.

"That may have been there ages," I said.

Jeremy took out his handkerchief and moistened it. Very gently he rubbed the mark; a rusty sort of dye came from it.

"And what'll you bet me that's blood?" he demanded, grimly. "Look at the floor here."

Beneath our feet were other darkish marks, not as if anyone had bled with any profusion, but the kind of marks you'd get from a cut wrist, or, as Jeremy pointed out, from a cut ear.

"Suppose Ralph to be standing here, and someone had come up behind and knocked him over the head, he might easily stag-ger, and bang up against the seat. You see." He gave a convincing illustration of his contention. "If you're taken unawares your knees automatically sag. That seems to be sound enough. The question is, who done it? Not Hilary. I should say someone came up behind him while he was talking. There isn't even any reason to suppose it was a plot. If Dennis, for instance, came up without warning and heard them, he might lose his head and sock Ralph one, and then, without realising how serious the position was, discover he'd done the poor devil in. Yes, I know we're getting away from the medical evidence a bit, but as that didn't agree I don't feel that matters awfully at the moment. I'm more inclined to think this was an accident, and that he was dumped in the pond in the hopes of pulling wool over the eyes of all of us. It seems such a rotten sort of night to choose for a deliberate murder."

"Then, if you're right, Hilary knows the position."

"She must. It must be ghastly for her. No wonder she won't say a word."

"Particularly if it were Dennis. But could it be? He was with us when Eleanor came to tell us about Hilary."

"But he went away before we dispersed; he's got legs like a kangaroo; have you ever seen him run? He covers the ground at the most amazing speed. I know he looks a leisurely sort of devil, but I'm not sure I wouldn't rather be up against Nunn if it came to a scrap than that fellow. Besides, he knows such a lot of dirty tricks; he's had me on my knees, remember, and I'm not likely to forget that."

"I wonder if Eleanor suspects anything; the trouble with the household at present is, quite half of them daren't be candid. Eleanor may have seen something, Dennis lolloping over the lawn, perhaps, and she wouldn't be able to speak. While Hilary's lips, naturally, are sealed. It would be rather satisfactory, don't you think, if we could get a bit of proof of any of these things?"

Jeremy agreed that it would. "All the same," he said, "I think we're on the right track. These marks here are quite clearly blood, and I don't see any reason for supposing they're animal blood. Animals don't make appointments in summer-houses as a rule, not when there's a whole wood, up and down stairs, to choose from. And we do know that Hilary was going to meet someone."

"We'd better not take Dennis into our confidence at the moment," I suggested. "Not if there's any likelihood of his being implicated. It would look pretty bad if he were, and the facts came out. I doubt if anyone would believe it was an accident. They'd regard Hilary as a decoy."

"I wonder if the police have made any of our discoveries or speculations," remarked Jeremy. "It's a pity we're all so much in the dark. If they are going to suspect Dennis, one would like to warn the fellow, though I daresay he's at least as capable of looking after himself as any of the rest of us."

We had no way of knowing what line the police were following up. They were skating all about the neighbourhood, paying us surprise visits every now and again, and asking further questions. Someone had come forward to say that on the night of the 15th he had noticed a car driving through the right-of-way between half-past eight and nine o'clock. Of course, cars frequently did drive there; the path wasn't good, but neither were most of the cars. Motor-cycles went there, too; there had been a loud outcry at first, as the path had been intended for pedestrians going to and from the works at Melford. But it was pointed out that a good many of these young men came on motor-cycles, and the right-of-way did save a great deal of time even for these. And when the motor-cycles began to be superseded by three-wheeled cars, and later by things that looked like disused buses on a small scale, with perforated windows and a general effect of mud and grease, there was no logical objection to raise. The right-of-way was wide enough to take them—it would have taken a Rolls for that matter—and as it wasn't much used, and no one lived near the road—the danger to pedestrian life was practically nil. So the cars of the workmen continued to go to and from Melford, and no one these days made any comment. The police's informant, however, said that he had noticed this car, particularly, because it was a rather better car than you often saw on that road, and inside was a man in evening dress, accompanied by a woman in a dark cloak. The car had passed him at some little distance from the pool. Another man had seen a figure wandering slowly along the road, hands behind his back, at about ten o'clock; he had been wearing a dark suit, and a hat tilted over his eyes; he gave the impression that he was waiting for someone. And a third witness remembered seeing two bicycles thrust in among some bushes quite near this spot; he had passed the place twice in the course of an hour, and each time the bicycles had been there. No one appeared to have heard any sounds or cries, no one had seen anything very important. But the police, in duty bound, took down all statements, investigated them, and where they were practicable made use of them. Meanwhile, they had broadcast a request for any information that might be forthcoming, and asked that if anyone had seen the figure of a man, apparently a tramp, coming through the Feltham property on the night of the 15th, he or she would come forward. In addition, the press was busy with the question of the conflicting medical evidence. Quite an interesting correspondence sprang up in the *Times*, eliciting at length a long, well-reasoned letter, inclining towards the official police view, from that veteran authority, Sir Willoughby Hare. So that the affair could be said to have created a quite appreciable stir, and we had a number of reporters coming and going, coming with hopes and departing with fleas in their ears, wanting photographs and news and above all, information about the position of Hilary and Dennis. Other people wrote suggesting that a reward should be offered, that possibly blackmail was involved and people who could tell the truth were being forcibly prevented from so doing; a lunatic came forward with a most elaborate confession that occupied some attention, as it was shown that he had at one time been comparatively intimate with Ralph, and had excellent reasons for wishing him out of the way. And Jeremy and I tried to get some kind of proof of our version of the affair.

3

Our luck, on the whole, was in. Three days after the discovery in the summer-house Eleanor said to me, "Tony, only God knows how long this is going on or how it's going to end. Personally, I feel as if we had been sheltering the police for years. Hilary's looking a wreck, and James is quite unapproachable. He doesn't say anything, but I know in his heart he blames me, for giving Ralph any foothold here at all."

I told her, rather uneasily, she was being ridiculous, but I, too, had noticed Nunn's attitude. It certainly wasn't conciliatory and I thought privately that Eleanor was very likely right, and he did lay the blame at her door.

"I'm not talking nonsense," said Eleanor, wearily. "I know James pretty well by this time. But it won't help to argue about it. I'm going to do some gardening; it's the best antidote to depression that I know."

I offered to come and help.

She said, "Would you? That would be delightful. Talk to me about something that has nothing to do with Ralph. And get me my garden-coat, will you? You know it, it's the one I've had for years and years, that will never wear out."

I said, "That old black thing with the caracul collar? My dear, it must be done for by this time."

Eleanor laughed. "Oh, no. It's like those invalids who outlast all their attendants. I had it cleaned the other day; I haven't worn it since. It's on those pegs in the hall, where it's hung from time immemorial."

I went to get it, remembering it well enough, since she had had it as a garden-coat for at least a dozen years. It was very long, very heavy, very shabby. It had a belt and large pockets and a deep collar. As I took it down something pricked me sharply, and withdrawing my hand I saw that there was a bead of blood at the base of the thumb. I examined the coat, and found a long black thorn in the collar. There was no need to ask where that had come from. There is only one tree in the neighbourhood where you can find such thorns, and that is the withered tree growing by the pond.

I was so much startled at coming upon this scrap of evidence that for a minute I stood stock still, forgetting Eleanor waiting in the garden, only trying to see what this meant. That Eleanor was involved in Ralph's death! I couldn't get any further than that. Eleanor! And there my imagination stopped dead. When it began to work again I reflected that the murder, if murder it was, had been the work of two people, and I wondered who had helped her.

Eleanor's voice called, "Can't you find it, Tony? It's on the same hook where it's always been. Are my gardening-gloves in the pocket?"

I put my hand into the pocket automatically. There were no gloves, but there was a slip of smooth grey paper covered with Ralph's writing. It was no concern of mine what he chose to write to Eleanor, but some impulse made me thrust the paper into my pocket, as I called out, "Yes, here they are. I'm coming, Eleanor. But you've smartened it up so much I hardly recognise the old friend."

For about an hour I gardened steadily, and we talked of various local matters, without touching on the one subject that filled both our minds. I wondered if I sounded very distrait, but she seemed satisfied enough, and as it drew towards dusk, she threw her trowel into the gardening basket, saying, "That's enough for one afternoon. Now, what about tea?"

I didn't get an opportunity of talking to Jeremy till some time that evening. I had glanced at the slip of paper, which said:

> "I have waited ten minutes and that is enough. Now you can come over at half-past twelve. Don't fail me. I've warned you what will happen.
>
> R. F."

I couldn't endure the thought that Eleanor had played into that brute's hands, and it occurred to me that, so soon as I had shown the paper to Jeremy, I should be wise to destroy it. I didn't want that to get into the hands of the police. When at last I got hold of him, he said in a slow kind of voice, "Do you realise what this is?"

I said nothing, and he went on, "This is our answer to one of the problems that have been racking us. Now we know why Hilary went into the garden at eleven o'clock, and why she tried to get away from Dennis during supper."

I said, "I don't see how you can be sure of that," and he replied, "Well, think over what you've just told me. This is Lady Nunn's coat, certainly, but you have her word that it's just been cleaned, that she hasn't put it on since it came back from the cleaners, and that it always hangs in the hall, on a peg where everyone knows where it is. On the other hand, you have Hilary saying she put on a coat when she went into the garden. What more likely than that she grabbed up this one, particularly as she must have been late? I don't know how much Ralph had threatened, but clearly it was enough to make her intend to go across at half-past twelve, as he suggested. That would be supper-time. I suppose she was to come back later, but it would be a tremendous feather in Ralph's cap to have forced her to meet him clandestinely, and very probably he had some plan in his head to make their meeting public, and force her hand."

"And you think he was deliberately hiding when she did come, so as to spin out the torment?"

"As to that, I don't know. I think we'd better get hold of Hilary, and have some of our suppositions on a firm basis."

Hilary was so much alarmed when we showed her the letter that many of our suspicions took firm root. She did know something, and she was terrified in case we got to know of it, too.

"You may as well make a clean breast of it," said Jeremy, curtly. "We're all having a very unpleasant time of it at present, and if you can help, you ought to."

Hilary muttered something about Dennis, and Jeremy said, "All right, we'll leave him out of it, if you like. Don't blame me, though, if there's hell to pay afterwards. He doesn't look to me the sort of man who likes being blindfolded."

Hilary said, "He mustn't know. Please, Jeremy."

"All right, I've told you we'll leave him out of it till you give the word. Now, come on. Tell us about Ralph. Did you see him in the end?"

"No. He wasn't there. I only found this note."

"And determined to come down at twelve o'clock?"

"What else could I do? You do despise me, Jeremy, don't you? Think I'm a horrible coward, but if you'd ever been blindfolded and set to walk along the edge of a cliff, with no hope if you made a false step, even then you wouldn't know quite how bad I feel. I can't explain the way it is with me where Father's concerned."

Jeremy said steadily, "If you didn't see Ralph, whom did you see?"

"No one. On my honour, I didn't."

"And you were wearing Lady Nunn's coat?"

"Yes. I was afraid of being stopped by you or Arthur or Uncle James if I went upstairs and fetched one of my own. Besides…" she hesitated and Jeremy finished up smoothly, "You thought you were less likely to be recognised if you wore that coat. It's very muffling, isn't it?"

"Yes," whispered Hilary. "I did think of that."

"Well, go on. What time, by the way, were you supposed to be at the summer-house?"

"Ralph said eleven."

"Did he write to you?"

"No. He wasn't taking any chances. He rang up during the afternoon. He sounded so strange and angry I was afraid of refusing him."

Jeremy said, "I bet you had a rotten night after the party. Because you didn't get away, did you?"

"No. Arthur saw to that. Jeremy, I want to ask you something. It's to be without prejudice. Do you think Arthur knows anything?"

"About Ralph?"

"Yes."

"Do you mean, do I think he had a hand in his death?"

"I don't know, but he's odd. He'll hardly speak to me, and he's so strange and gruff…"

"You can't expect him to be bursting with affection, can you?" said Jeremy, reasonably. "You've got us all into a lovely mess, and I daresay it'll all react against his interests. But as to whether he knows anything, I know no more than the man in the moon. Have you asked him?"

"Oh, Jeremy, don't be a fool! Do you suppose I dare ask Arthur things like that?"

"Then you are afraid…?"

"Yes. I am. He said in that quiet careless way of his that I could put the idea of marrying Ralph out of my head. And he meant it. He's the sort of man who doesn't make idle threats. I did warn Ralph, but he only laughed. We all think he's a bit of a milksop till we get closer to him. I don't believe either of you realise how strong he is really."

"He certainly seems to have impressed you," I murmured.

She said simply, "He frightens me, Tony. It's the first time I've found myself up against something I don't understand. Ralph's different; I know what he wants, and I understand the means he takes to get it. But when it's a man like Arthur, then you're up against something very changed. It's like being in the dark, with no landmarks."

Then Mrs. Ross came in, saying in the manner of a distracted but optimistic hen, "Oh, Hilary…" and Hilary said hastily, "I'm coming," and left us.

4

"We don't seem to be getting much forrader," Jeremy acknowledged rather gloomily. "Let's start theorising. We may get somewhere by the process of elimination. Put yourself and myself out of it. That leaves the Nunns and Hilary and Dennis, of this household, that is. The most likely person is Dennis, and I fancy Hilary is tormenting herself by a fear that he is responsible. Let's see what sort of case we can make out against him. Incidentally, I'm beginning to think I was probably wrong when I said it must be a two-man plot. I was thinking of the difficulty of one man carting the body from the summer-house to the pool, without scratching the face or tearing the clothes, but a fellow as muscular as Dennis, and in his good condition, could do it without turning a hair, I believe. The chief risk would be of someone passing at the crucial moment, but I don't suppose many people use the right-of-way after dark, and if they are lovers they wouldn't stay on the high road."

"You're assuming that Ralph was dead, I suppose? The medical evidence hardly supports that. Both Gudgeon and McKenzie said the blow on the head was superficial, and Gudgeon even thought it might have been caused by a stumble."

"It's possible that he was momentarily knocked unconscious."

"Then sudden immersion in cold water—and that pond's like ice in February—ought to have a contrary reaction. It would have brought him round."

"He might have been fairly far gone. My experience is that with these knocks on the head you can never be sure. He might collapse from shock, particularly if he'd been drinking at all. I know Baynes said he hadn't touched a drop all day, but we aren't compelled to take everything that virulent fellow said for gospel."

"Still, the police have examined the pond pretty carefully. The grass round the edge is quite long, and their conclusion was, I understood, that if anyone had tried to haul himself out of the pond by clutching at the grass, there would be signs of the effort. The grass would be torn up, for instance, and there was nothing of the kind to be seen."

"The only other solution seems to be McKenzie's suggestion of the wet cloth over the mouth and nostrils, and that argues wilful murder."

"Committed by Dennis? But when?"

"I should say not at eleven o'clock after all, partly because, according to this note, Ralph wasn't there then, and partly because I don't think he had the time. You can't murder a man and dispose of the body in ten minutes, and I remember now seeing him when I went back to the ball-room. I wonder if he could have got anything out of Hilary about the second appointment. He strikes me as a man who's apt to get his own way. Suppose he kept the appointment for her? How does that fit the bill?"

We considered the possibility, but came to the conclusion that it wasn't really satisfactory. To begin with, the doctors were of the opinion that Ralph died before midnight. And then, wouldn't Dennis's absence have created some comment? Besides, if Hilary knew the truth, could she keep up so excellent a pretence?

"She might," said Jeremy. "If you ask me, I think she's badly smitten where Dennis is concerned, has been all along in spite of all this damn-foolery about Ralph, and in that case, being Hilary, she'd act us all off the stage."

"All the same," I stuck to my point, "I call it thin. Can you suggest anything else?"

Jeremy thought. "If he didn't kill him at eleven, and I fancy we're agreed that he didn't, and it was too late after midnight (and as to that, I think we ought to accept the medical evidence), then what other opportunity did he have? Unless he settled Ralph's hash in advance, not being keen on taking any risks of a second local scandal. By Jove, Tony, that's an idea. Now we come to examine it, this," he tapped Ralph's letter, "strikes me as a bit unconvincing. To begin with, if Ralph was really crazy about Hilary, it's very questionable whether he'd take umbrage just because she was ten minutes late. He'd know how difficult it was for her to get away, and unless he was drunk, in which case his writing wouldn't have been so steady, he'd realise it would be next-door to impossible for her to escape twice in one evening. And there was too much at stake—because this time Ralph was in mad earnest about the girl—for him to take any unnecessary chances. Suppose she'd agreed to go off with him—anything is possible when you get two hotheads like Hilary and Ralph in juxtaposition—anyway, he must have known it was his one chance. Besides, what was he going to do for an hour and a half? And where did he get to? He didn't go home, and it doesn't sound to me like our Ralph to hang about on a cold night in a supremely uncomfortable disguise. No, no. Hilary didn't find him there, because at that time it wasn't possible for him to turn up."

"Because he was in the pond?"

"Where else? There's another thing. This paper. It isn't Ralph's kind of paper. It's a common joke that he writes on expensive paper if he's only making betting notes. Besides, this is a sheet from a writing-pad, and no man carries a writing-pad about with him. No, Tony, I'm getting it. This note was prepared in advance by the person who killed Ralph—deliberately killed him—and someone, moreover, who knew that Hilary was going to meet him at eleven o'clock."

"That means before the party began," I objected. "Then what about Baynes' evidence? If Ralph was killed so much earlier than we had supposed, then he must have left his house some time before half-past ten."

"That puts Baynes out of court," Jeremy agreed. "I wonder if he could have had a hand in it. It might be possible to find out something about his movements, if we're discreet. We don't even know whether Ralph made his cryptic remark about going to his death. Dear me, we seem to be getting very much involved. I wonder if we could find out whether a letter went from here to Ralph just before the party. He must have had some inducement to turn out at that hour; he's not the type of man who comes first to a party. Old Peters might remember. I don't doubt the whole village has been betting on what would happen on the night of the 15th. And if there was a letter from the Abbey, well, Peters must know their respective hand-writings. Could you find out, Tony, do you think? You know the villagers pretty well, and old Peters must have been going before you were born."

I agreed to do that. Then we went on with our suppositions.

"Are we still imagining that Dennis did the deed?" I asked. And then I stopped.

"What is it?" exclaimed Jeremy. "Come on, man. Don't make mysteries. I'm like Scotland Yard. I don't like 'em."

I said, softly, "The car, Jeremy, the car that was seen going up the right-of-way between half-past eight and nine. And the people in it."

"Well?"

"Has it occurred to you that of all the men on the night of 15th, Nunn was practically the only one who wore ordinary evening rig?"

"He was. And you think he was in the car?"

"Eleanor told me she was terrified that he would do something violent. And he came downstairs very late that evening. Mrs. Ross explained to me it was because Eleanor kept him out of the bathroom."

"She did, did she? Now why the deuce, Tony, do you suppose she would have taken the trouble to explain to you why her brother was late? You hadn't been commenting on it, I suppose?"

"No. I hadn't mentioned Nunn."

"But she wanted you to realise it was Eleanor's fault. You might, you see, have remembered later that he hadn't come down in particularly good time."

"What on earth are you driving at?"

"It's not what I'm driving at. It's the bulls-eye you've unwittingly hit. At least, I think you have."

"And what's that?"

"You've solved the problem we were sent down here to elucidate. By Jove, what a leg-up over Dennis."

"I don't know what you're talking about," I protested, rather irritably. "What have we solved?"

Jeremy's momentary hilarity dropped from him. His face was serious enough as he replied. "The identity of the Spider," he said.

CHAPTER XI

I

A T FIRST I WAS INCLINED TO TREAT THE NOTION WITH SCEPTI-cism. "It's nothing but a leap in the dark," I objected. "Why on earth, even if Nunn has got a quarrel with Ralph, you should pick on him as one of the chief criminals of his time—the thing's absurd."

"Not it," said Jeremy, staunchly. "Just consider the position for a minute. We came down here, at Philpotts' request, because he had every reason to suppose that the mysterious head of the gang was at the Abbey, and if not the head, then one of his lieutenants. We also believed that Ralph was involved, but we certainly didn't suppose he was the central figure. Consider the other personalities in the place. Who else is so likely to be responsible? You don't want anyone picturesque or noticeable. Nunn is the perfect type. He's middle-class and quiet and shrewd and respectable and rich; he has a great personality and, I should say, unusual organising ability. He hasn't a shred of nerves and probably not a shred of conscience. He knows a most unusual number of exclusive people, considering his position. I've heard from several friends of mine since I came here, and it's astonishing how many of them seem to have met Nunn, and not at the kind of houses you might have expected. I'm not saying the man isn't sufficiently unusual to have made a fair amount of headway on his own account, but he doesn't talk as if he knew any of these people intimately. Besides, how did he meet them? And another thing. It's odd, to say the least of it, for him to have rented the house where his predecessor took his own life. And one of the first things he does, having rented it, is to bar his own landlord. Now, you might argue two things from that. He might object to Ralph as a neighbour, as he declares he does, or it might be that he didn't want the County to suppose he was at all friendly with him. The fact that Ralph never came over here means nothing; both he and Nunn are frequently in town."

"And the whole thing was a blind? And he and Ralph were in the gang together?"

"I should say unquestionably yes. I wonder what the chap did in the war. Archie Fraser could probably find that out for me. I'll send him a line to-day. There must have been some kind of split between Nunn and Ralph, though, for Ralph to have started blackmailing Nunn's wife. I should imagine that if, as seems pretty certain, Cleghorne has been dead for years, Ralph must have had those letters for a considerable time. He wouldn't use them, of course, so long as his relations with Nunn were good, but when they quarrelled—possibly about Hilary—then Ralph played his winning card."

"You think that a man who hasn't scrupled to blackmail for years, would refuse to let Hilary marry his partner?" I asked.

"I daresay that wasn't Nunn's doing at all. It seems much more likely to have been his wife's. Lady Nunn is no fool, and her husband would have to throw dust in her eyes to prevent her getting suspicious. She may have come to him and said that at all costs he's to prevent a marriage between Hilary and Ralph. He had a lot at stake, remember. I think the trouble between them was genuine, not just part of a plan. Ralph wouldn't quarrel with a man as rich as Nunn if he could avoid it. And once that position arose, Nunn really had no option. Ralph's strength was that he had nothing to lose. His reputation was in shreds, and he possibly decided to marry Hilary, replace Nunn at the Abbey and settle down to respectability. That's quite comprehensible. It's the kind of thing men like Ralph, who have exhausted every emotional experience, do when they get bored. Byron, they say, would have been a monk if he'd lived to be fifty. Naturally, Nunn couldn't stand for that position. He wouldn't merely be unseated, he'd be positively in danger, and nothing could end that danger but Ralph's death. The man who has blackmailed knows better than anyone else the immense possibilities of such a field of activity. Nunn, if he had any imagination, and these big men usually have, it's part of their outfit for success, could look ahead and see himself getting gradually more and more under Ralph's thumb. And the notion was intolerable. So he had to get rid of Ralph, and this was an ideal time, when he had several of us on the premises who might be suspected of foul play."

"He meant it to look like an accident, though."

"He probably did. And if the luck had been a little more in his quarter, it would have been passed off as one. Even now a lot of people think the police are merely being nosey, as usual, and they clamour that the force is too large if it has to look for jobs like this."

"Is it your notion that he carried this out single-handed?"

Jeremy considered. "Sounds a bit difficult. Besides, you're forgetting. There was a woman in the car."

"You're not suggesting he dragged Eleanor into it, are you?"

"I don't think, for the sake of his own skin, he'd dare. After all, if this unromantic little husband of hers said casually, 'I've had enough of that kinsman of yours; I propose to do him in tonight; I want your help,' she might quite well protest. She might even refuse. It's on the cards that she'd try and warn Ralph. Oh no. This solves another problem that has perplexed me a little since I came here. You know what it is?"

"Well?"

"Think. How many households do you know where a widowed sister forms a permanent member? These households *a trois* hardly ever work out well. Look at the number of husbands who've been murdered by their wives' companions. Mrs. Belloc Lowndes has made a positive corner in them. And if a man keeps his sister with him, after he's got a wife to attend to his creature comforts, he must have some ulterior motive."

"Some men are quite daft about their sisters," I murmured. "I knew a Vicar once who stood on the doorstep in all weathers if his sister was late for tea."

"I don't precisely see Nunn doing that. Besides, was this lunatic of yours married? No? I thought as much. You can't have a wife and a sister, not in the same house, not for long, not without trouble."

"You're suggesting she was the Spider's accomplice?"

"Who could be better? You wouldn't suspect a woman like that. You'd look for some one who moved in different circles, someone less garrulous and more polished. Just consider the facts. We haven't been here long, but it's been long enough to prove that she has got a most peculiar attraction for men. It isn't looks or figure or intelligence; I suppose it's some kind of charm. Did you see her on the night of the party? She was surrounded by men the whole evening. Incidentally, she's an amazing dancer, even in that ponderous get-up. She could coax secrets out of them, if she wanted to, just as I daresay she could coax a hippopotamus out of its pond on an August day. And she's very clever; she gets your life-history out of you without any appearance of asking questions. I don't for a moment suppose she has anything directly to do with the blackmailing side of the business. And I daresay she doesn't even think it's very wrong. A woman like that has her own standards; I doubt if Nunn could find a more perfect contrast or coadjutor anywhere."

I had been thinking. "Baynes must be in this," I said. "Has he been in the plot from the beginning, do you imagine, or was he just bought over for the occasion?"

"He's been with Ralph a good many years, and if he wasn't born dumb, deaf, blind and imbecile, he probably picked up a lot about the business in that time. Besides, I can't quite see Nunn going to him and saying, I've a quarrel with your employer, and I'm proposing to murder him at nine o'clock to-morrow night. Here's a tenner to say he didn't leave the house till ten. No, I think Baynes was in the original scheme. That's probably been going on for years; you don't build up an organisation of that nature and efficiency in six months. In fact, if it hadn't been going on for some time, I don't see why Mrs. Ross continued to live with her brother after his marriage. I daresay they've all been gleaning a nice harvest ever since the war. That was a magnificent time for picking up secrets; you got men in their most expansive moods, learnt things that in the normal way would never have been revealed to you. There must have been a rich harvest for the social vultures after the Armistice. And, of course, if Ralph was going to reform, none of them was actually safe. He might not give any of them away, but they wouldn't feel secure. Besides, he'd have, in them, a pleasant source of income for the rest of his days, and a man of his tastes doesn't live on the small income Hilary brings with her. And on the small income Hilary brings with her. And now we come to the job of providing proof. That tracks very carefully, but they've probably left some clue, if we could stumble on it."

I said, "I might be able to find out from Peters if there was a letter from the Abbey for Ralph, making the appointment at the summer-house. Hilary has sworn she didn't write, so it wouldn't be hers. And Ralph 'phoned to her. That would be one thing, though I'm afraid we aren't likely to lay hands on any such letter, at this time."

"It would help a lot if we could come upon anyone who actually saw Ralph outside his house between, say, eight and nine o'clock."

"The police have been trying to get hold of such a man, but he doesn't seem to exist."

"It isn't everyone who hears what the police want; possibly a stranger, who hasn't been in touch with the papers, is wandering about somewhere with the very evidence we want. Anyhow, you try Peters and I'll write to Archie. Of course, Mrs. Ross was dressed ready for the party when she started. Nunn probably had blood on his hands or even on his shirt-front—I wonder if there's a clue there. We might try."

2

It wasn't so easy as I had supposed to get hold of Peters, and in any case I should have to drop my question casually, as otherwise I should merely rake up fresh local scandal. It occurred to me, in the interim, that Hook might be able to help. He would probably remember if a letter went to Ralph on the eve of the party, for, like everyone else, he was aware of all the moves in the game. He had been attached to the family for a great number of years, and was clearly devoted to them since he had abandoned a better job to return to Eleanor when she married again. Talking to him one evening, I said thoughtfully, "There's an ugly rumour going round, Hook, that you may have heard. It affects Miss Hilary."

The man looked deeply troubled. "The place is full of them, sir, if I may say so. You remember my telling you just before the party that people was coupling her name with Sir Ralph's in all sorts of loose ways. I don't know what this new one can be."

I said, "They're saying that she wrote to him, making the appointment that resulted in his death. I'm convinced that isn't true, but I'd like to crush it openly. You'd remember, wouldn't you, if there was a letter in her writing to Sir Ralph on the 14th?"

"I should, sir. To tell you the truth, being in the family so long and remembering Miss Hilary when she was no more than an infant in arms, I've been properly anxious about the affair myself. We all know the kind of reputation Sir Ralph had, and though one shouldn't speak ill of the dead, it did Miss Hilary nothing but harm to be mentioned in the same breath with him. And when she did write to him, and I've seen the letters lying as bold as brass on the table in the hall, I was sometimes minded to burn them. But, of course, it isn't my place to say these things, only, as you will understand, sir..." he hesitated. "Well," he began again, "I'm not a family man myself, as you know, and it's almost as if it was some girl of my own..." His voice was unwontedly deep and moved. I nodded.

"I know, Hook. Of course, there's the possibility it wasn't put on the table..." And indeed, if Hilary hadn't written it, the odds were it wouldn't be.

Hook debated. "That chap of Sir Ralph's might tell, if he liked," he suggested.

"I hardly think I can ask him," I protested.

"No, sir. Of course not. I wasn't suggesting such a thing, and it would put ideas into his head, if you did. I was only thinking that perhaps, if I chanced to run across him we might very likely stop and pass the time of day, and it might be possible to drop some hint without making it noticeable. Of course, you'd have to be precious careful with a fellow like that. But, if you like, sir, I'll see what I can do."

"I can trust your discretion, Hook, I'm sure," I told him. And then the post came in, and among the envelopes one addressed to Jeremy in Archie Fraser's writing.

Archie gave a comprehensive history of Nunn from the beginning of the war. It made very interesting reading.

It appeared that he had volunteered in 1914, when he was thirty-two. He went to France with the British Expeditionary Force at the end of that year and was wounded in the head the following spring. It was not a serious wound, and he convalesced at a Base Hospital, returning to the Front without leaving France. Just after this he got his commission as Second Loot, and was wounded for the second time. It was a body wound this time, a fragment of shell in the abdomen and he nearly collapsed. They sent him home in a pretty bad state, and he was nursed at the Officers' Hospital in Carlton House Terrace. This was June 1915; when he was discharged from the hospital his Medical Board decided he wasn't fit for overseas service, and gave him clerical work at the Ministry of Food in South Kensington, where, for six months, said Archie, he checked up the quantity of blood used in the construction of cattle-cake, and wrote letters about the distribution of strawberries and other soft fruit. It was obvious, however, that his gifts of organisation and intelligence were wasted in this subordinate job, and he seems to have pulled strings, for he was suddenly transferred from the Ministry of Food to a much more significant post at the Ministry of Munitions. Here he had a good deal of responsibility, and as time went on this increased, until he had a large department working under his orders. There had been one crisis when he had shown up a man in enemy pay who was sending out faked shells, and some very ugly letters had reached him. He hadn't turned a hair, apparently, and in consequence he was marked down for some recognition, and he'd had the O.B.E. in the next Honours List. Nothing, said Archie, bar influence could have effected that transfer; he ought to know, for he was himself invalided out in 1916, and spent the rest of the war in Government service, where he learnt to his cost that promotion is a slow job to the obscure young man.

"He had a sister to keep house for him," Archie's letter continued, "an amazing woman. They were always seen together. She was a widow, I don't know what had happened to her husband, probably he was killed in the war; anyway, no one ever spoke of him, and she and Nunn were practically inseparable. I met them both and you can take it from me that woman was magnetic. It wasn't that she tried to make you make love to her or stand treat to shows or dinners, but she was irresistible. I remember a woman saying to me that she was born to be a widow. She wasn't pretty and she couldn't dress, but you'd turn out on a wet afternoon to have tea with her—and you know what those end-of-the-war teas were like—where you wouldn't bother to go to dinner with half a dozen handsomer and more soignee women of your acquaintance. I fancy she was his chief asset with quite a lot of people, though you never heard rumours of her engagement, as you generally did with women who met a lot of men."

"It was a brilliant piece of statesmanship on Nunn's part," Jeremy observed, laying the letter down. "And luck as well. It isn't every brother who has a Meriel Ross in the family. And Archie's right when he talks about charm. She fairly drips with it."

He took up the letter again, but there wasn't much more of any importance. Archie said that Nunn seemed to know everyone and go everywhere; he had a marvellous head and no one ever saw him the worse for liquor. He had money, plenty of it, and though he didn't throw it away, no one ever described him as tight-fisted. People were always glad to have him as a week-end guest, and he seemed on excellent terms with people with whom he wouldn't have seemed to have much in common.

"And that's that," Jeremy observed, destroying the letter.

"Do you suppose Dennis has suspected any of this?" I wondered aloud.

Jeremy said coolly, "Well, if he hasn't, he can stay in the dark a little longer. We weren't sent down here to wet-nurse him. Dash it all, he's got my girl. He can't expect me to hand him anything else. Now, Tony, it's up to you. Carry on."

3

Everything, of course, from our point of view depended on our being able to prove some association between Ralph and Nunn, and this was particularly hard to do. Nunn had taken a stringent step when he refused to have his landlord over the threshold of the Abbey, and that seemed to indicate a deadlock between them. But what terms they'd been on before that, or if, indeed, they'd been on any terms at all, was almost impossible to learn. I sounded Eleanor on the subject. She said at once, "James didn't know Ralph. He met him once or twice, but I don't think he liked him, and he objected to his squiring Hilary, who was then only sixteen. That was the basis of the trouble between them. Of course, Ralph was away a great deal, but when he was at the Cottage he used to assume that he could come over whenever he liked. And the trouble was that when he did come over, he went out of his way to be insulting to James, talked about the country houses in the hands of corset manufacturers and jam merchants and so forth. And at last there was a final scene—I've never been sure what it was about, but I think it was Hilary—and James told him not to come again."

"And after that?"

"After that we had nothing more to do with him till the night Hilary was lost, that is to say, James had nothing more to do with him. I was seeing him and writing to him surreptitiously, about Cleghorne's letters."

"Nunn knew nothing about those letters until you told him? He hadn't been threatened by Ralph?"

"Oh, no. I never meant him to hear, but I think this time it wasn't a question of money, it was Hilary herself, and I must say it looked as if he might get her."

"That's all right," said Jeremy, when I told him, "but if she'd seen Nunn do it, she'd tell the same yarn. All her thought in this affair is for her precious husband, and has been from the beginning. I don't think you can count her an unprejudiced witness."

It was after this conversation that I managed to get hold of old Peters. I had known him many years ago, when he had a son about my age, who subsequently was killed in the war. There were other children, married or abroad, or scattered in their various jobs, and the old couple lived together in a very small, out-of-date cottage, where all the water had to be pumped up—the sort of cottage it's difficult to realise exists in these days of modern plumbing. Old Peters and his wife seemed delighted when I knocked at the door, and gave me the best place by the fire, and a cup of very thick stewed tea, with sweetened tinned milk. They said they could get cow's milk if they liked, but this was a treat. It was a bit of a shock to find they'd adopted town ways to this extent, and as I loathe sweet drinks it was all I could do to drink my mugful. The old couple talked and talked; they spoke of Hilary and of Eleanor and of Ralph; they spoke of all the changes that had taken place in the village during the last ten years; they produced photographs of their children and their grandchildren; they told me what a hard time Johnny was having in Canada, and how there was no dole out there; and they said that Lizzie, who was a lady's-maid, was in Italy and would go to Scotland when she came back.

And then Mrs. Peters added, "But let Mr. Anthony tell us his news. Have they found the fellow that murdered Sir Ralph yet?"

I said that we weren't sure it was murder, and in the talk that followed contrived to slip in my question about the letter, without arousing too much curiosity. Malicious people, I said, were asserting that Hilary had written to Ralph, luring him to his death, and it was all very unpleasant both for her and for Dennis.

Old Peters opened wide his blue eyes. "Ay, but she did, Mr. Anthony. I handed in the letter myself."

That was what we wanted to know. "When was this?" I asked. For there are three deliveries of letters daily at Feltham and Ravensend, one at about eight, one at midday and one at five. Letters for the first delivery must have been posted overnight, the last collection being taken at half-past six. Letters for the midday delivery can be posted by the nine-thirty collection for local addresses, and letters for the afternoon post can be posted up till half-past twelve.

Old Peters said, "You'll keep it quiet, sir, won't you? I wouldn't make things worse for the young lady."

And his wife chimed in, "Poor thing. I wouldn't be in her shoes now, that I wouldn't. She used to come in here quite a lot at one time, but lately she's too much occupied with other things. And though Sir James is a pleasant gentleman enough, it's not the same as having them you've always known, as belongs to the place, calling on you. Even Sir Ralph—well, you did feel he knew us, though he might be a bit wild."

"You can be quite sure I'm at least as keen as yourselves that Miss Hilary's name shan't be dragged into this show any further than can possibly be helped," I remarked, slightly nettled at their attitude. "But if you can remember what time you delivered the letter, it might make a lot of difference."

"It was in the afternoon," said Peters promptly. "I stopped and had a word with that chap, Baynes. Very civil to me he always was, whatever he might say about Sir Ralph and Miss Hilary in the court. We talked about the goings-on at the Abbey for that night. Sir Ralph, he'd been putting it round the village he was going to raise hell or worse, and us that have seen the family grow felt mortal fear'd what he might do. There's nothing a man like him 'ud stop at if he was so minded, my wife said, and we both remembered that French hussy he'd done for, and though she wasn't any better than she should ha' been, and French, which do seem to make a difference, still, we didn't like the idea that he might serve Miss Hilary the same. So I says to the fellow, 'Dessay you'll be glad, too, when this party's done and over?' and he says, 'That I will. Like a bear with a sore head the Captain is. Never left me alone a minute all the blessed day. I'll be glad to see his back this evening, and have a chance to call me soul me own.' Then I handed in the letter, and he put up his eyebrows, and said, 'Oh, my Lord, another of 'em. As if she wasn't going to see him to-night, too. Where's all this going to end?' Well, I didn't want to start naming Miss Hilary to him, so I said, 'Pity you can't keep him at home and save all the trouble,' and then I came away, but I was mortal fear'd. I mean to say, it isn't natural for a young lady to be engaged to one gentleman and be writing letters and meeting another, specially seeing how Sir James doesn't like him. But I didn't expect this end to it all, no, Mr. Anthony, that I didn't."

Mrs. Peters broke in in a wheedling voice, "Tell us, Mr. Anthony, you know how we feel about Miss Hilary, is there any talk of her being married to Mr. Dennis? It's a pity he doesn't get wed and get away from here, and they can settle down and let bygones be."

I said I didn't think marriage was being discussed at the moment, and got away, having learnt what I'd come for. It seemed to me impossible for Hilary to have written that letter, which must have been posted in Feltham (for Peters had spoken of its bearing the Feltham postmark) between half-past nine and twelve-thirty. Now Hilary had gone upstairs to put on her hat soon after nine, and we'd left the house before half-past. We had spent the morning buying her ridiculous bear and what she called "chicken fixings" for her party get-up, and it had been one o'clock when we came back. She hadn't posted a letter in Feltham, coming or going, so that seemed to me to let her out. Then I remembered seeing a number of letters in Nunn's writing on the hall-table, and cursed myself for a fool for not having glanced at the envelopes, though, as Jeremy pointed out later, you would hardly expect your host to be a first-class criminal, and there are even people who might take the view that the ideal guest does not pry among his host's correspondence.

I came away from the Peters feeling pretty pleased with what I had learned, though we still had to prove who had written the letter. As Jeremy had remarked, there didn't seem much likelihood of our being able to lay hands on the letter at this stage of the proceedings. Coming through the outskirts of Ravensend, where old Peters had lived since his last two children left the home and forced them into smaller quarters, I bethought me suddenly of a plea Eleanor had made me a couple of days ago. "If you're ever that way, Tony," she said, "I wish you'd go in and see old Nanny Finch. She's asked after you so often, and you know you used to be a great favourite of hers. This is the first time you've been at the Abbey, as she has reproachfully reminded me, that you haven't taken the trouble to go over and have a chat. She's such a dear old thing, and she doesn't see many people these days. Her own contemporaries are falling off, and she does so enjoy a chat. Luckily, Mrs. Gray and her family still keep up with the old thing, and a visit there is about the only excitement she has. You won't forget, will you?"

And now here I was within three minutes of the old dame's cottage, and not an inclination in the world to go near her. I wanted to get back and tell Jeremy what I had learned. On the other hand, it was too late for us to do anything else tonight and here was the opportunity ready to my hand. And the old lady had been very good to me years ago, making me cakes and buying me cornets of sweets. Moreover, she had a racy tongue and was excellent company. She hadn't, as so many people of her age do, fallen into decrepitude. Eleanor told me she could still walk, read and sew, that her memory was excellent, and no one enjoyed a long chat better. My steps took me up to the door of her cottage, and there I hesitated again. But while I debated within myself what I should do, a figure came to the window, carrying a lamp, and I saw it was Nanny herself. I was less sure whether she had recognised me, but I didn't want to hurt the old dear's feelings, so I pushed open the gate with my stick and walked up the narrow path, with its scrupulously neat border and its three bare little rose-trees in their circular beds in the lawn.

The old lady opened the door herself, delighted at her visitor.

"Come in, my dear," she said. "I'll make you a cup of tea in a moment. And how are you after all your travelling in foreign parts? Let me have a glimpse at you. Eh, and you're as lame as ever. The pity of it. Her ladyship's told you to come, I suppose? Aye, that's about the size of it." And so, with many exclamations and admonitions, she pushed me into the little front parlour, where a small fire burned, throwing its gay reflection on tall glass covers that shrouded pink and blue china figures, on sideboards decked with glass plates, and shelves edged with stiff white paper, cut into shapes, and where the round table was covered by a velvet cloth, edged with pom-poms, and there was an enlargement over the mantelpiece of the late Mr. Finch, a patriarchal old man, photographed in his best clothes, holding a black hat, as if asking for pence. The frame was ebony, inlaid with mother-of-pearl, and there were various beautifully penned inscriptions, in Indian ink and old English lettering, testifying to the virtues of the deceased. As a boy, this picture had fascinated me, as had also a reproduction of the Passion and Crucifixion, the three Figures miraculously inserted, on their crosses, in a green glass bottle. The bottle was still there, but the central figure had lost His Head, and one of the arms of His companions was broken. Otherwise, I could detect little change in twenty years.

"Now you didn't come over here specially to see an old woman?" Nanny began archly, and I said that I'd had to be in the neighbourhood on business, and thought I wouldn't postpone my visit.

"Eh, and I'm glad to see you," she sighed. "And which way did you come? Not by the short cut, surely?"

I said I certainly had come by the short cut; I'd always used it.

"Ah, but things are different now," she said, "with the poor Captain not dead above two weeks, and his murderer still roaming the countryside." No one about the place believed in the accident or suicide theory. "And a nasty man to meet on a dark night too. You never know what people like that won't do to you, if they get the chance. You take my advice, my dear, and stick to the high road."

I laughed. "This is the first crime we've ever heard of in connection with the right-of-way," I protested. "You mustn't regard it as a precedent."

"Things go in cycles," she returned, in oracular tones. "Anyway, you should keep to the high road till that dreadful man has been caught."

I said, "You couldn't be more in earnest, Nanny, if you'd seen him yourself."

She bent forward. "I have, my dear, and that's the truth. Though I don't say anything, because there's nothing I could do, and I'm sure I don't want a pack of interfering policemen bustling round my little house at my time of life."

"But how do you know it was the man?" I demanded.

She said, with serene assurance, "I know a wicked face when I see one, my dear. Besides, what was he doing wandering about in the dark like that? Honest men are in their homes at that hour."

"What hour was this?"

"Quite late it was, much later than I had any right to be. Though, for that matter, if I hadn't dropped off in front of the fire, I'd have been going over in the bus, and not walking at all."

"Do tell me," I invited her. "He didn't try and hurt you?"

"He might have done if I hadn't given him me half-crown, me beautiful new half-crown that I'd been keeping for Miss Isobel's Cathleen. You remember Mrs. Gray's Miss Isobel, her that I brought up as a little girl? Of course, I don't go out nursing now; ways have changed and they wouldn't let me have my way in the nursery. But in the old days I had a lot of little girls, but none sweeter than Miss Isobel. I always liked Mrs. Gray, too. One of those ladies that consider their servants. And now Miss Isobel's got a little girl of her own, they still let me come over to their parties, though it isn't the fun it used to be," she added, mournfully. "I don't understand the servants they have now. Such hoity-toity misses, all in silk stockings, that no good servant would have worn when I was in service, and silk underclothes and the pictures over at Munford every week. Still, I like to go for Miss Isobel, and Mrs. Gray, she comes to Miss Cathleen's parties and she's never too busy to have a word or two with me. Well, I'd been looking forward to this party for a matter of three weeks, and I'd got a nice bright half-crown for Miss Cathleen. I know when I was a little girl I got more fun out of a bit of money to spend than any kind of present. I was dressed good and early, so early I thought I'd rest a little before I started. Parties began at half-past three in the old days, and the Nannies came round at half-past six at latest. Now they don't begin till six or after, and it's ten o'clock before the children start going home. Even in a house like Miss Isobel's, which I shouldn't call new-fangled, they do that. Well, I didn't want to start till half-past five and I was dressed near an hour too soon, so I sat down by me little fire, thinking I'd rest, for I'm an old woman now, my dear, and I get tired easily. And it means stooping, putting on your best cashmere stockings and tying your shoes and so on. Well I must have dozed off for when I woke, goodness gracious me, the party had begun a long time ago. Eight o'clock it was. I could have cried. Me lovely party I'd looked forward to so. I jumped up as quick as I could, and tied on me bonnet and off I went. Nigh half an hour it takes me to get to the Grays' house by the road, and I'd missed the bus, that only comes by every hour. Then I remembered the short cut. I never have been by that short cut of a night before. I always say it's asking for trouble going out in the dark, and young women that do that kind of thing have only themselves to thank if they don't come back with a whole skin. But that day, being all flustered and so late, I determined I'd chance it. It was a clear night, and I thought I'd take the little lamp that Mr. Frank gave me two years gone, and my stick. So off I went, and I hadn't got very far before I wished myself back in me own house. For there, coming along the road towards me, was a man. And the last kind of man you'd wish to meet when you're alone and not so active as you were. I looked around, and there wasn't a soul in sight. Well, I couldn't do anything but stare straight ahead, and pretend not to see him. But as he got nearer, I knew he was going to speak to me. Don't ask me how, because I can't tell you, but all women that have their wits about them know when a strange man's going to make advances. I went on just as if he wasn't there, but he stopped me, and asked for some money. Said he wanted a night's shelter, and some food. I thought, You're as well-fed as I am, but I dursen't say so. You never can tell with these wild, rough men what they won't do. And it isn't as if it's only the young, pretty ones that gets set upon. There was that poor soul in the train, not many months back. There was her picture in the paper, and—well, my dear, goodness knows I've nothing to be vain about, now most of me teeth are gone, and I have this affliction growing beside me nose, but if I'd had a face like that poor body, I'd have hidden it behind a veil. And she hadn't any money neither. But she was set on and murdered, and all for no reason at all, from what the papers say. An inoffensive body, I've no doubt. So what with one thing and another, I was all of a shake, and I pulled out my purse and gave him what I thought was a penny. It wasn't till I got to the other end, hurrying all I could, for fear he'd come after me, I found that instead of a penny, I'd given him Miss Cathleen's beautiful new half-crown. I was upset, I can tell you. I hadn't another, and I had to make shift with a shilling, not a new one or anything, and I hadn't time to scratch her initials on it, like I'd done on the half-crown."

I said, "What was he like, this man who frightened you so?"

"He was a big tall man, dark, with a sort of beard from not shaving, dressed very ragged, with one shoulder higher than the other, and his hair was long and dark and all blown about." Then she described his clothes and as she spoke, word for word, she was drawing a picture of Ralph Feltham as we had found him on that fatal morning of the 16th.

"And what time was this?" I asked her.

"Oh, 'twas a quarter to nine when I got to Miss Isobel's, and would you believe it, the new-fangled servants they have there these days never so much as offered me a cup of tea or a bite to eat. All I got was some lemonade and a sandwich, made with some nasty stuff like liver. If I was head of a nursery I wouldn't have that kind of food on my table. No goodness in it, there isn't. Well, it must have been half-past eight or thereabouts that I met this murdering fellow, and he was making for the Abbey so far as I could see. Coming along the road he was, anyway, and as soon as I heard of the poor Captain, I thought to myself, So that nasty black murdering villain did it, after all. But, of course, I never said anything. And, after all," she added miserably, "I never see Miss Isobel at all. Gone out, she had, and it was her I'd gone for. Well, that's how life is, I suppose. I oughtn't to go on expecting at my age. But, you take my advice, my dear, and keep away from that dangerous road till they've got that man safe under lock and key."

She talked a good deal more, asking questions and giving me scraps of local gossip, but none of it was relevant to our case. I came away as soon as I could, and hurried back, by the right-of-way, of course, wondering how we could trace that half-crown. I found Jeremy pottering about in the front garden.

"Well, you've been a time," he said cheerfully. "Solved the mystery yet?"

I told him what I had heard. "By gum," he exclaimed, "the plot thickens, Watson, the plot thickens. That old lady's story is a bit of luck we couldn't have looked for. And what do we do now? The local police won't thank us for stepping in and teaching them their business. Besides, for all we know they're on the same track as we are."

"They haven't begun asking questions about the half-crown, so far as we can tell," I reminded him. "They might be glad to hear the story."

"Uncommonly glad," Jeremy agreed. "Shall you run down to the station and tell them at once?"

I said, "It seems to me we might take Dennis into our confidence at this stage. After all, we're down here in a sense as Philpotts' representatives, and he's his arch-representative, and Philpotts may not be too pleased if he finds we've been working quite independently. We aren't precisely the big noise at Scotland Yard—yet."

"Nor is Dennis—yet—so far as I can gather. Still, you may be right. We don't want to put friend Philpotts' back up, and it would be a thousand pities to lose another job of this nature on account of swelled head. Come and look for the chap."

CHAPTER XII

I

DENNIS WAS WRITING LETTERS IN THE LIBRARY. HE WAS SO much engrossed that he didn't appear to notice our arrival, and we stood for a minute watching his fine-pointed pen travel rapidly over the smooth grey sheets. He wrote a very personal hand, small, clear and characteristic.

Suddenly he looked up. "I beg your pardon!"

"Some chaps are lucky being taught to write when they're young," remarked Jeremy, with some envy in his voice. "Any spider can beat me when it comes to handling a pen. Look here, we don't want to butt in or poach on your particular preserves or anything of that kind, but we're interested in that affair on our own account, and we've managed to pick up some backchat that may be of some use to you, if you'd care to hear it. Besides, we want you to exert your influence," he added, candidly. "Tony and I haven't got any."

"If you can fill in any of the g-gaps I shall be infernally grateful," said Dennis, with that rather attractive deference of manner that I had noticed before. "I'm most horribly hung up. It isn't the s-solution that's baffling me. I've been p-pretty sure about that from the beginning, but I c-can't prove my theories. P-please be as detailed as you can, and go slow. These clever chaps never fail in the broad outline, but s-sometimes in quite trivial things they get let down. It isn't even their f-fault always, but something they c-could not possibly foresee."

2

I told my story and Jeremy listened, putting in a word now and again. Dennis occasionally asked a question, but though he had a pencil in his hand he made no notes. He drew a lot of designs on the writing-pad in front of him, regardless of the fact that the sheet was part of a letter. A castle he drew, and a row of cats with their backs to the audience, and a ship on some curly waves and various spherical diagrams. He was very particular as to the exact expressions my informants had used, and would ask me to stop and think twice. "You're sure he said thus-and-thus?" he would say. And I'd think and say Yes, I was sure, puzzling my brain to see why it should be of importance anyway. I cast surreptitious glances at Jeremy from time to time to see if he realised the way the wind was blowing, but Jeremy's eyes were fixed on Dennis, and he paid no attention to me, except to supplement something I had said, or query a precise remark. At last I finished. Dennis twiddled the pencil round and round in his fingers. Then he jumped to his feet.

"Do you think Lady Nunn will m-mind my using her telephone?" he asked. "I want to p-put through a trunk call."

I said I was sure she wouldn't, and he nodded and said, "Well, th-thank you awfully. You've dotted all my i's for me and crossed my t's. I c-couldn't have settled anything without you." And he went out of the room.

"He's a cool devil," remarked Jeremy, "what's the position now? Is he going to denounce the murderer or what?"

"I suppose he'll do something about Nanny's half-crown," I suggested dubiously, for Dennis had left me as much in the dark as Jeremy. "That point ought to be cleared up next."

"Perhaps he's going to make arrangements with the local bobby. Anyhow, let's wait."

Dennis was away for several minutes in the little lobby-like apartment across the hall, where the telephone was kept. Presently we heard the door swing to, and Dennis emerge. A moment later Eleanor said, "Oh, I've been meaning to come and talk to you. It's about Hilary. She's looking shockingly ill, and eating nothing. What can we do for the child?"

Dennis's voice replied, "It's the anxiety and strain. It seems to m-me quite natural. I'd be inclined to think her heartless if she could have a c-cousin murdered on the premises and not t-turn a hair."

"And she's to go on looking like this, and starving herself till the strain's over?" Eleanor's voice sounded tart.

"It w-won't be long now," Dennis promised her. "By the way, a friend of m-mine, perhaps two, is c-coming over to see me to-night. He's just been t-talking to me on the telephone. I hope I'm not taking t-too many liberties, but it might be important."

Eleanor said, "Of course, Mr. Dennis," but her manner seemed to freeze a little. Dennis said eagerly, "As a matter of fact, I d-do believe we're getting near the end. We're evolving a new theory, and I believe we're on the right lines at last."

Eleanor said, "I wish you would tell me," so he repeated Nanny Finch's story of the tramp and the half-crown. "So you s-see where that leads us to," he said, urgently. "Of course, we shall have to ask about the half-crown. I thought I might go d-down to the station in the morning. It was pure luck discovering that, because the old woman said she hadn't s-spoken of it to anyone, so it'll be n-news for them."

Eleanor said in an amazed voice, "You mean, you think he was murdered before the party began?" and Dennis replied, "That's the new theory, and I shouldn't be surprised if it wasn't the true one."

And not a word about me or Jeremy, if you please. Calmly taking the credit, stammering in his excitement. I was astounded.

"Did you ever hear anything so cool?" I whispered, in some indignation. "Bouncing us completely."

Jeremy shook with laughter. "Don't grudge him the credit," he whispered back. "Promotion may depend on it for him."

Dennis was still talking. "Dear old lady," he said, and his voice was as complacent as the purr of a cream-fed cat. "She'd no notion how much she was helping us with her story of her terrible fright."

"Did you tell her?" Eleanor asked.

"Oh, no. She said she d-didn't want a lot of interfering policemen bustling about her house. We didn't want to frighten her."

Then the door of the library opened and Dennis came in. "I say," he began, a little apologetically, "I hope you don't either of you mind, but I ran into Lady Nunn just now, and she seemed so upset about all this m-mystery that I told her about the half-crown, just to reassure her. I d-don't think she'll repeat it, and, of course, if there is anything in these suspicions of ours, the whole yarn is b-bound to come out."

Jeremy said heartily, "My dear chap, broadcast it from the dome of St. Paul's, if you think it would serve our purpose." I wondered if the fellow was afraid of losing caste with Hilary if he didn't occupy the spotlight. Then Eleanor came in saying, "What a beautiful fire! Oh, Mr. Dennis, were you writing? and am I interrupting you? I was going to suggest it was time for a drink before the dressing-bell goes."

"It's quite all right," Dennis assured her, drawing his writing-pad towards him, "I was only f-filling in time… By the way, I wonder if I could have m-my drink in here, and then I could get this letter finished to-night?"

Eleanor said Certainly, and Jeremy and I went down to the lounge where Nunn and Mrs. Ross had already begun their cocktails. Hilary joined us and we named our respective drinks—Hook mixed the best cocktail I ever remember having anywhere—and Eleanor told him to take Dennis's to the library.

"He's writing letters," she added explanatorily to her husband. "Oh, and Hook, he has some visitors coming presently. Show them into the library when they arrive."

Hook said, "Yes, your Ladyship," and went on mixing drinks. We dropped into casual conversation with one another. Nunn said he believed some neighbouring farmer was being accused of shooting foxes, and there was a devil of a row going on locally. Mrs. Ross said she believed Dennis was a policeman in disguise and was engaged in solving the murder under cover of being a guest at the Abbey. Nunn said he didn't much mind who solved it, so long as the affair was concluded. Mrs. Ross said she knew something of men, and when one went around as Dennis was doing at present, as pleased as a monkey with two tails, you might know he had something up his sleeve. Hilary fired up, saying, "If you mean that Arthur had a hand in Ralph's being killed, or in anything else discreditable, you can put the idea out of your head. You've only got to look at him to see he's good."

After the first moment of stark astonishment Nunn asked, a trifle grimly, "Does that imply, Hilary, that you've made up your mind at last about your suitors?"

Hilary blinked and said nothing (I believe she was shy), and the irrepressible Mrs. Ross exclaimed, rather scornfully, "Mind! The child's got no more mind than a weathercock that points in a different direction every day of the week."

Jeremy came to the rescue, saying affectionately, "And what could be nicer? You'd never have a chance of becoming bored, or of living in a stale atmosphere. Nothing wears a man down more than feeling he's got into a rut, and the atmosphere will never change. If you ask me, Dennis is a very lucky chap, and I hope he realises it."

"Oh, you young men!" said Mrs. Ross. "No wonder the girl's

unsettled. What chance does she get among the lot of you? You encourage her at every turn, in every new vagary she likes to indulge in. I suppose if she robbed the Bank of England you'd find some excuse for her."

"I should admire her flair," said Nunn gravely, and then Dennis's visitors arrived. One of them I knew slightly by sight, a tall, rawboned chap called Whistler, one of these chaps with independent means who start on a career and then drift into experimenting. Whistler had been a slum doctor at one time, but now he burnt the candle at both ends, no one quite knew to what purpose. However, he played a handsome game of bridge, which made him comparatively popular. The other man was a complete stranger to me.

Hook took them along to the library, and we continued our personalities. Mrs. Ross and Jeremy were capping one another's tall stories, Nunn and Eleanor were discussing some political problem about which they both felt strongly, and Hilary and I talked in undertones. I don't remember which of us was first aware of something unusual going on in the library; it wasn't that there was much noise, or any sound of struggle or loud voices; nothing to suggest violence, and yet quite suddenly we all stopped talking and began to listen.

Nunn said, "What's up?" and, not hindered by the delicacy that kept the rest of us where we were, went over to the library. An instant later Hilary had darted after him. "If it's anything to do with Arthur, it concerns me, too," she flung over her shoulder to Eleanor and Mrs. Ross, both of whom seemed inclined to stop her. The next minute we heard Dennis's voice, "Hilary, keep out of this, please."

Hilary said, "Jeremy, come here," and when he had come, and I with him, she said rebelliously, "I'll only go if you stay and see everything's all right. I haven't any idea what's up…"

"I know you haven't," Dennis interrupted, "that's why I told you to clear out. P-please go, Hilary. You're making things even worse than they're b-bound to be."

Hilary repeated, "I'll go if Jeremy stays." Dennis nodded, and his glance included me.

"Yes, p-please stay, both of you," he said. "And Sir James. That's all."

Neither Eleanor nor Mrs. Ross had attempted to follow our stampede; Hilary, looking crestfallen and snubbed, went back to the lounge. Dennis, rather surprisingly, asked me to lock the door. I couldn't make head or tail of the scene. Hook, with a bewildered expression on his clean-shaved face, was standing against the bookcase. Dennis stood on the farther side of the table, his partly-filled glass in front of him. Whistler stood at his side, and the stranger had taken up his position nearer Hook. Nunn was facing Dennis, and Jeremy and I had our backs practically to the door.

"I b-beg your p-pardon, Sir James," Dennis began—his stammer was worse than I had ever heard it—"for precipitating this c-crisis upon you. If I could have p-prevented it—in fact…" his hesitant officialdom broke down suddenly, and he continued in the vernacular. "I'm most f-frightfully sorry, but this is a thing that goes b-beyond your p-personal interests or m-mine. The fact is your butler's got a p-paper in my writing in his p-pocket, and I simply m-must have it."

Nunn looked up in the most pardonable surprise. "I don't understand, Dennis. Hook, what paper is this, and why have you got it?"

Hook said in his most official voice, "I don't understand Mr. Dennis either, sir."

The stranger took a hand. "Perhaps you'll allow me," he murmured, and with an unexpected movement he caught Hook's wrists between his fingers. Dennis moved across the room.

"Th-thank you. Sir James, I think perhaps it might help m-matters if you would read this aloud. I'm afraid," he added, with that queer desperate air of apology, "this is g-going to be most f-frightfully b-beastly."

Nunn, with a quite baffled air, read aloud from the grey slip that I recognised as coming from Dennis's writing-pad.

> "Now that it seems impossible to avoid discovery much longer, I may as well admit the truth. I killed Ralph Feltham. It was his own fault. He tried to double-cross me about Hilary. He should have known me better. We had worked together for years without anyone suspecting it. Indeed, I was constantly receiving official invitations to meet my prospective victims. He was a good partner, but he cheated me over Hilary. Besides, he was becoming dangerous. It was necessary for him to be removed. I thought, by leaving that note in the summer-house for Hilary to find, I had established an alibi, because, if Ralph had written it at eleven o'clock, then no one would think of his having been killed at nine. But now that the throw has gone against me, I am taking the only way out."

"And this amazing document is signed Arthur Dennis," wound up Nunn. "What on earth does it mean?"

"As a matter of fact, it d-doesn't mean anything," Dennis confessed. "I've s-spoilt it."

"Spoilt it?"

"The effect, I mean. By not cottoning to my drink." He indicated the glass in front of him.

"What's the matter with it?"

"Dr. Whistler is going to t-tell us that presently. I'm not quite sure myself, but I d-do know this. There'll be enough p-poison in that glass to k-kill two or three men."

Nunn looked at him hopelessly. Jeremy and I stood aghast and still uncomprehending.

"I'm afraid I don't get you," said Nunn curtly. "Are you suggesting that Hook—Hook!—has poisoned your drink?"

"I'm afraid I d-do mean that. I d-did warn you it was g-going to be a b-beastly b-business."

"But why on earth should he?"

"I knew t-too much. About F-Feltham's death, I mean. Let me explain. B-by the time Dr. Whistler and Detective-Inspector Benn arrived—oh, I haven't introduced you; my m-manners are all going to pieces; strain, I suppose—but that's Inspector Benn holding Hook's wrists—don't let go, Benn—by that time I ought to have f-finished my drink, when it would have f-finished me. They'd have found me fallen over the desk, or p-propped up against it, and by the time they'd recovered from their shock, and Hook had d-decided I was really done for, he'd have found also that p-paper lying on the t-table, explaining the tragedy. In the tamasha no one would have noticed that it hadn't been there as they came into the room."

"You're suggesting—let me get this clear, please—that Hook was going to commit a murder and stage a suicide? You still haven't explained why."

"B-because of Feltham."

"You mean, that Hook murdered Feltham?"

"I th-think so. In fact, I'm sure of it. He d-did it very well, but then I'd expect him to do anything he t-tackled very well. You see, this isn't my f-first experience of him."

"And then he wrote this balderdash?"

"Oh, no, n-no. I don't think he d-did that. I don't think he would refer to Feltham by his Christian name any more than I would."

"Then where did he get the paper from?"

"The same source as his instructions, all along the line. From L-Lady Nunn."

CHAPTER XIII

I

THERE WAS HYOSCINE IN THE DRINK FROM WHICH WHISTLER had taken a sample before any of us reached the library door. Dennis was right—he'd been right all along the line. There was enough of it to have killed every man jack in the place. Apparently Eleanor had a store of it, though we never discovered precisely how she got hold of it; Dennis said she was in touch with so many people that she could practically have demanded the Crown Jewels and been tolerably sure of getting them. And among the doctors in her power she wouldn't have much difficulty in getting hold of poison. Anyway, she had more than she'd given Hook to put in Dennis's cocktail, for when, at Nunn's request, she was sent for, in order that Dennis could repeat his story and she deny it, they found her dead in her room. She must have realised the game was up, and there was no hope for her. Hook bore the brunt eventually, and no one even tried to get up a reprieve for him, which shows how strongly the public, which can be sentimental enough about criminals, felt in this particular instance.

Nunn went through the subsequent proceedings like a man of stone. He had to give evidence, answer questions, make statements; he had to clear himself of the suggestion that he and Eleanor had been partners; he had to stand for any amount of obloquy. The affair cost him a tremendous amount both in prestige and in cash. I fancy it was due to Dennis that his name was completely cleared of every imputation of scandal before the wretched affair closed. The papers, of course, were full of it. The story of the Spider's activities became common property. Numbers of people whose relations had mysteriously made away with themselves during the past few years laid the blame at the Spider's door. In thousands of homes people felt as if at the eleventh hour they had been granted a reprieve. It was as if they could at last dare to draw breath.

Dennis wasn't mentioned by name in any of the newspaper reports. He looked, not triumphant, but sick and green when he had at length convinced Nunn of the facts. He told me privately that he couldn't look the fellow in the face. He seemed afraid to meet Hilary, too, as if she might turn and rend him. In short, he behaved as if he had something to be ashamed of.

Nunn spoke to no one, except Jeremy, and that was not until we were getting ready to leave the Abbey. He had been unapproachable, and I was wondering whether it would be possible to say a word before we went. Because I knew, if he and the rest of them didn't, that there had been another Eleanor besides the one who had lived on blackmail, and even helped to do her own husband to death (for Dennis convinced us of this also before he was through). There had been the woman who came down at five in the morning to see that a young subaltern had his breakfast before going back to France. It was odd, but that was the Eleanor I saw most clearly during those grim weeks following her death, and I had a confused notion that if I could make Nunn aware of her too, things might be more endurable for him. But, as if he sensed my intention, Jeremy said dryly, "Oh, don't be a funny ass, Tony. What is there for such as we to say to a man like that?" As we were going, Nunn held out his hand to Jeremy, and said, "It'll pass, Freyne. All things pass. It's only man who's indomitable."

2

"Do tell me," Jeremy said to Dennis, later on, "how did you know that drink would be poisoned?"

"It was their last chance," Dennis explained. "I had to get them red-handed; my case against them wasn't clear enough and this was the only way out that I saw. I don't know whether Lady Nunn had any idea that I'd found her out, but she realised that if we could prove that Feltham left his house, not at half-past ten but at eight, all the fat would be in the fire. She meant to prepare a cast-iron alibi by being in the house all the evening, from the instant the party started, but it was essential that everyone should believe Feltham was alive at—say—half-past ten. That note in the summer-house (written, incidentally, on my paper), was a very shrewd idea, because it misled practically everyone. But she had to take another risk. It was important that Hilary shouldn't be there to time, or the note would lose all meaning, so she had to detain her for at least ten minutes. You remember how she came to us in an agitated condition at eleven or a little earlier, saying she'd been doing her best to keep Hilary with her, but hadn't been successful? She did everything she could, except for that slip in the confession I was supposed to have written. There are only two or three people in the house who referred to Feltham by his Christian name, and I'm not one of them. And, by the way," he smiled deprecatingly, "I suppose it's horribly snobbish of me, but I was wounded at the idea that anyone could believe I'd prepare anything so melodramatic as that letter."

"Let's get this straight," said Jeremy, who is a single-minded young man. "You guessed it was Lady Nunn and Hook, but you couldn't prove it. What did you do to precipitate the crisis?"

"I told them I'd discovered about the half-crown, and that I proposed to talk to the police about it first thing in the morning. Now, from their point of view, it was of the utmost importance that no one should discover the half-crown. I don't say either of them had set eyes on it, but the police would jump on such a clue, and it was literally as much as their lives were worth to allow them the chance. So if they were going to act, they had to act at once. I thought of the drinks as being an ideal opportunity, so that when I said I'd have mine alone, it was simply a question of giving them plenty of rope, with the practical certainty that they'd hang themselves."

"And that," I exclaimed, "was why you took all the credit for discovering about the half-crown? We couldn't think…"

Dennis laughed. "Oh, you h-heard me?" he stammered. "Well, you see, I hadn't any choice. If Lady Nunn had realised that you and Freyne knew about the half-crown she wouldn't have done anything conclusive, because it wouldn't have been worth while. But, so far as she knew, I was the only person alive who could make that fact known to the police, and so I must be swept out of the way at once."

"And you anticipated the confession?"

"Well, if I was to be poisoned, it was obviously to be a case of suicide. And if you have a suicide, you must have a motive. In my case, the only motive that would be any use to them, would be Feltham's murder. It might have been a bit difficult for anyone to have put together a case against me, but in the face of a signed confession that would hardly count. As soon as Hook brought in the drink I tilted some of it into a phial, in case Hook got suspicious and overturned the glass, and then I waited."

"That," agreed Jeremy, "was very smart. But what put you on to Lady Nunn in the first place?"

"I've never been satisfied with the solution, if you can call it that, of the Feltham scandal, the first Feltham scandal, I mean. I know a lot of fools went about saying that Percy Feltham must be guilty because innocent men don't shoot themselves at the first breath of

suspicion, but that was all my eye and Betty Martin. Feltham had
no choice. He had to take his own life or stand his trial for treason.
And whether he was convicted or no, he was a ruined man. There
was a man whose work was his life, and when he'd lost the one the
other had no value for him. But, on the other hand, people were
right in saying that Cleghorne had an ally, and an ally who knew
more about the business than he did. Some of those facts could
not have come from him; he didn't know them. No one but Percy
Feltham knew them, and he never told official secrets. That went
against him at the time, of course; a chatterbox might have been
found guilty of indiscretion but not of wilful treachery. But everyone
recalled Feltham's reputation. They didn't remember, though, that
Feltham told everything to his wife. He had done it since their marriage; he rated her intellect very high; he regarded her as his partner
and ally. Really he thought of her in those capacities more than he
thought of her as his wife. And she did know as much as he knew
himself. He relied on her to a very great extent. So if anyone had
given the facts away, it was one of these two, and for every reason
I was convinced it wasn't Feltham. So you may say that I began
this business with a prejudiced mind. It might, of course, only be
coincidence that in the two biggest affairs of their kind that had
entered my experience she was a figure, even a central figure, but
I wanted some proof of that. She was Percy Feltham's wife and
confidante, and secret information was sold. She settled with her
next husband at Feltham Abbey—in itself an odd thing to do—and
Feltham Abbey was tracked down as being at all events connected
with this Spider scandal."

"We thought it was Nunn," said Jeremy, thoughtfully, "and the
odd thing is, we worked along much the same lines as yourself."

"I considered Nunn," Dennis acknowledged, "but he didn't
really fit the bill. You pitched on Mrs. Ross as his confederate, too;

I never suspected her. The woman talks too much, and she can't help showing off. It's part of her attraction, I know, but it would make her quite useless for this kind of work. You've got to have a cool head and unlimited powers of reticence. I got hold of the dossiers of about a dozen of the Spider's victims, and tracked them all down, and in each case I found that one of the two Felthams—Lady Nunn, that is, or the Captain—was intimate with the family. I hadn't a doubt that Ralph Feltham was in the ramp; it would be honey to the bear to him. And I knew several stories of his wartime activities. I don't doubt he was in the Cleghorne plot, too. You'll realise that a big gang movement like this one isn't built up easily; it requires a tremendous amount of machinery to ensure its smooth working, and every cog and nut must be thoroughly tested before being slipped into place. Lady Nunn, as Percy Feltham's wife, had gone pretty well where she pleased. She had unlimited opportunities for collecting just the kind of information that would be useful. And information of that sort retains its value. Of course, she had her spies and confederates. I had picked on Feltham as one, and then I examined the facts to see whether there was anyone who might be described as a bridge between the past and the present."

"And you found Hook?"

"I found Hook. The man had apparently had an excellent job, which he threw up to become Lady Nunn's butler, though it must have meant recalling an extremely painful period in his own life. Then came the story of Lady Nunn being herself blackmailed by Feltham. Now, to my mind that argued a recent split between the two. Feltham must have had those letters of Cleghorne's for years, but though he'd often been hard put to it for money, he'd never tried to raise it by those means. Not because he was scrupulous—he wasn't—but because he and Lady Nunn were on excellent terms, and it was a more paying proposition to keep in with her. But after the split, he produced the correspondence. I daresay she paid him handsomely; on the other hand, all he may have asked of her was Nunn's consent to the marriage. Lady Nunn, I'm sure, would have refused that. Knowing Feltham as she did, she probably felt a bit sick at the prospect of Hilary becoming his wife. And I daresay those were Ralph Feltham's terms. Once he'd married Hilary, he'd very likely have settled down, and the reformed criminal is the most dangerous person alive. So clearly he must be put out of the way. He was dangerous to Hook, too…"

"I still don't see how you can have been sure of Hook," Jeremy expostulated. "You might have suspected him, but it doesn't seem to me you had any evidence."

"I didn't, for a long time, do more than suspect him. But he showed his hand once in a very foolish fashion. He had said, you will remember, that he didn't speak to Baynes, but when you, Keith, were asking him about the letters, he said at once that it would be better for him to slip the question to Baynes. But if he wasn't on speaking terms with the fellow, it would be an extremely awkward subject to open up. And then, when I was thinking about Feltham's death, I became convinced that that note Hilary found was a forgery and that it had been waiting in the summer-house ever since someone had murdered him. You see, even I know the legend of the paper he uses, and this didn't fit in with the legend. Then I remembered it was Lady Nunn who prevented Hilary being in time. Well, if Feltham wasn't killed during the party, it must have been before it began. It wouldn't be safe to let Hilary find that note, with the chance of his wandering in inopportunely. I thought it was probably the work of two people—Feltham was a big man and he hadn't been dragged—and so I got back to the story of the unusual car in the right-of-way. I argued that a man taking that road between half-past eight and nine would have time to put Feltham out of the way, and get back to the house probably before any of the guests arrived."

"And Eleanor was late," I agreed. "Mrs. Ross commented on it, saying she was locked in the bathroom. It hadn't occurred to me that you can lock a door from either side."

"Or that a woman wrapped in an old cloak could probably slip into the house without attracting much attention. She could come up through the private gardens, and everyone would be dressing when she returned. And she could use that small private door into the house."

"It was taking a chance," argued Jeremy.

"All murderers take chances. It's part of the game. Hook took a chance when he banked on people identifying the man in the evening rig as a guest and not as a servant."

"What damned fools!" Jeremy cried. "I'd forgotten there are two sets of men who wear open-faced shirts in the evening, and the whole household knew that Hook—the careful, the meticulous Hook—had allowed his stocks to run low on an important night. The very last thing Hook would be likely to do. And in any case he wouldn't have gone himself, he'd have sent one of the underlings. Or even have telephoned."

"Yes, it was his candour that almost saved him," Dennis agreed. "He didn't attempt to hide his movements. He was a very cool, crafty, intelligent chap, the kind of man it's worth pitting oneself against." Again he offered us that deprecatory smile.

"Those bloodstains in the summer-house were a mistake," Jeremy observed. "I suppose if there weren't these accidents there'd be more undetected criminals than there are. If the car hadn't been seen that night, I suppose we'd never have brought it home to them."

"There's Mrs. Ross's Mills of God for you," Dennis protested. "You must remember that we always play a three-handed game—Fate insists on taking a hand in all these deals, and a lot depends on how she plays it. Generally, you know, in spite of the scepticism of the time and the public, she plays it on the right side. Still, it wasn't Hook who was the artist in this case. It was Lady Nunn."

A new thought struck me. "How did she make the appointment with Hilary?"

"Got you to drive her into Munford for the purpose. Mrs. Ross said she practically sacked that girl; she had to have some good excuse for getting out of the neighbourhood that afternoon. She managed very well; she couldn't have allowed for Mrs. Ross coming, but she got round that difficulty by saying openly that she must telephone the house about her failure to find a parlour-maid. And she did telephone the house, and Hook, who was waiting, answered the call. She told him whatever was necessary, and then asked to be put on to Hilary. You've noticed, of course, that she has a fairly deep voice at all times, and it wouldn't be difficult to pitch it a tone lower for the occasion. Besides, no one expects a voice to sound quite normal on the telephone, and these country wires, in particular, distort quite familiar voices. And then Hilary said the voice sounded strange and fierce."

"And she wrote the letter to Ralph making the appointment that ended in his death?"

"I should say, unquestionably. Peters, by the way, was a most valuable witness. He can't tell us what the letter contained; I don't suppose we shall ever know that, but it must have been pretty strong to have had much effect on the fellow. I daresay Hilary offered to elope with him; otherwise, why pitch the meeting so early? But Peters did tell us something supremely important. He said that in the course of his conversation with Baynes, the latter said he'd be thankful when it was time for Feltham to go out, as he'd been indoors the whole blessed day. Well, if that were true, he couldn't have telephoned Hilary, because there wasn't an instrument on the premises. That's why I asked you," he nodded towards me, "to be as detailed as possible, because it's in trifles like that that men give themselves away."

3

Jeremy got up and said he must go. He had a lot of things to see to. He had accepted an invitation to join a party of deep-sea diving—trust Jeremy to get in touch with something unusual and, probably, unprofitable. He stood by the windows for a minute, looking out on the lighted street, where the taxis, little beetles in orange and black, ran to and fro among the moving crowds. It was, I saw, going to be all right about Jeremy, though Hilary was going to marry Dennis, and he had to go back to his wandering life. He lived for the adventure of the moment and the anticipation of to-morrow. A settled life wouldn't really suit him at all. He had loved Hilary, but she wasn't the one thing in his life that mattered beyond everything else. Deeper than his feeling for her was the sense of the perpetual challenge of existence and his need to answer it. Already he seemed hardly one of our company. He was reaching out towards the unknown, the inexperienced, the so far unattainable. Rooted in life though he was, he was possessed of no local roots. One place was as much home to him as another. Part of him, indeed, seemed already to have sped away; he himself was already drawing the door of this last experience close behind him, turning his feet towards the future.

He turned to Dennis. "Good luck," he murmured. "You deserve it. I'll drink your health on the 19th."

Dennis, looking shy and becoming loquacious, stammered, "There's no such thing as deserving good luck, really, you know. Sometimes for s-some reason the heavens open and s-shower gifts on to men. It's all very s-strange. I haven't really got accustomed to Hilary preferring me to the r-rest of the world. I daresay I shall, though," he added philosophically. "I hope you're going to enjoy things."

"I expect so," Jeremy reassured him. "What would you like for a wedding present? A nice little octopus or one of those jolly fish with mouths like dust-chutes? Either would probably act as a Hoover. Next time you see me I shall probably be a travelling showman. It's more aristocratic than going on the movies these days."

He went out, and I was left with a bleak sense of loss. It wasn't Jeremy so much as Eleanor. She was wrapped up with the roots of my life; and I'd seen her lying dead. She had looked like a stranger, and it had almost knocked me off my balance.

Dennis said, "A nice chap, isn't he? I'd almost sooner have cut out anyone else. But that's how these things are. You know, I d-didn't think I had a hope when he appeared in the field. But the gods are more fair-minded than we ever allow. They even up the balances in an amazing way. He's everything I've always wanted to be, and yet Hilary d-doesn't want to marry him. It's very strange."

But as I came out into the brilliance, the mystery and the enchantment of the London night, leaving Dennis standing at his window, it didn't seem to me so strange after all.

HORSESHOES
FOR LUCK

"Luck?" said the stranger on my left. "tell that to the Marines. There's no such thing. It's nothing but superstition, and any sensible man will tell you the same. Look at these people that won't see the new moon through glass, throw salt over their left shoulder, won't walk under a ladder or sit down thirteen at table—are they any luckier than anyone else? You bet they aren't. I had a pal once, full of ideas about one thing being lucky and something else being fatal. He bought a pub., a free house it was, and he called it the 'Three Horseshoes.' Full of what he was going to do with it, make it into a regular hotel, with a garage and a bowling green. Bound to be lucky with a name like that, he thought. But the first week some loafer smashed up the bar, and the second week his wife skipped off with a commercial traveller, who hadn't even paid his account, and the week after that the barmaid helped herself to the till."

"He should ha' nailed three horseshoes over the door," said someone else. "You got to do these things right."

"That wouldn't ha' made a scrap of difference," said my companion scornfully. "There's no such thing as luck. What do you say?" and he turned expectantly to Inspector Field, who sat close by.

Field was ready for him. We used to discuss sometimes whether any man could have worked so many apposite cases as he seemed to have done, but if he hadn't, then he was the best novelist lost to the world since Edgar Wallace.

"Anyone can have horseshoes for me," he said promptly. "They're like that other superstition, that a man that's a gambler must be a good sportsman. It doesn't follow. Ever heard of Cheesehampton?"

Two or three men nodded. "They've got some very fine stables down there."

"It's because of those very stables I ever went down there. It was a hotbed of racing folk. The time I was there was just before Goodwood, and I was there because one racing man wasn't quite the sportsman you might expect.

"The day before I started we'd heard from the local police that the people at Cheesehampton were being bothered with anonymous letters. You keep getting outbreaks in various parts of the country and sometimes they're dangerous and sometimes not. Mostly they're the work of lunatics. All sorts of quite ridiculous people were getting them, people who had no more reason to fear the police than an archangel. It wasn't so much that the letters constituted blackmail—mostly they were too silly for that—but some folk were getting upset and it was felt generally that the thing should be stopped. Whoever was responsible didn't ask for money: he'd put his meaning something like this:

'You think no one knows what happened at Brighton on the 4th June last. But I do. Beware.'

It was like a story in a kids' magazine, but there must have been some truth in some of the suggestions, because people were jumpy. Even people who hadn't had letters were getting that way. Guilty conscience, I suppose. Quite often, of course, the man who got the letter didn't pay any attention; sometimes he thought it was a maniac, because what the letter contained meant nothing at all. But there were others, as I've said, who took it more seriously.

"Well, this had been going on for some time when the writer overstepped his mark. There was a big man there called Bayliss, a rabid racegoer with his own stables. Apart from horses he really hadn't any life at all. He wasn't married, never opened a book, never heard a note of music. It was horses with him all the time. I'd been at Cheesehampton only a few hours when he came in waving one of these silly sheets, in a state of great agitation.

"'Look here,' he shouted, 'I'll tell you who this fellow is. Read this.'

"So I read it. It was the usual thing, written on the same kind of paper in the same obviously faked hand. It said:

> 'If you do not withdraw Bluebeard from the race for the
> —— Cup, the whole world shall hear the truth about A.'

"'Who's A.?' I said, and he told me Alcock, his jockey, who was going to ride Bluebeard for the Cup.

"'What's this chap talking about?' I went on, and Bayliss looked murder and said: 'About a year ago I had a couple of horses running in a big race, and biggish odds on both. I backed one heavily myself, and wouldn't say anything definite about the other. She was a mare and very temperamental, particularly in wet weather, as mares often are. That was a drenching summer, and though she could make a very good pace if conditions suited her, she was no use unless she was pleased. Alcock was up that day, and if anyone could have coaxed a spurt out of her he was the man, but she was sulky, and even he could do nothing. A neighbour of mine, another racing man called Grey, whose property marches with mine, had a lot of money on her; he'd seen Alcock exercising her and knew she could make a fine pace. Of course, I didn't tell him not to put money on her—what man would? Anyway, I'm superstitious enough to believe that if you start warning people against your horse it'll get the inevitable reaction. The result was that Grey backed her heavily and lost a packet; afterwards he came round breathing death and swore that Alcock had pulled the beast. It was so vilely untrue that I was tempted to take action. I told him, anyhow, he could go to the stewards, but naturally he wasn't going to chance being run in for libel, and the damages would have been pretty heavy. I'm well-known round here and so is Alcock, and Grey hadn't a leg to stand on, and knew it. Still, he did what he could by dropping hints here and there, nothing definite enough to take up, but damned unpleasant for me, and galling as hell for Alcock. Fortunately, from my point of view, he's not a very popular chap, and no one paid much attention. But what I am afraid of is that if the yarn goes round often enough he may shake Alcock's confidence. The boy's got nothing to fear, actually, but if he gets the notion that anyone believes this ridiculous yarn it'll shake him to pieces, and he'll be no use to me or anyone else. And Grey knows that. Naturally, I'm inclined to back my own stable, but I'm not the only man hereabouts that knows that Bluebeard, with Alcock up, will sweep the field next week.'

"I hung around picking up scraps of local talk, and I was told that Bayliss hadn't overstated the case. One man said: 'If Alcock were on a rocking-horse he'd get somewhere,' which might be intended as a compliment, but made the story Grey was spreading sound a bit more likely than before.

"Bayliss told me he hadn't any intention of taking any notice of the threats, but all the same he wanted some assurance that no harm should befall his jockey. I asked him what proof he had that Grey had actually written the letters, and he had to admit that there was none.

"'Still,' he urged, 'no one else has a motive, while Grey's reeks to Heaven. He's running a horse of his own, and he backed him some time ago at very heavy odds. He's not a bad horse, either, but he won't stand a chance with Bluebeard and both of us know it. Grey's in desperately low water, and everything depends on his beast winning the race.'

"It appeared that Grey's horse was second favourite, but there didn't seem much doubt in the minds of those best qualified to know that Bluebeard would beat him, though it might be a close thing. I found out, too, that Bayliss's story of Grey being very deeply dipped was no more than the truth. So the position was pretty ticklish.

"'He'd get me warned off, if he could, but since he can't, he'll stop at nothing to put Bluebeard or Alcock or both where they can't threaten his security.'

"You can see for yourselves it wasn't a very easy position. I couldn't accuse Grey of being the author of the anonymous letters, but it didn't seem to me any harm going round to see him. After all, he might have had one himself. Grey was a laconic sort of fellow; no, he said, he hadn't been pestered; people with nothing to hide generally weren't, which shows you how much he knew about human nature, or life, for that matter. I must say I didn't take to him, a big swaggering sort of chap, too well dressed for me. I like tailor's dummies in a window, but nowhere else. Besides, his manner irritated me. You could see him putting a policeman in his place every time he opened his mouth. I came away feeling a good deal of sympathy for Bayliss, but reminding myself that a man isn't a bad hat because you don't take a fancy to him.

"Coming through the village I ran against Bayliss again, a lot more agitated than he'd been up to now.

"'Look here, Inspector,' he said, 'I've had another of these damned things; it's just come, and this time it's deadly serious.'

"The new letter read:

'You had better withdraw your horse while you have the chance. Alcock will never ride him.'

"'That's tantamount to a threat of murder,' said Bayliss excitedly, but, of course, I couldn't allow that.

"'Threat of bodily harm perhaps,' I agreed, 'or it might just mean there's some monkey trick on foot to keep him out of the way till after the race. You'd better keep an eye on him.'

"I wasn't able to get any definite evidence against Grey, but I thought I'd feel a lot more comfortable when the race had been run. Going back, I thought it all sounded a bit silly; this is England, not Chicago, and you don't kidnap men in broad daylight. But it didn't sound so silly twenty-four hours later when a man as white as paper came to find me and said: 'If you please, sir, there's been an accident. It's Alcock. They've just found him in a clump of bushes over by Milton Heath.'

"'What's wrong with him?' I asked sharply, and though I think by this time I expected the answer I got, I felt a bit sick when the fellow said: 'He's dead all right. Been dead for some hours. Mr. Bayliss is half crazy.'

"'Thrown?' I asked, and the chap looked sick in his turn and told me: 'Must have been. And Bluebeard lost his head—he was always an excitable brute; no one but Alcock could ride him—and trampled on him. His head's smashed…'

"I went along. They hadn't moved the body, because Bayliss, as soon as he heard, swore it was foul play, though it was as clear a case of a man being kicked by a horse as ever I'd seen. Alcock must have gone clean over the beast's head, we decided. Bluebeard had pitched him alongside a bracken clump, and the horse, either frightened by the accident or hurt itself, had done the rest.

"'It looks as though he saw Bluebeard meant trouble,' said Bayliss, who, I believe, was upset about the boy for his own sake, quite apart from losing the race. 'Look at the grass here; he must have tried to drag himself out of the horse's way. It's all crushed and trampled.'

"'Did he know this part of the country?' I asked, and was told that he brought the horse here every day.

"'Of course, I never supposed he'd come to grief, riding, and you can say what you like, Inspector, this isn't a natural death. Someone scared the horse crazy. He wouldn't have lashed out at his jockey if he hadn't been terrified out of his wits.'

"I suggested the usual things—a sudden shot, though who'd be shooting there I couldn't suggest—a piece of paper blowing under Bluebeard's nose, though there was no sign of any—but Bayliss wasn't satisfied. Bluebeard, he said, wouldn't have stampeded his jockey for a mere spasm of fright.

"All the same, it was difficult to see what else could have happened. The doctor said there could be no doubt about cause of death. Evidence showed that the upper part of the head had been crushed by a horse's hoof. He was a pretty grisly sight, and I was sorry for the boy's mother, who would have to attend the inquest.

"'Are there any marks of ill-usage on the horse?' I asked, and Bayliss said he was all right except for a pair of cut knees, but naturally he wouldn't be able to run in the race forty-eight hours hence. That was when I began to think that, after all, there might be something fishy about the whole affair. A fall on turf and bracken doesn't result in cut knees. Grazing and scraping—yes—but cuts—no. When I saw the horse I got more suspicious still; I'm handier with a motor cycle, I confess, when it comes to getting about, but even I know a bad cut when I see one. The place where the accident had happened was just over a slope where a few trees grew, and as I thought about it a new idea came to me. I walked up to the trees and began to examine them, and I found, as I'd half begun to expect, marks on the trunks of two of them, where the bark had been rasped very recently.

"'What's the matter?' Bayliss demanded, and he sounded as though I might have had a hand in the affair.

"'Just what I want to know,' I told him, and I began to hunt on the ground. I was remembering Bayliss's comment that the grass round the place where Alcock lay had been badly trampled. Well, I found the same condition here. Half a dozen men might have been stamping on it. Alcock hadn't threshed about much—the doctor was of opinion that he must have been killed outright by the blow—because there were no blood-stains anywhere, and in any case he had pitched several yards away from the trees. That looked as though it might have been trodden on purpose, and the purpose was to conceal footprints. You couldn't get the smallest trace from that mess. Presently, after about forty minutes, during which I thought Bayliss was going to break a blood-vessel—I found what I was looking for—two or three little chips of wire snipped clean at the edges."

"You mean, someone had stretched wire across the path to make the lad take a toss?" That was my neighbour who had talked about luck.

"Exactly. And it must have been someone who knew that Alcock would be coming hell-for-leather down that stretch. Well, that accounted for the cuts on the horse's legs, and whoever was responsible must have slipped out afterwards and cut the wire with a pair of tweezers. That got us on a certain way, proved that Bayliss was right when he spoke of foul play; but it didn't mean that Grey was the man responsible. Even when we found the wire that had been used, pitched in a pond near-by, it didn't help us. It was common or garden wire and anyone might have bought it, or had it.

"Bayliss nearly drove me off my head following me round and saying: 'It's murder, I tell you, murder. Bluebeard wouldn't trample his own jockey if he hadn't been frantic.'

"Someone suggested he might have had his back to the jockey and so didn't know what he was doing, but that wouldn't work either. The position in which the lad was lying showed that. The queer thing was that, if Bluebeard had been in a state of frenzy, he shouldn't have smashed in the whole head. It looked as though there had been just one blow and that he'd cantered back to his stable.

"Well, I thought of this and that, tested a theory and turned it down, and then I asked to see the horse. He'd come back all right on his own account, so it didn't look as though there had been a plot to kill him. I wasn't even convinced yet that whoever was responsible had intended to kill the jockey. After all, there was no need to do that, and murder's an ugly game, with ugly consequences for the murderer.

"At the stables the grooms were looking a bit askance at Bluebeard. Nobody likes a horse that kills its jockey; besides, he was known to have a queer temper at the best of times. I said I wanted to see his feet. For a minute no one moved, then Bayliss came shoving past me in a cursing rage and lifted the great feet, one after the other, for me to examine. As he stood back, saying: 'Well?' I felt myself sweating.

"'You're right, sir,' I told him. 'There's more than a toss to this. It's murder or I'm a Dutchman.'

"You see, there wasn't a trace of blood on any of those four hoofs. And yet Alcock had been killed by a blow from a horse, and the wound was too deep, too frightful, for no trace to be left on the shoe.

"Bayliss was still shouting that Grey was behind this, and I went off to inquire into Grey's movements, though I had to handle the affair pretty carefully. I hadn't an iota of evidence against the fellow. I asked him whether he'd been in the neighbourhood of Milton Heath that morning, and if so, if he'd seen anyone hanging about, but he told me he'd spent his time at the golf club, going round on his own.

"'I don't want to find myself one of these fellows who turns up beaming to find that every other chap is unfortunately paired off, or is feeling groggy and not up to play,' he told me, 'and it seemed to me my eye wasn't quite as straight as it used to be.'

"Several people remembered seeing Grey at the club, and one man agreed that he had lunched with him. I asked if he'd employed a caddie, but it appeared he hadn't. He felt he might foozle half his shots, he explained, and he'd feel less of a fool if he were by himself. Well, that was reasonable enough. Few men are heroes to their caddies. I inquired about Grey's stable, but it appeared none of his horses had been out that morning, and he hadn't hired a hack. Besides, he'd been on the golf course, and a man can't be in two places at the same time. The only thing I did discover that might conceivably help was that the course ran quite close to the place where Alcock had been found.

"I thought and I thought. Suppose he'd timed himself to be at this particular spot at the time when Alcock would probably be passing? Even so, how could he have been responsible for the jockey's death? He'd been carrying golf-clubs, certainly, but Alcock hadn't been killed by a golf-club, but by a blow from a horse's hoof.

"And then, suddenly, I knew what had happened. Don't ask me how. If it wasn't for these gleams of inspiration the life of a policeman would be harder than it is, and it's hard enough, heaven knows, what with criminals being so unsporting and detective writers giving them so many hints. I went down to see the village blacksmith.

"'Shod any horses for Mr. Grey lately?' I asked him.

"'One,' he told me. 'A mare. About a week ago.'

"'Going a bit lame, wasn't she?'

"'Well, no, not that I could see. Don't know what he wanted her shod for, come to that.'

"But I knew. Grey had come down himself, which was a bit unusual, for he was one of these high and mighty chaps, who think themselves a cut above the rest of the world. After that I went up to Mr. Grey's house, choosing a time when he wasn't there, and told the servant that I was expected and I'd wait. They put me in the library and I routed among his books and found what I'd expected. Mind you, in a way I don't know that I wanted to find it, because even a policeman doesn't like to think of what humanity is capable of. But I was right. I even got the weapon in due course, as ugly an object as ever I've seen." He took a pencil out of his pocket and began to draw something on the back of an envelope. "Know what this is?" he asked us.

Well, there wasn't much question as to that. It was a stick like a club, with a horseshoe on one end. When we began to understand, we knew what he meant when he said he'd half-hoped he wouldn't find it. There was a famous Continental criminal called The Spider, who'd liked making use of it. Paris was his happy hunting-ground, till they ran him down at last. His method was to get a couple of horseshoes and fasten them on to a wooden club, and you had as murderous an implement as any criminal could desire. Grey had read his story, and seen in it a fine chance to put Alcock out and secure his own future. He must have waited till the boy came past, took a toss over the wire, and then walked in and deliberately murdered him.

"But was that necessary?" we asked. "Wouldn't it have been enough if he'd incapacitated Bluebeard? Why risk his neck in that foolhardy fashion?"

"He couldn't afford not to put the jockey out of the way," Field told us, with a shade of contempt for our slower intellects. "Alcock would know the horse hadn't come down by himself. And Grey had got to clear the wire before anyone discovered his share in the plot. He literally didn't dare let Alcock live. And I suppose he thought he was safe enough. Any doctor would have sworn death was caused by the kick of a horse. There'd been a horse on the spot, a queer-tempered horse at that. Grey thought Bluebeard would get the blame, and he'd save his own skin. He was steeped in debt and worse; if he couldn't put up a considerable sum of money he'd have got five years, and I suppose he thought it was worth risking his life. He planned it all pretty carefully; the anonymous letters began arriving long before any hint of danger threatened Bayliss and his jockey. A more feeble criminal would have sent one to himself, but he didn't make that mistake. But it's a fact that no criminal ever remembers everything, and what Grey forgot was that there would be no blood on Bluebeard's hoofs. Or perhaps he thought no one else would think of that. And so," he wound up, passing his tankard to be refilled for the third time, "when I hear about horseshoes being lucky, I remember two men who were killed by them, as you might say, and it's not the kind of luck I'd appreciate, even if it came my way."

THE COCKROACH
AND THE TORTOISE

"TALKING OF COCKROACHES," OBSERVED INSPECTOR FIELD, guilefully bringing the conversation round to his own subject, "reminds me of a queer thing that happened to me once. It was a good many years ago; I was a sergeant in the K District. That's a fairly well-to-do part of London, and most of the cases we had were shoplifting and bag-snatching. Not much scope for an ambitious man, but there's generally a chance if you keep your eyes open. One morning I was on duty in the station when I heard a scuttering movement outside and a woman burst into the room. She was a little thing, very plainly dressed, rather taking if you like 'em small, with big eyes and curly lashes. She stood there, staring, and panting as if she'd been running in a race.

"I thought she was another of these people who've had their bags emptied while they left them on the counter in order to look at a sweetly pretty thing in the bargain basement. But it turned out not to be that at all. In fact, it was one of the strangest things that ever happened to me." He polished off his tankard and shoved it across the counter. "I was so sure it was a shop-thieving affair that I'd already picked out the right form. Forms are more useful where women are concerned than you'd ever guess; seem to impress them that there's something serious going on.

"When I began to ask what was wrong, though, she just gasped at me: 'I want you to help me. I want some advice. I never meant to come here, but where else am I to go?'

"Well, of course, that wasn't precisely what I'd expected, but you soon learn in a job like ours not to be surprised at anything, so I said as nicely as I could that we'd be glad to help her, and she went on in a jerky sort of voice: 'Of course, I know the proper thing would be to go to a lawyer and make him do something. But I daren't. I don't know any. Only Harry's, and he wouldn't be safe.'

"Harry was her husband, she explained. I told her there were other lawyers, but she said: 'I wouldn't dare trust them. If I picked a dishonest one, and a lot of them are rogues, for I've heard Harry say so, I'd be even worse off than I am now. So I thought perhaps the police could do something.'

"'You'll have to tell me a bit more,' I encouraged her, and bit by bit, a word here and another there, I got the story out of her. It was what I'd begun to expect—blackmail—and for the commonest of reasons where a woman's concerned.

"'It's wicked,' she kept saying, 'simply wicked that I should be tortured like this, just because I was a fool for a little time.'

"I could see at a glance it wasn't any good telling her that life doesn't play a bit fair, and that lots of people are tortured for being a fool for less than an hour. Some of these murderers, for instance, who're driven half crazy before they strike. But she wasn't the type of woman to appreciate a point like that, so I just let it go and asked her to tell me what was wrong. It was an ordinary affair enough. She'd got playing about with some young fellow while her husband was away, and now the chap was making trouble. Well, that's quite a common position, too, though I knew she wouldn't believe me if I told her.

"'He's trying to get money out of me,' she went on in an incredulous sort of voice, as if she despaired of making me believe in the existence of such a monster. 'I've told him again and again that it's no good—I haven't got the money—but he says I can get it out of my husband. Which, of course, is just what I can't do. As it is, he's beginning to complain of my extravagance, says I never used to ask for extras like this, and do I think he's made of money? I've sold all my jewellery, and pretended it's being reset, but I shan't be able to keep up that pretence for long, and when Harry finds out he'll start making inquiries, and everything will be ruined.'

"'You haven't thought of telling your husband?' I suggested, and I thought she was going to faint dead away.

"'He'd kill me,' she said simply. 'And though sometimes I feel I wouldn't mind being dead, I couldn't bear to think of him being hanged because I'd been a fool.' She admitted that quite frankly. This fellow—she referred to him as Gerald—had just been a diversion. She was young and not bad-looking, and like a lot of young pretty women she'd got into a mess as soon as her husband took his eye off her. But she insisted that it was Harry who mattered.

"'He's real,' she said. 'Gerald was only a game. I never meant any harm.'

"I sometimes wonder," added Field in parentheses, "whether some of these women would do worse if they meant to play the devil generally. Most likely not, seeing the way women are. Well, she'd tried to shake this fellow off, but he was sticking closer than a brother, asking for more and more money.

"'Have you got any of his letters?' I asked her, and she said she hadn't, but if I wanted one there were sure to be more and she'd bring one along.

"'He never wrote the other kind,' she went on, 'though I used to write pages to him. He's kept all those, and he's making me buy them back. The worst—I mean, the ones that Harry would think the worst—are the most expensive. I don't feel as though there were enough money in the world to pay for them.'

"I was sorry for her, of course, but I don't mind telling you I was a bit disappointed too. Just at first, when she began, I'd got an idea she might be one of those cases that do a fellow a bit of good. These domestic blackmails don't get you anywhere. I asked her the usual things—how long had she been giving this Gerald money—and she said: 'Six months. And I can't give him any more. But lately he's begun to torture me in a new way. He follows me when I'm out; he hangs round the house, so that the servants must notice him. The other day, when my husband and I were walking together, he came across the street towards us. I thought he was going to speak to me. I think he just wanted my husband to notice him, to warn me that he would have no mercy. He's cruel and wicked, and you must help me.'

"I asked her for Gerald's full name, and she hesitated.

"'I don't want him to find out I've come to you,' she said.

"'Your best plan will be to suggest a rendezvous next time he asks for money,' I told her. 'Meet him there, and we'll catch him red-handed.'

"She looked horrified. 'I couldn't. My husband might find out.'

"I thought that most probable, but she wouldn't hear of making a clean breast of it. She wasn't afraid of a divorce—there would be no question of that, she said—but her life would cease to be worth living.

"'It would be just a prison for the rest of my days,' she assured me. 'And he would turn our child against me. I will never, never do anything wrong again, but somehow you must frighten this man away without Harry finding out.'

"I couldn't argue about her husband, of course; there are men like that, taking a pride in cutting off their noses to spite their faces, and go about mutilated for ever afterwards.

"'If you won't tell your husband and you won't give me this man's name, what do you expect us to do?' I wanted to know.

"She said she didn't really know, but that sometimes she thought she'd kill herself.

"'I shouldn't do that,' I warned her. 'But, if you should be in earnest, don't come and tell the police about it first. It's a criminal offence, see? And you'd be making me accessory before the fact.'

"But it was easy to see she didn't care about that. I could be sent to prison for five years and she wouldn't even notice it. Any more than she wanted to proceed formally against this chap who was bleeding her white.

"'You ought to think of the community,' I told her. 'Why, he may be sucking another lady's blood at this minute.'

"She tossed her head. 'That's nothing to do with me. And, anyway, he isn't. Because he's been following me about ever since I left my house this morning. That's why I came in here, because I thought it was the one place where he wouldn't dare show his face. Even he wouldn't be brazen enough to storm a police station.'

"Outside the door someone whistled, and then a very tall man, dark and clean-shaven, walked in; he had those deep blue eyes you see in some Irish families, and when he saw the lady he began to laugh.

"'So this is where you'd got to,' he said. 'I must hand it to you for nerve. Putting your head into the lion's mouth and trusting to his British chivalry not to snap.'

"She stood up; she was a tiny little thing, really, and for a minute I thought she was going to faint. She leaned against my shoulder and one hand clutched my arm. But when I said I'd fetch her a glass of water, she said No, it was all right, she didn't want anything, I wasn't to go.

"'I've been telling the police about you,' she told the new-comer defiantly.

"He only laughed again. 'Tell me,' he urged. 'I always like to learn.'

"'The officer says you could get seven years.'

"I gasped a bit, because I hadn't said that, though it might be true. It depends on the judge.

"The man threw back his head and roared with laughter. 'That's a good one,' he said, 'but you always were fine at telling the tale. All right, Sergeant, go ahead. Make your arrest. Incidentally, you might let me know the charge. That is, if you know it yourself.'

"I said in a wooden sort of voice: 'This lady wishes to charge you with blackmail,' and instead of laughing again he turned to my companion and remarked in a soft sort of voice: 'So I'm a blackmailer, am I? I will say, Fanny, you do think up good stories. How much have I had off you?'

"I was beginning to feel uncommonly foolish; if this lady had been hazing me it might put me a long way back with my superiors if the truth came out, but before I could speak the woman he called Fanny went on in indignant tones: 'You can't deny you've been following me about all the morning…'

"'Like hell I have,' he agreed heartily. 'Well, wouldn't you, if she'd pinched a stone worth four thousand out of your house?' He was talking to me now. 'I don't know if you've heard of the Pendleton Emerald? I'm Pendleton.' He fished in his pocket for a card. 'I'm taking this emerald abroad this afternoon, as Fanny knew, and she meant to get her claws on it. I will say one thing, her gang generally does get what it wants. I got a 'phone message this morning calling me up in a ghastly emergency, and off I went hell-for-leather. When I arrived I found my man knew nothing about it, and I realised I'd got Clapham Fanny on my track. This isn't, I may add, the first shot they've made to relieve me of responsibility for the jewel. Of course, you know all about her; so do we. She's a familiar name to every dealer and fence between Hatton Garden and Amsterdam. I came haring back in a taxi just in time to see another taxi going away from my house. I just caught a glimpse of a lady stepping into it and—well, you can see for yourself she's not a lady you'd easily forget. I knew I hadn't a moment to wait; in that taxi were Clapham Fanny—and my emerald. I was so sure I didn't even stop to open my safe. I knew she'd done that job for me. My man, Baynes, is pretty reliable, but he's no match for an old-timer like our friend here. She'd sent the message, of course—or one of the gang had. It wasn't a woman's voice.'

"He stopped to get his breath, and Fanny said contemptuously: 'That's very clever of you, but this is a police station. They know your sort here.'

"'Well,' he told her, 'the proof of the pudding's in the eating. Where are my blackmailing letters?'

"'Do you suppose I kept anything so dangerous?' she asked him. She did look rather handsome in a rage.

"'Even more to the point,' the fellow went on, 'where's my emerald?'

"'I don't believe you ever had an emerald,' she scoffed. 'It was clever of you to follow me in here, when you realised I was going to the police at last, to try and spoil things, but you lose this time.'

"'Do I?' If he was bluffing, he was a remarkably cool card.

"'If I'd stolen your emerald do you think I'd be in a police station?'

"'Ever hear the story of the cockroach that was set before the tortoise as a *bonne bouche*? It took one look at the tortoise and gave one leap and concealed itself under the creature's armpit— the safest hiding-place it could find. I don't want to sound rude, Fanny, comparing you with a cockroach, but—well, you see my point?'

"'Perhaps the Sergeant's a bit quicker than I am,' Fanny retorted.

"'Oh, come off it,' said my fine gentleman. 'Hand over that emerald—unless you want to get about five years.'

"Fanny faced him with her chin in the air, her hands gripped round the neck of a little black silk bag she was carrying. 'I haven't got your emerald,' she said. 'I don't know anything about your emerald. I don't even like emeralds. They're unlucky stones. This is simply another of your crooked attempts to get a living.'

"'My dear, be a sportsman,' Mr. Pendleton urged her. 'You haven't been out of my sight since you left my house, except for a second when I got caught in a traffic jam. It isn't likely the taxi-driver has the stuff; you wouldn't let it out of your sight. Therefore, you have it on you. Hadn't you better confess you're beaten? If you won't listen to reason,' he added regretfully, 'I shall have to charge you, and you'll be searched, which will be most humiliating. You do see that, don't you?'

"However, she stuck to her guns that she knew nothing about the thing and hadn't got it, though she was more frightened now. I could feel her trembling.

"'All right,' said Mr. Pendleton. 'Then I'll charge you with the theft.' And he turned to me.

"I hadn't any choice. I had to have her searched, and off she went with a woman searcher, and I felt pretty uncomfortable altogether.

"I didn't gather that my companion felt much more happy. 'I don't like this,' he told me. 'I've a lot of admiration for that girl. She takes chances and she generally brings them off. Silly of her not to admit she had the stone.'

"I wasn't feeling quite so certain myself; after all, he hadn't stopped to examine the safe. It looked to me uncommonly as though he'd walked into the trap Clapham Fanny had laid for him, and that at this very moment the rest of the gang was making its getaway with the emerald. But I had the sense to say nothing about that.

"'If it turns out that you're mistaken you'll find yourself in a tight pair of shoes,' I suggested, but he only laughed and offered me his cigarette-case.

"'She's got it all right,' he said. 'She hoped I'd weaken, that's all. Just you wait.'

"Well, we waited, and presently the searcher came in and said she'd examined Fanny from top to toe, and the only jewel she had was the big paste diamond on her left hand.

"Well, thought I, this about cooks the goose, and then Fanny herself came in. She was in a towering rage, no doubt about that. Her eyes were burning and she said, in the sort of voice that makes husbands remember there's a job of work they left unfinished at the other end of the town: 'Well, Mr. Pendleton, and what happens now? Perhaps I can't give you in charge for blackmail, but I can give you in charge for slander, and false accusation, and I hope it ruins you.'

"My gentleman hadn't turned a hair. He was still leaning against the door, with his hands in his pockets, and all he said was: 'Then, if you haven't got it on you—and I must take the searcher's word for that—it's somewhere in this room. The point is, where?'

"He didn't move, but I could see his eyes going round to every possible place. 'There's no need to look on the picture rail,' I told him. 'The lady hasn't been alone for a minute, and all the time she was here she was talking to me.'

"'You remaining stationary,' he suggested. 'Well, that narrows the field certainly.'

"It seemed to me it narrowed it so much it was scarcely a blade of grass, let alone a field, but before I could say so he'd dashed forward and caught me by the arm. While I was wondering what the game was he'd plunged his other hand into my pocket, and when he brought it out there was something in it, something that seemed to fill the room with a bright light. I hadn't had much to do with jewel crimes, but even if I had the Pendleton Emerald would probably have dazzled me just the same. Like a green fire it was, as he stood there, flashing it this way and that.

"'I ought to have guessed when I saw you standing so much nearer the law than is normal or safe,' he teased the girl. 'It was very long-sighted of you. I suppose you thought I'd never look for you in here; and then, when you realised I wasn't altogether a fool, in spite of my appearance, you disposed of the emerald in the one place where no one would think of looking for it. Oh, you're a very pretty cockroach, my dear. Well, what's the next move?'

"I admired the woman then; she must have known she was on a hot spot, but she didn't turn an eyelash.

"'You can have me arrested—if you dare,' she said. 'Though it mightn't be too comfortable for the Inspector here. After all,' and here she burst out laughing, 'nobody saw me park the jewel.'

"He roared at that. 'Jolly for you, Inspector,' he said.

"I didn't altogether like the way things were shaping.

"'Do you wish to make a charge?' I asked him.

"He shook his head. 'Haven't the time. I told you this jewel has to accompany me out of England this afternoon.'

"'It doesn't take all day to make a charge,' I assured him in my driest tones.

"'I'm afraid, if I do make it, I may never live to make anything else,' he explained. 'Fanny has a husband—and even a public school education doesn't seem to give these gangmen any respect for the police.'

"He grinned, said, 'So long, Fanny,' and to my disgust out she went a good deal cooler than when she came in.

"I was properly angry now. 'You'd no right to do that, sir,' I told him. 'She may be robbing someone else's safe within the hour.'

"'That's their luck,' he said.

"'You ought to have given her in charge,' I insisted.

"'That's her luck,' he told me. 'I mean, her husband's her luck, of course.'

"'There ought to have been an arrest,' I said again.

"'That's your luck.' He'd gone before I'd properly understood what he meant. I was beginning to think: 'That's life; just a lot of beginnings that don't lead anywhere,' when one of my colleagues came in with some photographs in his hand.

"'Keep a look-out for these,' he said, putting them down. 'Some gang got away with the Pendleton Emerald this morning. Old Sir Joseph's foaming at the mouth, and seeing what a squat bald little chap he is, it isn't safe for him to work overtime at that game. It seems it's worth a lot of money—four thousand, the experts say—and he was got out of his house by a trick this morning, and then the thieves turned up as calm as you please, on a pretext of answering some advertisement, tied up the butler, and picked the lock of the safe as easy as kiss your hand.'

"'Do they know who the chaps were?' I asked.

"'A man and a woman. Here are the pictures. Someone saw them in this part of London. How they got away with it in broad daylight takes some explaining. One thing, you'd know him again.'

"He put the pictures on my desk. Hers wasn't very flattering, but I'd have recognised his anywhere, that tall dark fellow, with the big shoulders and long chin. I suppose she thought someone had hit her trail, so in she came, parked the jewel as calmly as you please in case questions were asked, and then he popped along to warn her the coast was clear. It was all very prettily done."

"Did they get them?" someone asked.

Field shook his head. "I did hear the emerald was seen round the neck of a lady in Central Europe some time afterwards, but that might be just gossip. Anyhow, Sir Joseph died of apoplexy within the month, so it wouldn't have been much use to him."

We all felt a bit delicate about putting the final question. Finally, the barmaid, braver than the rest of us, or perhaps just more curious, asked: "And what happened when the story came out?"

Field looked at her disapprovingly. "When you're as old as I am," he told her, "you'll understand there's times when it's positively unhealthy to know more than your superiors. Gives them a wrong impression, and an ambitious man—and I was ambitious in those days—doesn't make mistakes like that. But it's an odd thing," he wound up, pushing his tankard across the counter, "and I daresay these new-fangled psychologists would find some indecent reason for it, but since that time I've never been really partial to a tortoise."

ALSO BY LUCY MALLESON,
WRITING AS ANNE MEREDITH

Adrian Gray was born in May 1862 and met his death through violence, at the hands of one of his own children, at Christmas, 1931.

Thus begins a classic crime novel published in 1933 that has been too long neglected – until now. It is a riveting portrait of the psychology of a murderer.

Each December, Adrian Gray invites his extended family to stay at his lonely house, Kings Poplars. None of Gray's six surviving children is fond of him; several have cause to wish him dead. The family gathers on Christmas Eve – and by the following morning, their wish has been granted.

This fascinating and unusual novel tells the story of what happened that dark Christmas night; and what the murderer did next.

ALSO AVAILABLE

Fancy yourself as a golden-age detective?

In these pages lie the clues you will need to crack the most impenetrable of cases. Culprits lurk between the lines of word searches. Imposters are unearthed in anagrams. A keen eye and a quick wit are your best tools for eliminating the suspects in a range of puzzles, suitable for all ages and levels.

For seven years, the British Library has brought neglected crime-fiction writers into the spotlight in a series of republished novels and anthologies. Updated with brand-new puzzle styles and including the very latest British Library Crime Classics titles, there are even more ways to solve the mystery in this sequel to *The Pocket Detective*.

BRITISH LIBRARY CRIME CLASSICS

ALSO AVAILABLE

Many of our titles are also available in eBook and audio editions